I0525529

The String Serial
Volume 1

First String – Part One
Second String – Part Two
Strung Out – Part Three

THE STRING SERIAL VOLUME 1
Copyright © 2016 by Andrea Ring

All rights reserved. No part of this book may be used or reproduced in any manner whatsoever without written permission except in the case of brief quotations.

This book is a work of fiction. Names, characters, places, and incidents are either the product of the author's imagination or are used fictitiously, and any resemblance to persons, living or dead, business establishments, events, or locales is entirely coincidental.

Originally published in 2016 by Square Gorilla Press.

ISBN 978-069273044/

Cover image:

Copyright © 2016 Michael Ring and Hannah Reams

First String

The String Serial
Part One

Andrea Ring

Dedication

To my mother, Laurinda Claus, who is the only person on the planet who thinks I'm funny.

Chapter 1

I sit sullenly in Dr. Steinburg's office, staring at my painted toenails. Va-Va-Va-Voom, the red polish is called. I hate the color, and know it only makes my white skin look whiter, but Matt loves it when my nails are red.

Loved it.

"Why do you think your mother is so worried about you?" Dr. Steinburg asks.

I sigh. "No big mystery. My husband left me, and she thinks I'm depressed."

"Are you depressed?"

"Not pill-popping depressed," I say. "I get up, go to work, pay my bills."

"So you don't think you need to be here."

I sigh again. "You've been treating my mother for fifteen years, so you know how screwed up my childhood was, and that's reason enough for me to need to be here. But if fifteen years weren't enough to cure her, I'm not sure you're that good at what you do."

"Try me," he says. "Your mother is paying for the sessions. What have you got to lose?"

I finally raise my eyes to his. "I'm sure she's told you everything. What do you want to know?"

"Tell me about your marriage."

I shift in the overstuffed chair. "Big question. Matt was my childhood sweetheart, literally. I loved him and that was it. We got married two days after graduation, and now, ten years later, here we are."

"Here you are, where?" he asks.

"Here. Divorced. He left me for a teaching assistant in his department at the university. That's it."

"Were there signs that he was the unfaithful type?"

I shrug. "Not really. I never...I thought..."

Dr. Steinburg looks at me patiently. He makes no move to speak. And tears gather in my eyes for no good reason.

"He was my rock," I say softly. "I had all this chaos at home...cokehead dad, doormat mom, arguments and brawls and weeping spells and days where my mother refused to get out of bed...and there was Matt. He rescued me. And then he dumped me."

"Tell me about Matt."

"He's...kind. Generally, I mean, mostly. Nice. Polite. He has a quiet voice, so different from my dad. He never yells. He can get mad, but it's a quiet mad. He'll look like he's about to burst, and then he'll meet my eyes, and it's like the anger just washes away. He was so respectful of what I needed. Always."

"Except for the fact that he left you for someone else."

I laugh. "Yeah, well, there's that."

"He must have had some flaws," Dr. Steinburg says.

I think about it. "He wasn't that great at communicating," I say. "I mean, I always got the feeling that he was holding back and not sharing every thought in his head."

"Why do you think that was?" he asks. "Because, obviously, he was hiding a great deal."

I shrug again. "I don't know."

Dr. Steinburg leans back in his chair. "You know, often, we choose what we know. You knew an abusive, drug-addicted father, and it would have been easy for you to choose the same for a husband, because that is your known. But you went the opposite direction. You chose a quiet, polite man. One who refused to even yell when he was mad so that he wouldn't upset you."

I nod.

"There's something very noble about that."

I crack a smile. "Thank you."

"But...it didn't work. Something was off. Do you think he tried too hard not to upset you?"

I blink. "What do you mean?"

"Maybe, sometimes, he needed to yell. But perhaps he felt stifled because he knew he couldn't yell at you."

I press my lips together. "So you think he left because he couldn't be himself?"

"I don't know without talking to Matt. But, let's say he did yell. What would you have done?"

"He yelled," I say. "Twice. He was allowed to yell."

"Twice. In how many years?"

"Seventeen," I say. I force myself not to add the extra two months and twelve days.

"And how did you react?" he asks.

"How does anyone react when their husband yells?"

I get the stare again.

"I cried," I finally say. "He always said he hated to see me cry."

Dr. Steinburg hands me a tissue, and I take it and dab at my eyes.

"Let's leave that for now," he says. "So Matt was your first boyfriend?"

I nod.

"First kiss, first lover, first everything?"

I nod again.

"Have you dated anyone since?"

I laugh. "It's only been six months. I can't just turn off seventeen years of loving someone and date someone else."

He nods. "How long do you think you need to wait?"

"I'm not waiting for anything," I say. "I just…"

Patient nod. Patient stare.

"I don't know what I want," I finally admit. "I had Matt. That's all I thought I'd ever have, all I thought I ever wanted."

"What is your idea of the perfect man?"

I picture Matt in my head. "Dark hair, brown eyes, kind voice. Nice."

"Is that a description of Matt?"

I wrinkle my forehead. "Well, why not?"

The sarcasm hangs between us.

"What do you like to do in your spare time?"

"We used to go to baseball games. We had season tickets for the Angels. And we always had people over, you know, for barbecues, so I would cook and entertain. We used to ride our bikes around town."

"Do you still do those things? Now?" he asks.

"No."

"Do you want to do those things?"

I just stare at him.

"Let me offer something," he says. "I think you grew to be an adult only in the context of your relationship with Matt. You were Matt's girlfriend. Matt's wife. And it's a wonderful thing to be in a relationship and care about your role in it, but you didn't take the time to think about who you are as a person. An individual. Who is Hope Russell?"

I laugh nervously. "Do I have to answer that?"

"I don't believe you can answer that," he says. "Not yet. But that's why you're here. I don't think you're depressed. Sure, you're sad, and you have a right to that. Seventeen years out of twenty-eight is a big chunk of your life. You're starting fresh. You have to figure out what you want out of life without Matt in it."

My eyes sting. "I don't know how to do that."

"So here is your assignment," Dr. Steinburg says. "I want you to explore your interests. Take a class, or join a club, find something that interests you and try it out. It doesn't matter whether or not it sticks. You just need to do something for you."

"You think that will help me get over the love of my life?"

"It's a start. And the second thing I want you to do is have a wild affair."

My mouth falls open. "You want me to sleep around? When I've been with one man my entire life?"

"I'm not suggesting a one-night stand. I'm saying you need to give yourself permission to try things out. Including men. You've known exactly one, but there are a zillion different men out there, each with the capacity to teach you something about yourself. Every relationship doesn't have to be a lifetime commitment. A relationship can be that, of course, but look at it like shopping for a car. You don't just buy the first car you see. You compare prices, you test-drive them, you ensure they have enough cup holders. There are a lot of great cars out there, but they're not all a great fit for you."

He rises just as the hands of the clock slide to ten minutes 'til three. I take the hint and rise with him.

He smiles. "How about we give it a month? I'll have my receptionist call you to schedule."

I nod. One session a month. My mother's gone cheap, and I can only be grateful.

Chapter 2

My phone rings as I slide into my car.

"Hey, Ma. The session went fine."

"Did he put you on Prozac?"

I roll my eyes. "I'm not depressed. I told you that. He wants me to find a hobby."

"A hobby? He's up to his old tricks. I tried that in 2005."

I smile. "Did it work?"

"I spent $1000 on golf lessons, and all I got were a few calluses for the effort. Honestly, Hope, you need drugs."

"Said no mother to her daughter ever," I say. "I'm hanging up. And he's your therapist. Maybe I should try someone else."

"No!" she says. "No. I trust him. Forget I said anything. Follow his advice. I just…I hate to see you so sad."

My body sags. "I know. Listen, I've gotta run. I'll see you for dinner tomorrow."

"Don't be late! See you then. Bye!"

"Bye, Ma."

I throw the phone into my purse and start my car. My mother.

She means well. Truly. Finally. I give her credit for it, but sometimes…she's a bit much. Like she's making up for years of bad parenting. Which she is.

We're at a good place now. She's attentive to me, and takes care of herself, and we can actually talk. I've let go of my resentment for the years she spent placating my dad and putting us both in harm's way. I barely remember the fights anymore. I can watch two actors arguing on TV, as long as it's a comedy, and not feel like I need to run.

Matt always hated that. He'd put a movie on, the latest thriller or action thing, and he wanted me to watch with him. I tried. But if violence came on, or voices were raised…I didn't even think about it. My feet hit the floor, and my body stood up, and I'd be out of the room.

I pull into a parking space and look up. Without realizing it, I'd driven to the Tustin Town Cinema.

Who is Hope Russell? Dr. Steinburg asked me.

A girl who runs, I think.

I grab my purse and exit the car. Watching a movie isn't exactly a hobby, but it's an activity. Something to do on a Saturday afternoon. And Dr. Steinburg mentioned that—*What do you like to do in your spare time?* I was too embarrassed to say I play Free Cell on my computer or clean the house.

"One ticket, please," I say to the pimply-faced teenager behind the glass.

"Which movie?"

I look up at the marquee. There's the latest Disney flick, some slasher crap, a Nicholas Sparks romantic tragedy…

"*Navy SEALs to the Rescue*," I say. "Is that one violent?"

"The SEALs don't tap dance, as far as I know," he says.

"Right. Great. I'll take it."

Chapter 3

The theater is mostly empty when I enter. I take the seat nearest the exit and take a deep breath.

The first time a gun is fired, I literally jump in my seat. And the blood...my stomach rolls.

I rush out of the theater and into the open, gulping fresh air and trying to calm my heart.

"You okay?"

I startle and turn.

"I'm sorry, hey, I'm really sorry," a guy says. "I didn't mean to scare you. I saw you run out. Are you okay?"

I shake my head. "Fine. I'm fine. I just don't like those kinds of films."

He smiles, and it's kind of lopsided. "What kinds of films?"

"The bloody kind."

"Then why'd you see it?"

I smile back. "A personal challenge of sorts. I'm really fine."

He's staring at me a little too hard. Not in a creepy way, but it's...uncomfortable.

"Well, I appreciate the concern," I say. "I should get going."

I turn to go, but he stops me with a hand on my arm, which he quickly snatches away. "Wait. I'm Sam. I just...you were gonna watch the whole movie, right? So you don't have anywhere you need to be."

I raise an eyebrow at him.

"Maybe I can buy you a cup of coffee."

"A cup of coffee."

He grins. "Yeah. And a muffin. Or maybe a scone. You look like you could be a scone girl."

I laugh. "What does a scone girl look like?"

"Pretty," he says. "Beautiful brown eyes. Soft, hesitant smile. Red toe nails." He looks pointedly at my feet.

I wiggle my toes. "I'm divorced," I say, and then I cringe. Why the hell would I say that?

He laughs. "Scone girls are awkward, too. In a charming kind of way."

I blow out a breath. "I'm an idiot. And woefully out of practice at this."

He holds out his hand. "Like I said, I'm Sam. I can call you Scone Girl, but I'm sure your name is sexier."

I shake his hand. "I'm Hope."

He grins. "I knew it."

Chapter 4

"I'm a grad student at UC Irvine," Sam says. "History. You?"

I sip my chai latte. It has a weird taste, but whatever. Sam asked me what I wanted, and when I couldn't decide, he decided for me.

"I have my bachelor's in English," I say. "I'm a copyeditor for Nikon. I write their technical manuals."

"Do you write anything besides technical?" he asks.

"Novels, you mean?" I say, and he nods. "No. I keep a journal, but I've never felt that creative."

Sam leans forward. "You said you were divorced, right?"

I pick at the lid of my coffee. "Yeah."

"All great artists are fueled by their personal angst," he says. "Maybe you should try to tap into that."

I cringe again. "I'm sorry. Is it that obvious? My angst?"

He smiles. "It was the first thing you told me about yourself. I'm guessing it's on your mind. How long has it been?"

"Six months."

"And I'm guessing you haven't dated anyone since?"

I laugh. "I haven't dated anyone else, ever. I'm not just out of practice—I've had no practice."

Sam takes a sip of his coffee. "You need to get laid."

"What?" I say, laughing in discomfort. "That's a little presumptuous."

He laughs, too. "Just an observation. You need to move on."

I wave a hand. "What about you? You're single, I'm guessing."

"No, but my girlfriend's cool with it. She lets me pick up sexy strangers at the movie theater."

My eyes widen. "Oh. I, uh…I don't think—"

Sam laughs again. "I'm kidding, Hope. I'm single. Totally single."

I blow out a breath. "Shit. I thought you were serious. Wait. You think I'm sexy?"

He grins. "You could be."

I roll my eyes and we both laugh.

"So history," I say. "Why history?"

"Mostly 'cause it doesn't feel like work," he says. "I get to read and write fantastic real-life stories." He points to a pile of papers sitting on the table between us. "Although teaching history is a different animal. The way my students write about it is painful."

"You're implying you're a poor teacher," I say.

He holds his hands up. "The semester just started. I can't be blamed yet. I'm actually an awesome teacher."

I sit back. "Teach me something."

Sam meets my gaze, and a soft smile creeps to his lips. "I think you need extra attention. Private lessons. Definitely private."

He has crazy blue eyes, the kind that are so light they look otherworldly. But his lashes are dark, his eyebrows strong. His hair is a bit too long, like he has better things to do than get a haircut. He's not my type, I don't think, but he's not unattractive. In fact, I love his smile. It's boyish, charming and roguish and endearing all at the same time.

"I don't know if I'm ready for that," I say. "I'm flattered, I mean, I haven't even looked for this, but I just don't know."

"Stand up," he says.

I pop to my feet. And then I feel completely foolish. Why did I simply follow his command?

He stands up next to me and takes the coffee from my hand. He sets it on the table.

"Don't think about it," he says. "Just go with it."

"With what?"

He leans into me. Too late, I realize what's happening, and I find myself frozen in place. Sam's lips meet mine, and I'm as stiff as a statue.

He pulls back an inch, and his breath fans my face. "You're not trying. Look at my eyes. Listen to my voice. We're just two people, making a connection."

My hands are shaking. I clench them into fists, and I stare into his eyes. He smells…not bad, just different. When I kissed…when I kiss someone, I have an expectation of the scents, the feels, the sights. This is just strange.

Sam places his lips on mine again. I take a deep breath, and his scent fills my lungs. I soften my lips and mold to him. His hands come up and cradle my face, and his touch makes my eyes sting. I place my hands on top of his and grip tight.

He shifts his stance, and I feel his hips bump mine. He opens his lips, just a bit, and I open mine. Our tongues meet on a sigh, and suddenly his lips crush against me, and I tilt my head, and we're glued together.

"Wow," he breathes against my mouth. "Better."

I grin. "You think?"

He steps back shaking his head. "Damn, I'm good. I knew you were sexy."

We take our seats, and Sam pulls out his phone.

"Can I have your number?"

I hesitate, and he grabs my hand across the table.

"I have class in thirty minutes, or I'd stay," he says. "Let me take you out."

"You want to take me on a date?"

He smiles. "If you'll let me."

I don't know what to say. I have no idea what I want. And I just kissed a stranger. In public.

"There's a concert tonight, at the Galaxy. A bunch of us are going. How about that? Totally casual, big group, no pressure. We can just hang out."

"What kind of music?"

He looks at me with that goofy smile. "I'll try not to be offended that the kind of music might actually sway your decision. It's an 80s cover band. If you're feeling bold, you can dress up."

I take out my phone and hand it to him to exchange numbers. "Scone girls can be bold. When we try."

Chapter 5

There's a long line of people outside the Galaxy when I arrive. I almost turn around and go back to my car—I mean, what am I doing? This is like a Punk'd episode. Get the meek little girl to show up and watch her thrash around helplessly, looking for the cute boy who lured her here.

But as I hesitate, I see Sam emerge from the crowd and jog over to me. His hair is plastered up in a Flock of Seagulls wave, and he's wearing a worn Duran Duran t-shirt. He gives me a hug before I can move.

"So glad you made it!" he says. "You look great."

I smile at him. My best friend Martika helped. I didn't want to go too out there, but she convinced me to wear the blue eye shadow, the side ponytail, and the resurrected Guess jean skirt I saved six months to buy when I was twelve. "Thanks for asking me. Love the hair."

Sam grins. "Come on. Looks like they're letting everyone in." He takes my hand and leads me over to the line.

"Do we have good seats?" I ask.

"No seats. Standing room only. This way I get to see you dance."

Oh good Lord.

"Hey everyone," Sam says as we hit the line. "This is Hope. Hope, this is Dave, Jack,

Mandy, Sarah, Owen…and that's Sophie." Everyone says hi, and I try to smile back. Dave reaches into a paper bag at his feet and pulls out two beers. He hands one to each of us.

"Hurry," Dave says. "You have just enough time to pound one before we go in."

Sam clinks his beer to mine. "Bottoms up."

I look at the beer. It's the same IPA that's stocked in my fridge at home, waiting for Matt to come drink it.

Sam chugs, and I think, *What the hell?* I put the bottle to my lips and drink.

I finish before Sam does, and his friends cheer. Sam raises an eyebrow at me, and I blush.

"I don't drink that often," I say. "Just trying to be bold."

He laughs. We throw our bottles away as the line moves forward, and suddenly we're inside.

Music blares. Lights flash. Sam squeezes my hand and leans into my ear. "Awesome, isn't it?"

If you like this kind of thing, I guess. It's overwhelming, like I'm inside a disco ball. But is it awesome? I don't know how to feel about it. I've never been to an actual concert…not since I was a child.

We settle in the middle of the crowd, and the band takes the stage. It's so loud I can barely hear myself think, let alone talk, but Sam keeps hold of my hand, and somehow, we're connected without even speaking.

Thirty minutes ago, I was embarrassed at the thought of dancing. But when you're in a crowd of people, all with the same purpose, it's impossible not to go along. I find myself jumping and cheering and singing, and Sam holds me from behind and grinds his hips into mine, and I lean back against him and rest my head on his chest, and he leans into my neck and kisses me softly.

I've never thought of 80s music as particularly sexy, but something about this night has my body humming. And I haven't felt that since high school.

When the concert ends, I don't know what to expect. Maybe a goodnight kiss, hopefully a request for another date. Just to see. I mean, I don't even know Sam, but it couldn't hurt to see.

He walks me to my car and then takes me in his arms. He gives me a soul-quaking kiss.

"Come home with me," he breathes into my ear.

I pull back. "To your house?"

He nods. "It'll be good, Hope," he says. "So fucking good."

I bite my lip. "I'll go, but I can't promise. I mean, I don't know how far I can promise to go."

He grins. "Got it. I came here with my friends. Can you drive?"

I nod. "Tell me the way."

Chapter 6

Sam has a one-bedroom townhouse near the university. It's fairly neat and the furniture looks new. I don't know what I expected, but it wasn't this.

"How old are you?" I ask him as he throws his keys on the kitchen counter.

"Thirty," he says. "I know it seems a little old for a grad student, but it took me a while to figure out what I wanted to do. I spent six years as a studio musician."

"Really?" I say. "What instrument?"

"Guitar."

My heart beats faster.

"Do you miss it?"

He grabs two beers from the fridge, pops the tops, and hands one to me. "I still play. But the musician's life is rough. I prefer a steady job."

"Would you play something for me?"

He leans on the counter and grins. "You're gonna make me work at seducing you, huh?"

I take a sip of beer. "Seeing as I'm not fully committed to being seduced...yes."

"I thought the hair would do it."

I laugh. "Oh, the hair is sexy. It's definitely not that."

"I thought the dancing would do it," he says. "Aren't all women turned on when they dance?"

I smile. "I've heard that. But for me...honestly, Sam, I have no idea."

"He really screwed you up, didn't he?"

I frown. "It wasn't him. It's just that he's the only experience I have. We had this life, and this relationship, and I just went with it."

Sam sips his beer. "What did he do to turn you on?"

"Nothing," I say automatically, and then I laugh. "I mean, we were at the point where he didn't have to do anything. The love was just there."

He looks at me, and it almost looks like pity. Like my relationship with Matt was pitiful.

Maybe it was.

"Have you felt anything, even a little twinge, all night?" he asks.

I look away. "That's embarrassing."

"Why?"

"I can't talk about it," I say. "I'm not used to talking about it."

"But that's a good thing," he says. "You need to do things completely differently. You need to try new things. And I can help."

I shake my head as he comes to stand before me. "I don't know why you're even bothering," I say. "I sound pathetic to my own ears. This is way too much trouble for you."

"The payoff is worth it," he says, brushing my hair from my cheek.

"What's the payoff?" I ask.

He shrugs. "In the long run, who knows. But for tonight, it's this." And he pulls my body tight against his, and I can feel his erection, firm, against my hip.

I gulp.

He sets my beer on the counter and presses into me again. "If I do something that feels wrong, just tell me. I want this to be all about you."

"Why?" I say. "Why would you do this? You don't even know me."

"That's how I get turned on," he says, nuzzling his mouth against my neck. "If it's good for you, it'll be amazing for me."

He slowly strips the clothes from my body. I pull his shirt over his head and throw it across the room. When he reaches behind me to unsnap my bra, I push him away.

"I want to explore you first," I say.

He grins and leads me to the bedroom. He climbs on the bed and leans back against a mound of pillows.

"Whatever the lady wants," he says.

I can't believe this moment. I'm here, in my underwear, staring at a half-naked man who is not Matt.

Matt was all athletic muscle. Years of baseball and soccer and weightlifting had bulked him up and sculpted him. That body is the only one I know.

Sam's body is completely different. He's lean, like a cat. His chest isn't as hairy. His stomach is flat, and his hipbones protrude, but he doesn't have the ab definition I'm used to.

"I like your body," I say aloud, and when Sam laughs, I mentally slap myself.

"Good."

I kneel next to him on the bed and run my hands over his chest. He groans as my hands roam lower, skimming his hipbones.

"You could take off your bra," he says with a grin. "I mean, if you want."

"I'm working up to it," I say.

My hands move to his jeans. He lifts his hips, and I work the buttons loose. I slide the jeans down his long legs and gulp again.

He's wearing boxer briefs, totally sexy. Matt preferred…ugh. I growl. Why the hell am I thinking about Matt now?

Sam. Sam is the man in front of me. Sam is the one who wants me. Sam.

He kicks off his jeans and puts his hands around the waistband of his underwear. "You ready for this?"

I nod.

The underwear comes off. And I'm staring at a cock so thick I don't think I can get my hand around it.

"Wow," I say. "Holy shit."

Sam laughs. "That's the best reaction I've ever gotten."

"I...wow."

I stare at it. It twitches. I reach a hand out and slide it down the length of him.

"Christ, you're killing me," he says.

"In a good way?"

He smiles and closes his eyes. "The fucking best way."

I've always liked giving head. There's something powerful about it, about being in control, about giving pleasure rather than taking it.

But oral sex on the first date? What kind of girl does that make me?

Who is Hope Russell?

Maybe I am a slut, and I just never had the chance to express it.

I grip his cock tight and bend forward. But Sam pulls away from me and pushes me gently backward.

"I said this was all about you," he breathes into my mouth. He kisses me hard, and I relax under him.

Before I know it, my underwear is off, and Sam is kissing my stomach. I fight not to laugh, but my stomach muscles are shaking.

"Does that tickle?" he asks, licking my belly button.

"A bit."

He lifts his head. "Then laugh. If that's what you're feeling, do it."

"Laughing isn't sexy," I say.

He shakes his head. "Laughing is the sexiest thing you can do."

"But I don't want to hurt your feelings."

"You can't," he says. "I know this is taking a lot of trust for you, and I want you to feel that from me. Whatever you do, whatever noise you make, however you touch me, it's all good. We're doing the most intimate thing two people can do. Let's have fun with it."

"I'm having fun," I say. "I hope you know that."

He laughs. "I think you're still stuck in your head, and that's okay. But by the end of the night, I'm gonna get you out of it or die trying."

"And how are you going to do that?"

Sam gives me that goofy grin. Then he slides down until his head is between my thighs, and he buries his mouth against me.

"Oh, God," I breathe, and a million thoughts rush through my head. I fight to banish them. I tell myself to be in this moment.

I feel Sam's five o'clock shadow rubbing against my thighs. I feel his thumbs pull me apart. I feel his tongue as he licks down the very center of me in long, firm swipes, flicking my clit on every upstroke.

My inner right thigh twitches. It's never done that before.

"Tell me what you like," he says, his breath cool against my moist flesh. "Tell me when I hit the spot."

I can't speak. I dig my fingers into the sheets and grip them tight.

He concentrates on my clit with his tongue, and puts two fingers inside me. I cry out as they sink deep.

I feel my orgasm building. My thighs shake, and my fingers clench, and my head thrashes.

He notices that I'm close, I think. He backs off, moving his thumb to caress my clit while his mouth moves lower. And lower.

"What are you doing?" I say.

"Just go with it."

"But I—"

Sam suddenly lifts his head. He moves his hand to his mouth and pulls out a tiny torn piece of toilet paper.

My mouth falls open in horror. "Oh my God." I sit up and cover my breasts, and it feels like I might throw up.

He laughs. "Hope, calm down. It's fine."

"Fine? It's not fine! I can't believe...I'm gonna go die now." I move to get off the bed, but he puts his hands on my thighs and keeps me there.

"You can't be embarrassed," he says with a grin, and I stuff my face in the pillow. "Well, okay, you can, but you don't have to be. It's no big deal."

"Yes, it is," I mumble into the pillow.

"Laugh about it," he says. "I am."

I lift my head and bash his chest with the pillow. "That's for laughing at me."

"Come on," he says. "Give me one little giggle. I know you want to."

He makes me smile. I try to fight it, but I can't. My lips split, and laughter bubbles out of my throat, and in my effort to suppress it, I snort.

Sam laughs out loud, and I join him. He tackles me back against the pillows, and we laugh into each other's mouths.

Until we're kissing. My arms are around him, and I'm feeling every slope, every plane, every dip of his body, and he sneakily slides back down between my legs and licks me with pointed tongue.

"Sam," I breathe, and he goes lower, pushing my legs up higher until my ass is totally exposed, and I dig my heels into the mattress and he licks me where I never even contemplated being licked.

My clit tingles. And he's not even touching it.

"God," I say. "I've never...I've never felt that."

He puts a finger inside me, and then moves it to that lower entrance. "You've never done this?"

I shake my head, and he smiles.

"Just relax. Let all your muscles relax. You'll like it."

He licks my clit again and probes with his finger. I can tell I'm too wound up, too tight, but I can't make myself relax. Just the tip of his finger manages to go in, but as he licks, and my orgasm builds once again, my muscles unclench of their own free will.

His finger slides in. All the way in.

Oh. My. God.

And my orgasm hits, and my hips buck, and Sam concentrates on my clit, and pumps his finger, until every last drop of pleasure is squeezed out, and my body spasms, and his finger withdraws, and I didn't realize how filled up I felt until it's gone.

He lifts his head and I look down at him. He's smiling, but he has blood on his lips.

"You're hurt!" I say, sitting up and leaning toward him. I put a finger to the blood and show him. "You're bleeding!"

He licks at the blood and grabs a tissue from the nightstand. "Bit my tongue. But it was worth it."

"Did I do that?" I say.

He smiles. "When you came. I didn't expect it. My fault."

"It's my fault," I say. "I'm so sorry."

"No apologies. You came harder than anyone I've ever been with. I'm taking it as a compliment."

I blush. "You were...incredible."

"It was the ass, wasn't it?" he says, running a hand down my leg. "You liked it."

"I didn't expect to," I say. "I can't believe I let you do that."

"I can do it again."

I smile. "I think it's your turn."

"You don't have to," he says. "I mean, you can, if you want, but you don't have to."

"I want to."

We trade places.

I give as good as I got.

I've already met Sam's friends, but the concert didn't really count. I didn't get to have a conversation with any of them, and I doubt I could tell you what any of them looks like. I was pretty much in awe of the music and only focused on Sam.

But for date number two, Sam's invited me to pizza and a ball game at his place. Baseball I can do. It's one of the few topics I know inside and out.

I'm the first to arrive, and I think Sam planned it that way. He greets me with a bone-crushing hug around my neck first, and then a slow, wet kiss. But both are awkward because my hands are wrapped in oven mitts, and I'm holding a hot crockpot.

"Let me set this down," I say against his lips, and he laughs.

"Sorry. Got a little carried away. I see you and I have to touch you."

I blush and hide it by running to the kitchen. I set the crockpot down and slide off my mitts.

"Queso," I say. "My special recipe. I just have to run back to my car and get the chips."

"Grab a beer and relax," he says, moving to the door. "I'll get them."

He's out the door before I can blink. Wow. Matt never offered to help bring groceries in. Even when I returned from Costco, and he watched me lugging in a case of water, ten pounds of laundry detergent, and box after box...he just sat there, his eyes glued to the television.

Then again, I never asked for help.

Sam comes back in. "Did you get a beer?"

I shake my head. Frankly, I forgot about it.

He moves to the fridge and hands me a bottle. "Do you think it's poor etiquette to dive into the queso before the guests arrive?"

I smile. "I'm a guest, and I've arrived."

"Excellent point." He tears open the bag of chips and lifts the lid of the crockpot. He digs a chip in and shoves the whole thing into his mouth. His eyes close, and his lips lift in a smile as he chews. "Man. You're a queso goddess."

I laugh. "That's the best reaction I've ever gotten."

He slits open one eye and grins. "Eat a chip so I can kiss you without worrying about my queso breath."

I smile, take a chip, and scoop up a big bite. Before I even finish chewing, he's on me, pressing his entire body against mine, and backing me up against the fridge. His hands roam, and my body grows warm.

"I could marry you for your queso, you know that?"

"Man cannot live on queso alone."

"This man could."

I laugh.

The door opens, and two people spill in. Sam smiles at me, pecks my cheek, and moves to his guests.

"Dave," he says, slapping the guy on the back. "And the lovely Sarah."

"I burned the wings," Sarah says, "but we brought them anyway. Maybe someone wants to torture themselves."

Dave smiles. "I told her we could just order them along with the pizza, but she was feeling domestic."

"You make that sound like a dirty word," Sarah says. "*Domestic.*"

"You guys remember Hope?" Sam says.

They both turn to me. "Hey, Hope," Sarah says. "Nice to see you again."

"You, too," I say. "You know, the wings don't look that bad."

Dave snorts. "Are they supposed to be black?"

"I personally don't mind that," I say, "but for those that do, they can just peel the skin off."

Sarah looks triumphant. "I told you we shouldn't just dump them."

I laugh. "Are you learning to cook?"

"I don't know that I'm actually learning anything," she says, "but I'm trying."

"May I?" I gesture to the wings.

"They're your taste buds," Dave says, and Sarah pokes him in the stomach.

I grab a wing and take a bite. Yes, the burnt char taste is bitter, but I can taste the sauce, too, and it has good flavor. "They're good," I say. "Did you make the sauce?"

She nods. "I wasted two pounds of butter."

"You cooked them with the sauce?"

She nods again.

"The sauce burns," I say. "That's the problem. Cook your wings first, then coat them with the sauce."

"You cook a lot?" she asks.

"Yeah. I love feeding people."

"Dave's birthday is next week," she says to me quietly. "Would you help me? I want to bake him a cake."

I smile. "Love to."

We exchange numbers and set up a time. Sam and Dave have moved the queso and chips to the coffee table, and they're totally silent, shoving chips into their mouths. On the TV, the teams are announced and the first batter steps up.

"Do you like baseball?" I ask Sarah.

She shrugs. "I've gotten used to it since Dave and I moved in together. It's a good excuse to hang out with friends."

"I used to go to almost every Angels home game," I say. "It wasn't really my thing, either, but my ex loved it."

"When'd you guys split?" she asks.

"About seven months ago. Sam's the first guy I've dated since."

"Sam's a good guy," she says. "I met him in college, and we hit it off right away. Not in a sexual way, just as friends. He's had a tough time finding someone."

"Why's that?"

She smiles. "He tends to go for the chemistry and ignores everything else. Chemistry is great, I mean, you've gotta have some chemistry...but it doesn't last. There has to be more, you know?"

I nod. "Are you saying he's mostly dated bimbos?"

Sarah laughs. "I try not to be mean about other women, but...yes. Dear God, were they all beauties with no brains."

"Then why the hell is he dating me?"

Sarah looks at me, startled, I think, by the honesty in my question. "You've got both," she says. "Maybe he hasn't figured out how much substance you have yet."

I laugh. "Thanks for that. But seriously...I'm not that special-looking, and I'm not saying they're recruiting me to MENSA or anything, but...is he just looking to get laid?"

She takes my hand and squeezes. "I've totally screwed up by telling you all that. Ignore me. Sam is a good guy. He deserves someone like you, and I think he's serious. He really wanted us to hang out with you today. That says a lot."

I nod. "Enough second-guessing then. What do you do?"

"First grade teacher," she says. "You?"

"Technical writer," I say. "First grade? You must be a saint."

She smiles. "I love it. I absolutely love my job. It takes some patience, but that's my gift. I can't cook, but man, I can tie shoelaces and wipe snotty noses and sing 'Happy Birthday' all day long."

I shake my head. "I've never even been around kids. I'd have no idea how to do any of that. Well, I can tie a shoelace. And I can sing. But I'm totally jealous."

"You've never been around kids?"

"Nope. Only child, very little extended family…even my ex's family hadn't gotten around to having kids yet."

"You should come to my class and help out one day. I mean, if you want." She laughs. "It's an experience."

I grin. "I just might have to try that."

Sarah moves to the bag of groceries they brought and pulls out a wine cooler. "You want one?"

I hold up my beer. "I'm good for the moment."

She shakes her head. "I've tried, but I just can't drink beer."

"Hey," Sam calls. "If you guys want queso, you better get over here. We're demolishing it."

Sarah and I move to the couch and sit with the guys.

"I don't know why they started Billings," Sam says, referring to the pitcher. "The guy's older than dirt."

"He has the best ERA on the team," Dave says.

"But that's only because he's played so few games," I say. "Hernandez is slightly higher, at 2.4, I think, but he's started at least fifty more times. I think they're saving his arm. Oh, and two of Oakland's starters are lefties. Billings does better than Hernandez against lefties."

I dip a chip. Everyone's gone quiet. I look up, and Dave and Sam are staring at me open-mouthed.

"I didn't know you knew that much about baseball," Sam says.

I smile. "Now you do."

"I don't know anyone who knows that much about baseball," Dave says, shaking his head. "Not that's female, anyway."

Sarah slaps his arm. "Why does it surprise you that a woman knows about baseball?"

"Do you know anything about baseball?" he asks her.

"You know I don't."

"Proves my point. I know I've shacked up with a feminist, but you can't ignore reality. Men are more into sports. Accept it."

Sarah scowls, but she doesn't argue.

Pizza arrives, along with Owen and Mandy. Sarah and Mandy eventually wander to the kitchen, and I feel out of place. I mean, I could watch the game, I'm happy to watch it, but I don't have to. I could hang out with the girls. Maybe I should be hanging out with the girls.

I move to get up, but Sam stills me with a hand on my thigh. "I was just gonna get another beer," I say. "You want one?"

"I'll get it," he says, bounding to his feet.

I sit back and a commercial comes on. Dave scrapes the bottom of the crockpot with a bunch of chip crumbs.

"How'd you get into baseball?" he asks.

"My ex," I say.

He shakes his head. "I need to meet this guy and learn his tricks. I can't get Sarah to sit down and watch a whole game."

"The trick is to give her an incentive," I say. "The game is not an incentive. But if you rubbed her feet while you watched the game, I bet she'd stay."

"I usually eat during a game," he says. "Rubbing feet and eating is kind of gross. Give me something else."

"Pick a body part that she likes to have rubbed," I say.

Dave laughs. "I know a few of those."

I laugh, too. "Or maybe when the commercials come on, turn your attention to her. If she's doing something for you, do something for her. Like a throw a load of laundry in the washer."

He stares at me like I've just spoken a foreign language. "Did your ex actually do that?"

I smile. "Always."

"I love Sam, but dude, that guy had skills."

I laugh again. "We were together since the sixth grade. I had years to train him."

"Sixth grade…shit. I can't even imagine that. One woman for literally my entire life? That takes some balls."

"Balls?"

"Yeah," he says. "Marriage is the biggest commitment you'll ever make, right? The biggest decision? And to have confidence that your junior-high self knew what the fuck you wanted out of life? Damn. I wish I trusted myself that much."

I sigh. "Well, since we're not together anymore, I guess you could say we didn't know what the fuck we wanted."

Dave gives me a sympathetic smile. "His loss is Sam's gain."

"You think so?"

He nods. "And Sarah's, too. I'm actually thinking about doing the laundry."

We both laugh.

Chapter 8

Dr. Steinburg eyes me as we take our seats. "You look different," he says.

"I met someone," I say. "I left here that Saturday, and I couldn't think of anything I wanted to do. A hobby, I mean. I had no idea what I was going to do, but I ended up going to a movie. I don't know if my mom ever told you, but I can't watch violent movies, or family drama, anything where people hurt each other. I've never been able to watch that stuff. So I thought I might try it."

Dr. Steinburg chuckles. "I wasn't expecting you to torture yourself, Hope. Facing our fears and our phobias can be a good thing, but sometimes it's an unnecessary thing. How'd it go?"

"Not too well," I say. "I saw that Navy SEALs flick, and I lasted about twenty minutes. But I met a guy outside the theater. We had coffee and then we went to a concert. He's…nice."

"Just that one date?"

I shake my head. "We've been out six times this month. We're getting to know each other."

"I think that's great," he says. "Have you been intimate?"

"A bit," I say. "We haven't actually…you know, but we've done some things."

"And how do you feel about that?"

I twist my hands in my lap. "It was weird. It is weird. If I think about it too hard…it feels like a betrayal."

"To whom?"

I shrug. "Me, I guess. Being only with Matt was part of who I was. I was proud of that. It felt loyal and virtuous. But I gave that part of myself away."

"You had to," he says. "If you want to find love again, you had to give it up. And there's nothing wrong with that. You can still be loyal and virtuous."

I nod. "I know. I just…I think working myself up to actual sex is going to be tough."

"Why is that?"

"It means that Matt and I are really over."

Dr. Steinburg's eyes soften. "You and Matt are over, Hope. He's moved on. You deserve to do the same."

"I'm trying."

He smiles. "Tell me about this new man. What do you have in common?"

"Well…he's a musician."

Dr. Steinburg raises an eyebrow.

"I know. I know what you're going to say. But that's what he used to do. Now, he's a history PhD candidate. He wants to teach and write."

"Have you told him who you are?"

I purse my lips. "That's not who am I."

"It's a part of you," Dr. Steinburg says. "You can't deny that."

I don't say anything.

"You are the daughter of one of the most highly regarded guitar players of all time," he says. "You should embrace that."

"I'm the daughter of a drug addict who beat my mother, beat on me, and died of a drug overdose on the toilet. That's how I remember it."

"Do you still play? Your mother has told me how nimble your fingers are."

I shrug. "I haven't lately."

"I don't bring this up to dredge up old memories or hurt you," he says. "But sometimes we need a new perspective. You don't have to hold your father up as a hero, because we both know that would be a lie. But he was gifted. He passed that gift to you. If that is the only good thing we can take from him, then I think you should take it."

"What does this have to do with anything?" I grumble.

"You have a new man you are getting to know, but you haven't let him in. You've only known him a month, so of course, you haven't shared everything, but it's going to start weighing on you. You don't have to share the bad. Share the good."

"What do you mean?"

"Correct me if I'm wrong, but…music is your life."

"My mother talks too much."

Dr. Steinburg smiles. "It's just something to think about. This new man will never know you unless you share the important things."

Chapter 9

I think about my session on the drive home. What does Sam really know about me?

Nothing. I haven't even been able to tell him that I prefer Corona to that hoppy IPA crap, or that I take my coffee black, no chai. He knows my father is dead, but I haven't shared anything about the circumstances.

I haven't picked up a guitar since Matt left. I used to play every day, five times a day, but now...my music's wrapped up in Matt. All my memories, of sitting outside classrooms, waiting for a mother who was chronically late to pick me up, strumming away on my guitar...of Matt sitting with me, waiting, often walking me home...of playing for him before bedtime, after dinner, around the bonfire at the beach...

I get home and go to the spare bedroom. I take my bass off its stand.

There are certain songs I just can't play yet. And that's fine. As Sam likes to say, I need to do things differently.

I choose a Duran Duran song, which reminds of Sam. "Come Undone" has a bass line— it's actually played by the keyboardist, but it sounds like a bass line—so I play it.

An hour passes before I even realize it. Damn. I missed this.

I put the bass back and take my phone out of my pocket.

"Hello, gorgeous, I was just thinking about you," Sam says when he answers.

I smile. "I know we were gonna have dinner with Dave and Sarah, but would you mind a change of plans?"

"Yes, you can come over and cook naked."

I laugh. "Actually, I thought maybe you could come to my place. I'll cook for you, and...there's something I want to show you."

"I get to see the Scone Girl's house? For real?"

"I think you've earned it."

Sam laughs. "Done. I'll call Dave. What time?"

"Whenever you're ready."

∞

Sam arrives at six with a bottle of wine. He gives me a lingering kiss and holds up the bottle.

"I don't know what we're eating. I hope it goes with red."

"Whatever you like," I say, carrying it to the kitchen. Sam follows me, swiveling his head to take in my house.

"Wow. Was your husband rich?"

I shake my head. "Actually…that's part of what I want to show you tonight. I didn't make anything fancy, just lasagna, so we have time while it cooks."

Sam smiles. "Does it involve lace? Or silk?"

I laugh. "No. More like steel and wood."

He pulls me to him. "I knew you were kinky like that."

I laugh and kiss him. Then I take his hand and lead him to the couch. "Stay here."

I go to the spare room and grab two guitars. Then I stand before him.

His eyes go wide. "Is that a Martin?"

I nod. "A 1929 Martin Vintage. They only made 15 of them."

He tears his eyes away from the guitar and looks at me. "I didn't know you knew about guitars."

"I'll get to that. And this is a 1963 Fender Stratocaster. My dad left me these."

He stands. "May I?"

I pass him the Fender.

"This has seen some serious playing. Did your dad play?"

"A bit."

He examines the guitar. "I can't...I almost don't want to play it. It's like you can feel the music just by touching it."

"I always thought that," I say. "Somehow, you can hear the guitar just by looking at it."

Sam lowers himself to the couch and pats the seat next to him. I sit.

"What do you hear, Hope?"

"Russell is my married name," I say. "Did I tell you that?"

He shakes his head.

"My maiden name is...Cruz."

He blinks at me.

"And I play. I mean, you can't be Joe Cruz's daughter and not play. And I should have told you. When we went on that first date, and you told me you were a musician, I should have said something. But I just don't talk about it."

Sam looks at his lap. "Do you still play?"

"Today was the first day I've played since my divorce. I was thinking about you, and I wanted to tell you...but before that, I played every day. Music is a big part of me."

He raises his eyes to mine. "Why not just say that? You know how important music is to me, too."

"That made it even harder," I say. "When I hear people worship him like he's some kind of god...you know how he died, right?"

Sam nods.

"Imagine that. He was a drug addict. And he had a temper. My mom and I had to live with that."

"God," he says. "If I remember right, you're the one who found him, didn't you?"

I nod.

Sam pulls me against him. I'm not sad, exactly, since all I have is bone-deep hatred for the man. I guess I'm more ashamed. And then I'm frustrated, that every person on the planet sees my father as great when only I know the truth.

"Seems like you got the best of him, baby," Sam says into my hair. He kisses my head and pulls back. "Can I hear you play?"

I smile. "What should I play?"

"What do you know?"

"If I've heard it, I can play it."

Sam laughs. "Shit. Okay. Play your favorite song."

"I don't think you'll know it." Sam raises an eyebrow, and I laugh. "Okay. I'll be super impressed if you know it."

He rubs his hands together. "A challenge."

Something hot gleams in his eyes. My body shivers. I pick up the Martin and set it on my lap.

I play the introduction of Depeche Mode's "Stripped." I want to sing along, but that would give the song away.

Sam leans back and closes his eyes.

"It's not meant for guitar, is it?" he asks.

"Keyboard," I say, still strumming.

He opens his eyes. "Depeche Mode."

I stop playing. "I can't believe you know it."

He frowns. "I'm a musician, too."

I blink. "Did I offend you? I didn't mean to."

"No." He gets to his feet and walks to the kitchen.

I set the guitar down and follow him.

"I did. I offended you."

He shakes his head. "Can I get a drink?"

"You want me to open the wine? Or I have Corona."

He laughs. "Corona? Isn't that a little light for you?"

I bristle. "It's what I prefer."

He turns his back on me and sits down on a stool at the island. "Corona's fine."

"What's wrong?" I ask. "What did I do?"

"You're finally opening up," he says, not meeting my eyes. "I just never thought this was what you were hiding."

"I haven't been hiding," I say. "I've just never had to open myself up like this. We've only known each other a month."

"A month where you met my sister, and you heard me play, and you've met my friends...I thought I was okay with all that. With you being...coy. But I guess I'm not."

"What does that mean?"

He laughs. "You like fucking Corona. Every time we've eaten together, have you been holding your nose? Every time we've kissed...have I been doing it wrong?"

"You're blowing this out of proportion," I say. "You knew I didn't open up easily. But I haven't lied. So I prefer Corona. So what?"

"I'm surprised you even drink, with Joe Cruz for a father."

I narrow my eyes at him. "Get out."

"Jesus, Hope, I didn't mean it. Not like that."

"I said, get out."

"Hope—"

"No!" I yell. And the loudness of my own voice startles me, but it also gives me courage. "Do you know what it took for me to invite you here tonight? Nobody knows! Nobody knows the real me. Fuck, I don't even completely know the real me! And you're throwing it in my face!"

Sam scrubs a hand over his face. "I'm sorry."

I sag in place. "Don't be. This is the real you, your real thoughts. I shouldn't...I can't be mad at you for that. I mean, I don't like it, but at least you're being honest."

"I like you, Hope. A lot," he says.

"But not the real me."

"I'm just getting to know the real you," he says. "It's a shock. I have to fit these new pieces into the puzzle."

"Okay," I say. "Call me. I mean, if you want to."

"Call you?" he says. "You think I'm leaving? I'm not. I just need a minute to process."

"Oh."

"I thought we'd finally be having sex tonight."

I stare at him and cross my arms over my chest. "So I get real on you and spill some serious shit, and now I've ruined the mood. Silly me."

"That's not what I meant," he says. "I spent the last month playing songs for you, and even writing songs about you, and now I find this out and hear you play...I feel like an idiot."

"You wrote songs about me?" I say. "Wait. Why do you feel like an idiot?"

"You don't know how good you are, do you?"

"Good at what?"

Sam shoots to his feet. "Are we having the same conversation? The guitar! You're fucking brilliant!"

"I...you only heard me play that one song."

"That's all I took," he says. "It's the most comfortable I've ever seen you. You had this look on your face...I've never seen that look."

"What look?"

"Perfect contentment. Everything's right with the world. You're in love."

I nod. "That's how I feel when I'm playing."

"I want you so bad," he says, and then he takes a deep breath. "Honestly, you don't know the real me, either."

Something cold slithers down my spine. "What do you mean?"

"I've been holding back a lot with you. I didn't want to scare you or push you."

"You mean in the bedroom." I make it a statement and he nods. "So...what have you been holding back?"

"I'm not gonna tell you unless you can handle it," he says. "I'm so turned on right now, I'm afraid that if we start, I won't be able to stop."

"You can't say that and expect me to agree just like that," I say. "What if you want to do something horrible?"

Sam scratches his chin. "What's your definition of horrible?"

"I don't know," I say. "Pain. I don't like pain."

He shakes his head. "I'm not into that."

"Bodily fluids. Other than the usual."

Sam grins. "I have no plans to pee on you."

I blow out a breath. "Thank God."

He moves to me and runs his hands down my arms. "I just want to ravage you. Hard and fast, music blaring, with no time for either of us to think. I want to get lost with you."

I almost ask him why. I mean, yeah, maybe my guitar playing was a turn on, but he saw something in me even before he knew I played. I desperately need to know what it is that he saw.

But I don't ask, because Sam has been so patient with me. This is the first thing he's truly asked for since we met. And I want it, too. I need it. I have to move on.

I lead him to my bedroom and put on some music. Foo Fighters' "Everlong" blares through my radio.

I strip my shirt over my head and unclasp my bra. I slide my skirt to my ankles and press myself against him.

"Is that a yes?" he asks.

"Don't talk," I say. "Just do it."

Chapter 10

There's nothing here but us, Sam and me, and Dave Grohl's perfect acoustic guitar.

Sam sheds his clothes and bends me over the bed. He cups my ass and then rips my thong right off me.

Damn. Those were expensive.

I clench my teeth. *Stop thinking!* He wants me so badly he fucking tore my underwear off! Concentrate on that!

He licks a moist line down my spine. It's kind of gross. I mean, his spit is drying on my back, and it's making me shiver. In a cold way.

He gets to my ass crack, and as his tongue swirls around, I giggle. It tickles. I look over my shoulder, and he gives me a smile.

The smile I love.

He nibbles at my hips. "I want to watch you," he says.

"Watch me what?"

"Play with yourself."

He flips me over and I scoot up closer to the headboard.

"Um."

"Touch yourself, Hope," he says.

I thought we were going to make love. I prepared myself for that. But this…this is different.

I tentatively rub my breasts. Sam watches me closely with hungry eyes, and he seems to be enjoying it. Okay. I can do this.

I move my hands lower. Sam grips his cock as my hand slides between my thighs. Now I'm the one watching closely.

Matt and I…we didn't do this. Okay, maybe we tried it once or twice, but it wasn't a part of our regular repertoire. I don't like to be watched. Who the hell knows what kinds of faces I'm making?

"I want to touch you," I say. "Please. Don't make me watch from over here."

He chuckles. "You're embarrassed again."

I nod.

"I've seen you come," he says. "Several times. You know why I want to watch you?"

He's still rubbing his cock. And I can barely concentrate on anything else. "It turns you on."

"Nope. I mean, it does, but I want to see the way you like it. I want to know exactly what to do."

Something in me softens. Sam's always been like this, encouraging me to express myself, to be myself, but in this moment, he doesn't have to. He can just get laid. And he's putting that off for me.

"If I'm gonna do this, I need to be able to see you, too," I say. "All of you. Can you stand up?"

Without comment, Sam crawls off the bed and stands where I have the perfect view.

"Can you come like that?"

He squeezes his cock. "Fuck yeah."

I lean back and close my eyes. The music washes over me, and I let it fill my head, pushing out every nasty thought, every doubt, every bit of insecurity.

I caress my neck with one hand and squeeze one breast with the other. I pinch my nipple, roll it between my fingers, pull on it until I feel that bolt of lightning shoot down between my legs.

My other hand roams over my chest, down my belly, and to my thighs. Mmmm. I lick my lips. I open my eyes and watch Sam stroke his cock in an easy rhythm.

I open my thighs wider and slide one knee up. My fingers find my clit, and I pinch it. I flick it while my other hand flicks my nipple. I lick my lips again and slide one finger deep inside myself. Then two.

I slide them in and out, and my breath comes faster, and I watch Sam's rhythm pick up. His thigh muscles are rock hard. I abandon my breast and move that hand to my clit.

I rub it with two fingers while I pump the others in and out of my pussy. I rub faster, and Sam moves in sync with me, and I moan as my orgasm builds, and Sam moans, too.

And suddenly he's on top of me. His tongue tangles with mine, and he lifts my leg up over his shoulder, and I feel his condom-wrapped cock rubbing on my inner thigh.

"Now," I say into his mouth. "Now. Fuck me now."

He reaches down and guides his cock. I'm so wet that it slides halfway in with one gentle push of his hips.

"Tell me if it's too much," he says. "Tell me—"

"It's not," I say. "More. Give me all of it."

He props himself up with one arm and reaches the other between us. His fingers find my clit, and he rubs me as he sinks his cock deep.

I gasp. It's not painful, exactly, but it is. I've never been stretched like this.

He starts out slow, moving his hips in circles to give me time to adjust. And he keeps working his fingers, sending shivers down to my toes.

"I'm close," I say. "So close. Fuck me, Sam."

He draws out slowly, and then pushes into me hard. My clit throbs.

"Again," I say. "Again."

So he does it again. He takes back my mouth, and sucks on my lip, and I cling to him, my hips meeting his, our tongues entwined, until an orgasm rolls out from the center of me and sets every nerve-ending on fire.

I cry out.

Sam moans into my mouth, and pumps into me harder, and suddenly lifts his head, crying out, too. He collapses against my chest, and I laugh.

He pushes up and looks down at me with a grin. Then he kisses me.

"You're amazing, you know that?" he says.

"I was pretty good, wasn't I?"

We both laugh.

"Did I hurt you?"

"Not even remotely," I say. "I would have said something."

"Would you have?"

"I know I'm not great at expressing myself, but I don't let myself be hurt."

Sam rolls over onto his back and pulls me against his chest. "Is it too soon to say the L-word?"

My heart thumps and I swallow hard. "We agreed to be honest, right? To the best of our ability?"

He nods and turns his head to me. "I think I love you."

I don't know what to say. I like Sam. A lot. I might love him. Maybe. Quite possibly.

"I think I might love you, too," I say.

Sam laughs, and we just cuddle.

Chapter 11

I wake to my body throbbing. In a good way. All is dark, and Sam's spooning me, his hands gently rubbing my breasts, his cock an insistent ache against my ass.

I flip over and take his mouth with mine. Our hands roam, and I move on top of him.

"Condom," he says. "In my jeans pocket."

Thank God he remembered that. That's one mistake I do not want to make when I'm only possibly sorta maybe in love.

I shuffle through the clothes on the floor, trying to find his jeans. But I'm completely blind.

"I need a light," I say. "Shield your eyes."

"No way," he says. "Not when I have the chance to see you naked."

I smile and flip on the light. I find his jeans and fish in the front pockets. "Got it," I say, and when I hold the condom up, Sam's eyes widen.

I look in my hand. It's not a condom. It's a little baggie of white powder.

My hands begin to shake.

"Hope."

"Is this…what is this?"

He hops off the bed and grabs the baggie out of my hands. "It's no big deal. Sometimes I like to party. It's not a regular thing."

I sit on the bed, and Sam kneels at my feet. "I meant what I said. I love you."

"Don't," I say. "Don't do that. I can't. I'm sorry, Sam, but I can't."

"It's not—"

"I don't care!" I scream. "You knew, I told you who I was and what I went through, and you fucked me with a fucking bag of cocaine in your pocket!"

He looks up at me, and his eyes have turned glassy. "I'll stop. I'm not addicted. I'll never touch the stuff again."

"No," I say. "I can't do this. I won't do it. You need to leave."

He climbs to his feet. "Can I call you tomorrow? Maybe you'll feel differently."

"I won't."

I watch him dress, and I follow him out. At the door, he pauses and puts a hand on my cheek.

"I'm sorry," he says.

I nod. "Me, too."

Chapter 12

Dr. Steinburg listens politely while I tell him of my disastrous affair with Sam.

"You should be immensely proud of yourself," he says. "You cared about this man. It would have been easy to give in, but you didn't. You stood up for yourself."

"The shitty part is that he was good for me," I say. "He was a good person. He genuinely cared about my feelings."

"You need to be strong," he says. "The drugs are a deal breaker."

"I know," I say. "I have no intention of getting back with him. It just…I think I'm a different person now. In a good way. He helped me come out of my shell."

"That's what happens when we meet new people, even the bad eggs. We learn about ourselves. We grow. Are you open to another relationship?"

"Actually, I'm itching for one," I say. "It was nice to have someone to talk to and to do things with. I miss Sam, but it's not an ache like it was with Matt. I think I can try again."

"And what about the hobby? Any movement on that front?"

I smile. "No. But I've picked up my guitar again. Does that count?"

Dr. Steinburg shakes his head. "Something new. Something adventurous. Something you've never tried. How about rock climbing?"

I laugh. "Rock climbing? There's no way. I can't even do a pull-up."

"How about surfing?"

"When I was five, my dad made me watch *Jaws*. It scarred me for life."

He frowns. "I swear, if the man weren't already dead, I'd strangle him."

I grin. "Thanks."

"How about yoga?"

"My mother does yoga. If she found out I was doing it, she'd insist on going with me, and I have no desire to see my mother in yoga pants."

Dr. Steinburg chuckles. "Then give me an idea. Just one."

I sigh. "Fine. I'll go rock climbing."

Chapter 13

I dragged Martika with me, and now I'm regretting it. She's an absolute stud. Four years in the Navy honed her body, and two hours in the gym every day keeps it hard as a rock. I'm fit, but I still have some jiggle. And now I'm standing at the bottom of the wall next to her, and I've agreed to climb first, and all I can think about are the hundred people here, mostly men, who will be watching my ass.

Martika leans into my ear. "Your ass looks great," she says.

I smile at her. She always knows exactly what I'm thinking.

"Just don't fall," she says. "That would be embarrassing."

"Thanks for the pep talk," I say, giving her a jab with my elbow. Martika just grins.

"Any time you're ready," our instructor says.

"So I just...climb up the wall?" I ask. "I mean, that's it?"

Rock-climbing-master-of-the-world Jeremy laughs. "Pretty much."

Martika pushes me forward. I stumble and glare at her. And then I straighten my spine and march to the wall.

I grip two of the handholds, and Jeremy appears at my side.

"Think about what you're doing," he says. "This is physics. If you hold on here, at shoulder height, you won't have the leverage you need to pull yourself up. Try these two, up higher." He physically removes my hands from the grips and places them on two up higher. "Good. Now, go."

I put a toe on one of the lower thingies, and I push myself up. My other leg flails, trying to find a grip.

I hear Martika giggle, but I'm dangling from a wall and have no way to glare at her.

"Here." Jeremy takes my dangling foot and guides it to a grip. "You got it?"

I'm splayed like Gumby. "Now what?"

"Move your hands up one level," he says. "Then move one of your feet up."

I move my left hand up to a higher grip. But to move my right, I have to hang on with my left arm, and it's about as strong as a wet noodle. So I lean into the wall, all my weight on my toes, and throw my right arm up. Luckily, my hand hits a grip, and I cling to it for dear life.

"Great! Now your legs."

Um.

No one told me it would be this awkward. My knees are at right angles to the wall, and my cheek is smooshed. I feel like a fly splattered on a windshield.

"Hey, Martika."

I freeze. I'd know that voice anywhere. What the fuck is Matt doing here?

"Hey, asshole," she says. Ah. That's my bestie. "You can go now."

"Really?" he says. "We've known each other since sixth grade. I know you and Hope are close, and I'm glad she has you, but it takes two to end a marriage."

"Not when one of the people in that marriage is fucking someone else."

"I guess that's it then," he says. "You're not interested in the truth."

And then Jeremy yells, "Come on, Hope! You can do it!"

Christ.

"That's Hope?" Matt says. "On the wall?"

I imagine Martika nodding and thinking to me hard, *Come on, baby. Go. Climb! Show him what you've got!*

So I grit my teeth and move one foot up. Then I push with all my might and boost myself up. Dangly leg manages to find a hold, and I pause, panting.

"Yes!" Jeremy cries. "Again!"

Again. Right.

There are no holds above me. Now I have to go left or right if I want to go up.

There's no way I can let go with my hands. I need a boost from my legs first. So I put an awkward leg out and up about three feet away from me, and now I'm doing the splits. My inner thigh screams at me.

"The purple one!" Jeremy yells.

Purple…purple…I don't see a purple hold, except for the one my splayed leg is on. Maybe that's what he means. So I move my other foot to the same purple hold, and now I'm sideways on the wall, my arms are shaking, and my fingers are getting slippery.

"Help!" I yell.

"Just let go," Jeremy calls. "I've got you."

But there's no way. Something in me won't let go.

"Let go, Hope!" Martika calls. "You can start over."

I want to, I do. I want my feet on solid ground. But my body won't respond.

"Hey. It's okay. I'll catch you."

I look down. Matt is standing just below me, maybe two feet away. I've only climbed eight feet off the ground.

Sigh.

So I let go. I only drop about a foot before Jeremy's expert belaying arrests my fall, but my feet swing down from their sideways perch and clip Matt in the side of the head. He crumples to the ground.

∞

Martika laughs hysterically as we get in the car.

"I got it. I got the whole thing! Holy shit, was that funny."

I pull out of the parking lot, and laughter bubbles in my throat. I don't want to laugh at Matt's misfortune, but it was kind of funny.

"You are not posting that on Facebook," I say.

"Hell, yes, I am," she says. "You have to see the position you were in. I've never seen anything like it. You were Spider Woman."

I drive as she watches the video on her phone. Again. I hear myself scream and a loud thud as my legs hit Matt and he falls.

"So what time tomorrow?" she asks.

"What time for what?"

"Uh, barbecue. Our house. Benny's friends are in town for the reunion. Stop me when it actually clicks..."

"Right. My mom's torturing me with a friendly tennis game at the club. I'll have to go home and shower...say, five o'clock?"

"No later," she says. "Everyone'll be at our house at four. I promised them the human karaoke machine."

"I'm never invited as a guest," I say. "I have to fill in as the fourth in the tennis match, or be a machine. What happened to saying, hey, Hope, come on over, hang out, and have a burger with us?"

She waves a hand. "If I thought you could just come over and hang out and be social, that's exactly what I'd say. But if you don't have a guitar in your hand, you won't speak. I'm helping you."

I sigh. "And Benny's doing the cooking? Do you think that's a good idea?"

She shrugs. "As long as my husband does it, I don't have to."

"Good point. Except that he actually wants to keep his friends, right?"

Martika smiles at me. "You keep an eye on the burgers, and I'll keep the beer flowing. By the end of the night, they'll love us."

Chapter 14

So it's been a year since I picked up a racquet, and I was never that good anyway. But as the result of Dr. Steinburg's Bright Idea of 2002, my mother and I have to spend quality time together every Sunday. In fourteen years of this, I've picked the activity twice. Every other time, I've been left to go along with whatever harebrained scheme my mother managed to think up.

Tennis might not seem that harebrained, but when you consider that it's a mixed doubles match with her latest conquest as her partner, and that conquest's son as mine...yes. Harebrained.

I arrive exactly on time, but the three of them have already warmed up.

"Finally," Mr. Conquest says as I enter the court. "I thought we'd have to start without you."

I pointedly look at my watch. "My mother said three. It's one minute to."

"Did I?" my mother says, coming over and kissing my cheek. "I'm sure I said two-thirty."

I bite my tongue and hold out my hand. "Nice to meet you. I'm Hope."

Mr. Conquest shakes my hand. "Randall. And this is my son, Chet."

Chet. Jesus. These country club people don't even realize how ridiculous they are.

"Hey, Chet," I say. "You play a lot of tennis?"

Chet, with his perfectly coifed blond locks and his killer white smile, nods. "I played for Princeton."

I look at my mother. "And you told them that I haven't played in quite a while, right?"

"Of course, dear. But you're an athlete and you have my genes. You'll pick it right back up."

On what planet am I an athlete? Yes, my mother is a great player and is athletic, but I took after my dad. Maybe I should show them my rock climbing video, just to set the proper expectation.

Randall tosses my mother two balls, and they deftly disappear up her skirt. "Ladies first, Rosie," he says.

Ugh. My mother hates being called Rosie. It's Rosalyn. Rosalyn.

"Such a gentleman," she gushes, touching his chest. Ugh.

Chet and I make our way to our side of the court.

"I'll take backhand," he says. The strongest player always does, so I have no objection. But he could have asked me.

"No warm-up for me, huh?" I say.

My mother positions herself at the baseline and bounces the ball. "I'll take a few practice serves," she calls. "You can warm up that way."

Super.

She tosses the ball in the air and slams it my way. It hits the service box and goes by me before I can move.

"Good one!" I yell.

She serves and aces me again. I sigh.

"Are you ready?" Chet says. "Get on the balls of your feet. She's not serving that hard."

I give Chet my signature glare.

My mother hits another serve, and I lunge for it. The ball pings off the frame of my racquet and sails over the fence.

Chet sighs. My mother looks away.

"Okay," she calls. "This one's gonna count."

Great.

∾

Randall's like a big fat gorilla of a wall at the net. He actually stands in the middle, diving for every ball he can reach and slamming it at me.

This is not proper etiquette. When you play mixed doubles, yes, the men tend to make up for the women's weaknesses, but they are also supposed to hit to each other. When the helpless, weak woman on the other side is standing at the net, you do not hit an overhead at her. Period.

But no one told Randall that.

My mother slices a rather weak second serve to Chet, and since he's caught moving in the wrong direction, he barely manages to get the tip of his racquet on it and loop it over to his dad. I sigh and run backwards, knowing the ball is coming back at me.

Of course, I don't move fast enough. The ball hits the court about two feet in front of me and shoots up straight between my eyes, knocking my sunglasses off and my visor askew. I give them my back and try not to cry.

"You okay?" Chet says, actually putting a hand on my shoulder.

"Give me a sec," I manage.

"Shake it off," Randall calls across the court.

Shake it off? What kind of cretin is this guy?

It's my serve. Chet hands me my glasses, and I straighten my visor.

"Your face," he says. "Do you need some ice?"

"Thanks for the concern, Chet, but I'm shaking it off." He shakes his head and goes to his position at the net.

I get my first serve in and run to the net. My mother throws up a loopy ball, and I slam it with my forehand.

She claps her hand with her racquet. I actually hit a winner.

Now I'm serving to the gorilla.

I focus. I gather all my strength. I'm gonna hit it as hard as I can and hope for the best.

I actually hit a damn good serve, and Randall dumps it in the net. "Let!" he calls.

I look at Chet. *Let?* I mouth. There's no way that serve touched the net. Chet shrugs.

Fine.

I bounce the ball. I gather my strength again. And I fucking blast the serve.

And with a loud crack, it thuds right into Chet's back and he stumbles to the ground.

"Ow!" he cries. I run to him and kneel beside him.

"I'm so sorry," I say. "Are you okay?"

He shakes his head, and I watch a tear drip onto the court. "I'm not okay! It hurts!"

"Let me look at it." I lift his shirt, and sweet Jesus—he already has a purpling welt. "I think we need some ice."

Randall bounds over the net and to his son. "Chet? Tell Daddy where it hurts."

I pop to my feet and look at my mother, who has wandered up to the net. *Daddy?* I mouth. She shrugs.

Chapter 15

I'm running late. It's already ten 'til five when I race into the house and start the water for my shower. I throw my glasses and visor on the bed, strip off my sweat-soaked clothes, and head into the bathroom. But as I'm sliding open the shower door, I catch a glimpse of myself in the mirror.

Holy crap.

I lean over the counter, close to the mirror. I have an imprint of the edge of my glasses in my forehead and right between my eyes, and both my eyes are purple. I can't go in public like this!

I find my phone and call Martika. I can hear music in the background.

"Hey, where are you?" she says.

"I can't come," I say. "I got hit with a tennis ball in the face. I'm purple."

"Are you in pain?" she asks. "Do you need to go to the emergency room?"

"No," I say. "I'm fine, but it looks like I've been on the losing end of a bar brawl."

"But you're not in pain?"

"Well, the bruise is sore, but no."

"Then come," she says. "It'll be fun."

"Martika."

"Come on, Hope! Play the cool rock star. Put on some concealer, wear your shades with the mirrored lenses, and show some cleavage. No one will be looking at your face."

"Martika."

"Please," she says. "I think I'm liquored up enough to sing a Barry Manilow song. Pleeeease?"

"I'm not playing Barry Manilow," I say.

"Yes! Hurry up!"

ജ

The party's in full swing. I can hear the laughter and music as soon as I get out of my car.

Benny's ten-year high school reunion is tomorrow night, and he invited a bunch of the out-of-towners here tonight. Martika's just about peed her pants in excitement. She can't wait to hear stories about nerdy Benny in high school.

I let myself in and almost bump into a wall, even though this place is like my second home. These damn sunglasses are too good. I grab a beer from the fridge and head out to the patio.

Martika squeals when she sees me. She gives me a big hug, bumping the guitar I have slung across my back.

"Thank you," she whispers in my ear. "I needed backup."

Ah. I should have known. Even in your own home, it's awkward to host ten people you don't know at all, but who know your husband.

"Can you see the bruise?" I whisper to her.

"Nope. You look divine. And much cooler than most of the people here."

"Are they not being nice?" I ask.

"No, they are," she says. "I shouldn't have said that. But you'll see what I mean."

Benny comes up and gives me a kiss on the cheek. He reeks of beer, and he's not a big drinker. But reunions tend to be tough to get through without alcohol.

He takes my arm and steers me to the center of the crowd.

"Everyone, this is our good friend, Hope!" he yells. The chatter stops, and everyone turns in our direction. "Turn off the music, Marti! Hope's gonna play!"

"Uh, everyone seems to be having fun, Ben," I say. "I can play later."

One of the men in the crowd approaches. He's tall, dark skinned, with wire-rimmed glasses and an untucked Oxford shirt. He's holding a glass of white wine, and he points it at me.

"Let's hear what you've got."

"Do you play?" I ask him.

He smiles. "I dabble."

I unsling my guitar and hold it out to him. "You first."

Benny claps and someone whistles and several others cheer. "Charles!" somebody cries.

"Come on, Charles," I say. "Light it up."

Charles holds up his hands to quiet the crowd. "I know one song. And I'm gonna give it to you." He looks at me. "Do you sing?"

"When the mood strikes."

He grins. "Let's see if we can get you in the mood."

Charles settles himself in a chair, and everyone gathers around. Chair legs scrape on the concrete, and Ben drags a bench closer. I sit on the concrete next to Martika, and Charles nods at me.

"It's Hope, right?"

"Yep."

"Let's see if I can give Hope something to sing about."

He thumps the guitar with the flat of his hand in a steady rhythm. Everyone claps along with him.

Where is he going with this?

And then he plays, strumming one string at a time, "Seven Nation Army" by The White Stripes.

I smile. It's the first "real" song a beginner learns because it's so easy and repetitive. Not to take away from Charles. The guy's got rhythm, and he knows how to work a crowd.

So I sing.

Martika pulls me to my feet, and we dance. Or thump. That's about all you can do with this song, but it's satisfying anyway. Benny joins us, thrashing his head and making a fool of himself. An endearing fool.

Charles laughs as he finishes the song, and he waves at me to take a bow.

"Nice," I say to him. "Very nice. You rocked it."

He stands and hands me the guitar. "Now I'm dying to hear you play. Let's hear your version of the same song."

"No way. I can't improve on it. I'll play something else."

Charles just shakes his head. "You're being polite."

"No, you were great. What else should I play?"

He raises an eyebrow. "You take requests?"

Benny throws an arm around my shoulders. "She does. Anything. Name any song. She'll kill it!"

God, I love Benny.

"How about KT Tunstall? 'Black Horse and the Cherry Tree'?" Charles says.

"I love that song!" Benny says.

"You gonna be my drums and my backup vocals?" I ask him.

Ben pumps a liquored fist in the air. "Yes!"

৪৩

I'm hot and sweaty, and I can feel the concealer caking on my face. Charles hands me a fresh beer, and I take it from him gratefully.

"So when does your album come out?" he asks.

We take a seat on the bench and sip. "Thank you for the compliment."

"I'm serious," he says. "I'd pay good money to listen to you."

I shake my head. "It's only a hobby."

"Jesus. What do you do for a living?"

I swallow my beer. "Technical writing. You?"

"Propulsion engineer. Way less exciting than it sounds."

I shift one leg under me on the bench. "Rockets or jets?"

"Rockets," he says. "Not many people know to ask that."

"Don't ask me anything else about it," I say. "That's all I know."

Charles smiles. "How long have you known Benny?"

"Five years," I say. "Since he and Martika started dating. I met her in the sixth grade. You?"

"Kindergarten," he says. "We both grew up in the same shitty neighborhood, but both of us pulled ourselves out. I admire the hell out of the guy."

"Me, too," I say. "He's great for Marti. She's very lucky."

Charles slugs his beer. "Are you married?"

I shake my head. "You?"

He smiles. "Not a lot of women in my field. I thought I'd have plenty of time after college to start my career and find someone, but it hasn't happened."

"Life rarely goes where we expect it."

He gives me a searching look. "Sounds like there's a story there."

I shrug. "I'm currently in the process of finding myself. I only recently realized I'm missing."

Charles laughs. He's got a great laugh. "You're an incredible musician. Why aren't you doing something with it?" I stay silent. "Or is that a personal question?"

"It is, but...my dad is Joe Cruz. The music's in my soul, but I'll be damned if I walk his path."

Charles stares at me. And then he slowly nods. "I can understand that."

"What about you? When did you start playing guitar?"

"Last week," he says. "I always wanted to learn, but we didn't have the money when I was young, and then I got too busy…I'm making time. Time for the important things."

"I can understand that."

We smile at each other. And then Charles shakes his head.

"What?" I ask.

"I feel like the universe is playing with me. I finally meet a hot woman with brains who I'm interested in, and she lives halfway across the country."

My cheeks grow warm. "Thanks."

"If I even knew I could be out here every month, I'd ask you out. Hell, I'd skip the reunion for a date with you."

I lean forward and kiss his cheek. "I'd say yes."

Then he puts a hand up to my cheek. "Can I take the glasses off?"

"Uh. Actually…it's kinda funny. I was playing tennis today and I got hit right between the eyes. It's not pretty."

"I bet I don't even notice," he says.

I debate…and then I nod.

He slides my glasses off and we stare into each other's eyes. And then Charles kisses me softly.

Mmm. He's warm and soft and perfect.

"If you ever get back out to California, look me up," I say.

Benny stumbles over to us, interrupting. He slings an arm over each of our shoulders from behind the bench and leans in close. "Marti has told me it's time for bed. She's already there. It's midnight, and she has to work in the morning."

Charles and I exchange a smile. "Walk me out?" I say.

I kiss Benny goodnight, and out we go.

"I'm not tired at all," Charles says as he walks me to my car. "It's two in Houston. I should be out."

"Me either," I say. I turn to him. "Thanks for the talk. And the songs. I had a great time."

"Me, too," he says. "I meant what I said."

"Well." I take a deep breath. "We could continue. Talking, I mean. At my place."

He blinks. "You're sure? I don't know when I can visit. If I can ever visit."

"I understand."

He smiles. "I have my rental car. I'll follow you."

ଡ

I make us each a cup of coffee, and we settle on my couch.

"Big place for one person," he says.

I nod. "Hoping to fill it with a family someday."

"How many kids do you want?"

"Ten."

Charles's eyes go wide, and he laughs. "Shit, that's a baseball team."

I laugh with him. "I was an only child. It was lonely. I want a big, loud, messy family. What about you?"

"I'm the baby of seven," he says, "so I'm leaning towards two. A nice, neat, round, manageable number."

"Seven," I say. "What was that like?"

"Chaos. I had three extra mothers with my overbearing sisters, and my brothers just wreaked havoc. Two were dead before they could graduate high school."

"I'm so sorry."

He shakes his head. "It's not what you think. Sickle cell anemia. Runs in my family. Even though we were poor, my parents stayed together, and they ruled with an iron fist. If I stepped a toe out of line, I was punished. But it worked. All five of us went to college. We're all successful. I hope I can give my kids the same thing."

"They sound like amazing people," I say. "I love to hear stories of happy families."

I sip my coffee, and Charles cocks his head. "Was yours not happy?"

"No. My dad was a drug addict. He beat me and my mom. But hey, I got a steady stream of guitar and piano lessons out of the deal."

Charles sets his coffee down and takes my free hand in his. "You have beautiful hands."

I smile at him. He puts his lips to my knuckles and kisses them softly. My stomach flip-flops.

I set my own coffee down and shift closer to him. Our knees bump. Our eyes meet. My stomach rolls again, like I'm flying in a roller coaster, and I lean in and place my lips on his.

Charles is slow, lazy, almost, in the way he kisses. He takes his time, deepening the kiss and pulling me closer before he opens his mouth and gives me his sweet, soft tongue.

Oh. I melt into him. He holds my face in his hands and works that tongue slowly, so slowly, exploring every part of my mouth. I run my hands up his neck and into his hair, and he sighs into my mouth.

It's the slowest I've ever made love, and it's delicious. Charles takes his time, exploring my neck, my breasts, my stomach, my thighs, until we're finally on the bed, and he's over me, moving his hips in a slow, sensual rhythm that thrills every part of me.

Our mouths never part. In one smooth motion, he's deep inside of me, and we move together, two people who've connected on every level, who are connected, and he makes love to me for hours, literally hours, until we fall asleep welded together.

I wake alone, late for work, but I don't care. There's a note on my pillow.

You're walking your own path, Hope, and I'm so lucky to have stumbled across it. Call me. Any time. I'll dream about this night forever. Yours, Charles

I hold the note to my heart and force myself out of bed.

Chapter 17

"So update me on the last month," Dr. Steinburg says.

"I went rock climbing," I say. "It was okay, but not for me."

"In the interest of honesty," he says, "I have to tell you…your mother sent me a link to the video."

I sigh, and he laughs.

"At least you tried."

I nod. "I did. And I met someone else."

"Wow," he says. "I can't believe it. I mean, I can, but—"

I laugh. "I get it. I can't believe it, either."

"Do you want to share?"

"He's a friend of a friend and…I'll just admit it. I slept with him the night we met."

"And?"

"And he lives in Houston. His job doesn't allow much travel. We've been emailing, though."

"Is that what you want? A long-distance relationship?"

"Not really, but we don't have a lot of choice."

"Except that your job allows for travel, at least on weekends. And you have the money to go."

I nod. "I know."

"So something is holding you back."

"It's not him," I say. "He's...close to perfect. Smart and funny and sweet and easy to talk to. But my life is here. I don't want to move."

"Is that a deal breaker? Moving?"

I shrug. "I don't know. I want to say no, but the thought of leaving...it makes me sick."

"Why?"

"I don't know."

"If you say 'I don't know' one more time, I will throw you out," Dr. Steinburg says, his voice firm. "You are an adult, and you have a sound mind. Use it."

"But I honestly don't know," I say. "How do I figure out if moving is what I want?"

"You weigh the pros and cons," he says. "Do you want to be with this man?"

I nod. "I could be. If he were here, we'd definitely be dating."

"Can you live with only seeing him once or twice a month?"

I close my eyes and lean my head back. What do I really want? What can I live with?

"I think I met him too early," I finally say. "I haven't got my life figured out yet, and there are too many big decisions that would need to be made with him. I'm not ready for him."

Dr. Steinburg smiles. "That's a good answer."

"It is?"

We both laugh.

"You're making progress," he says. "And you're getting stronger. But you're not there yet. I think you should take any relationship slowly. Now, what about the guitar? Are you playing every day?"

I nod. "New stuff. Not the old, but I'm hopeful I'll get there."

"And why can't you play the old?"

"It just reminds me too much of Matt."

"Let's talk about that. What was right about your marriage?"

"We knew each other," I say. "I mean, all the little stuff, the quirks and the insecurities and the pet peeves and the likes and dislikes."

I get the stare and a nod.

"And...we were both supportive of each other. Of what we wanted to do in our lives. And I was comfortable with him."

"So to recap, you said WE knew each other, and WE were supportive, and that YOU were comfortable. What about Matt? Was he comfortable? And don't even think about telling me you don't know."

I shrug. "I thought so. But since you put it in my head that maybe he left because he couldn't be himself…no. I don't think he was comfortable. He walked on egg shells around me, didn't he?"

"You tell me."

I nod. "He did."

"Let me ask you something. Why did you never get help for your issues?"

"I couldn't face it," I say. "I was embarrassed, ashamed, angry, hurt. I just tried to ignore the whole thing."

"Did Matt ever encourage you to get help?"

"He tried. He even paid a psychologist to come to our house once. I just refused to talk."

"So what made this time different?"

I take a deep breath. "I needed a way to get my music back."

Dr. Steinburg refills his coffee mug from the pot on the table between us. "Did you and Matt have a conversation at the end? Did he explain why he left?"

"It wasn't much of a conversation," I say. "He said he loved me, completely, but that he needed to move on. He said we'd gotten married too young. I found out two weeks later that he'd been seeing someone."

"Do you think he was being honest?"

"You think he didn't really love me?" I ask.

"No, I don't think that. But I think there's more to the story. From what you've told me, Matt hated to hurt you. Perhaps there were other reasons he needed to go, but he was afraid to tell you. Do you think this is a possibility?"

Tears gather in my eyes. I nod.

"Do you think you're strong enough to hear the truth? If Matt were willing to give it to you?"

"I don't know" is on the tip of my tongue. But that's a lie. I do know.

"Yes."

"Then that's it. You need to ask him. If you don't know what went wrong, how can you fix it?"

Chapter 18

I gather my courage and call Matt at work. I figure he won't be able to tell it's me calling, and maybe I have a shot at speaking to him.

It goes to voicemail. I leave a bland, not-desperate message, asking him to call me back.

Martika calls just as I put my phone down.

"Hey. How's therapy?"

I smile. "Good. Going good."

"Benny just got off the phone with Charles. He says he's gonna try to come out next month."

I sit down and put my head between my knees. "That's good."

"What's wrong?" she asks. "I thought you liked him."

"I like him a lot," I say, lifting my head. "I think I just moved too fast."

"A rendezvous once a month is not what I'd call fast."

"No, but he's a keeper. And I'm not ready to keep anyone."

Martika doesn't say anything. I can hear her washing dishes.

"You're right," she finally says. "You just need to have fun. No commitments, no strings."

"Does that sound like me?"

She laughs. "I thought we didn't know you. You could be anyone. Maybe you're Batgirl."

I smile. "I'd rather be Wonder Woman."

"That's it!" she cries. "Thank you!"

"That's what? Thank you for what?"

"I need a birthday present for Ben next week. I'll buy him rope."

"Rope?" I say with a laugh. "Why the hell would you buy him rope?"

"So I can tie him up. It'll be a blast."

I shake my head. "Benny's a lucky man."

"Isn't he, though?"

I laugh again. "My mom's probably having a hissy. I was supposed to meet her ten minutes ago."

"For what? I thought you always see her on Sundays."

"Dinner with Randall," I say in best British accent. "He wishes to dine as a family."

"Is Randall *Daddy*?"

I giggle. "Yep."

"This should be fun. Is his wussy son joining you?"

"But of course. He must be present to pull out my chair and so that I have something to dab at with my napkin."

Martika cackles. "Let me know how it goes. And wear the heels. Why did you buy them if you never wear them?"

"I'm going. Thanks, *Mom*."

"Bye."

&

Dinner at the club, promptly at eight. So of course my mother makes me arrive at seven.

We order drinks and sit at the bar while we wait.

"So what's up with Randall?" I ask. "It's not getting serious, is it?"

"What shoes are you wearing? You're like a giant."

I hold out one leg and we both look down. "Hooker heels. Marti made me buy them."

Mom wrinkles her nose. "Really, Hope, do you have to use that language?"

"What fucking language is that?"

"Shhh!" she whispers furiously. "We're not at a saloon! Lower your voice."

I lean into her. "Why are you acting like this, like you actually like this place? Dinner at the country club? That's not who you are."

"I'm having fun with a nice man," she says, straightening her lapel. "Nothing wrong with that."

"You don't need his money."

"But why should I spend mine if I can spend his?"

I stare at her. And then we both laugh.

She waves a hand. "I'm not serious. He's not even that rich. But he treats me well. So he's an ass on the tennis court. Everyone has flaws."

"Some more than others," I say, and she swats my arm.

"Be nice. Chet is quite accomplished. You might have something in common."

"Doubtful."

"He's been coddled all his life, and he is a product of his childhood. You should recognize each other."

"No one ever coddled me."

My mother sighs. "Why are you being so difficult? They're both nice. Give it a chance."

"So you want me to chalk up their poor behavior to Randall's competitive nature and Chet's childhood?"

"You nailed him," she says, lowering her voice. "Randall sent me pictures of the bruise. It was awful."

I try to keep the smile off my face. "Do you still have them?"

She looks stealthily about the room, ensuring we're alone. Then she takes out her phone and starts scrolling.

"Here."

I rear my head back. "Holy Christ. I did that?"

"I told you you were athletic."

"Poor guy. No one deserves that."

The bartender takes my empty iced tea glass and gives me another. "No one deserves what?"

My mother holds up her phone. "Look what my daughter did. On a serve. Hit her partner square in the back. He cried."

The bartender winces. "Anyone I know?"

Mom opens her mouth, but then closes it and puts her phone away. "No. Pity. Hurt so bad he may never play again."

The bartender grins at me and goes back to his work.

"He may never play again?" I say. "Where do you get this shit?"

She smiles. "It's fun. You're right, I don't really belong here, so I can be anyone I want. It's like acting. I always wanted to be an actress."

"Since when?"

"Since always," she says. "You don't know every little thought I've ever had."

"Thank God."

"Oh. There they are. Sit up straight. They're coming."

I hike my skirt a little higher and twist my stool sideways. It never hurts to show a little leg.

❧

Randall kisses my mother's cheek and then kisses mine. "You both look beautiful," he says. "I'm sorry about your…" He waves a hand at me. "I get a little carried away when I play a game. Call me the stereotypical male."

"Guess I should bow out of the after-dinner Monopoly, then," I say, and he laughs.

"I'm truly sorry. Thank you for having a sense of humor about it."

Chet steps up. I give him my hand, which he squeezes, and then he leans in for a cheek kiss anyway. He smells expensive.

"How's the back?" I ask him.

"Sore," he says. "But at least I can hide it."

"I picked this dress because it's the same shade as my bruise," I say. "At least I match."

"Our table's ready whenever we are," Randall says. "Shall we?"

Mom slides off her stool and takes his proffered arm. Chet offers me his, and we head back to the dining room.

Chet pulls out my chair for me. I smile at him, and he slides it in smoothly under my butt.

We take our menus from the waiter. "What do you recommend, Chet?"

"The salmon is excellent," he says. "The scallops, too. Do you like seafood?"

"Sometimes," I say.

"What are you in the mood for?"

He suggested salmon and scallops. So I'm debating between them, but they aren't actually what I want.

"Beef, I think."

Randall chuckles. "Where will you put it, in that dress? Try the house salad with shrimp."

I glance at my mother. I get nothing.

"I think I'll have beef, too," Chet says, looking hard at his menu. "The short ribs melt in your mouth."

"I need potatoes with that," I say. "Should I go mashed or au gratin?"

"You pick one and I'll order the other," he says. "We can share."

I smile at him and close my menu. "What do you do for a living?"

"Real estate attorney," he says.

"Chet just made partner last year," Randall says. "The youngest at the firm."

Our waiter steps up and asks for our drink order.

"Margarita," I say. "Blended." My mother and Randall look at me in horror.

"Make that two," Chet says.

Randall orders a bottle of Chateau St. Something for them to split, and as soon as the waiter leaves, he leans across the table.

"I'm sorry, but you'll have to do without the free chips and salsa."

"How do you know about those?" I ask. "You mean, you've been to that type of place before? Mother, did you know this?"

Chet fights to hide his laughter behind his napkin.

My mother narrows her eyes. "Please stop. This is supposed to be a nice family dinner. We don't have to push each other's buttons now, do we?"

"What's your business, Randy?" I ask.

The muscles in his jaw clench. "I specialize in second-hand parts for automobiles."

I can't think of single comeback for that. "Sounds interesting."

"He's been in television commercials," my mother says.

"Oh. Really? Which ones?"

"For my business," Randall says. "Just some local spots."

"Would I have seen them?"

Chet smiles. And then he sings. "Grab and go, so you don't get snowed, it's the Grab and Go Junkyaaaard!"

I laugh. "No way! You're the Junk Man!"

"Laugh all you want, but it's a very lucrative business."

"I'm not laughing at you," I say. "You have to admit, those commercials are funny."

Randall cracks a smile. "If you remembered the jingle, they did the trick."

The waiter returns with our drinks and takes our order. While my mother and Randall talk, I'm left with Chet.

Which has turned out to be far more entertaining than I anticipated.

"So what do you do?" he asks.

"Nothing important," I say. "I'm thinking about a career change."

"What would you like to do?"

"Music," I admit.

"Tough one," he says. "I can see you've been raised with money and class, but it's exhausting, isn't it? I wish I had the kind of creative talent that would allow a career like that."

"You do?"

He laughs. "Why the surprise?"

"You just seem to fit in here very well."

"If you hadn't ordered the margarita, I would have thought you fit here, too."

I look around. "Yeah, I grew up with money. I can fit in here, but like you said, it's exhausting."

"What do you want to do with music? Do you sing?"

"Some. I write songs and play the guitar, the bass, keys…mostly guitar. But I don't know if I want to do my own stuff or write for someone else."

"Thirteen years of piano lessons here," he says. "In some ways I'm grateful, but I never connected to it."

"You learned the classical stuff?"

"Exclusively," he says.

"What kind of music do you like?"

He leans into my ear. "Country."

I smile. "Maybe you should learn some country songs."

"Only if I wanted to give my father a heart attack."

"How good are you?" I ask.

Chet smiles. "I can play Beethoven's 'Hammerklavier' pretty well."

I laugh. "That's some major shit, right there."

"Have you ever played it?"

I grab his hand and pull him up. "Let's try something."

"Where are you two going?" my mother asks.

We push our chairs in. "We'll be right back," I tell her.

I lead Chet over to the piano in the corner of the room. I slide onto the bench and pat the seat next to me.

He shakes his head. "We can't do this. They'll kick us out."

"Not if we're good," I say.

He reluctantly sits. "You are outrageous."

"If they make us leave, I'll buy you a beer and hot wings."

Chet laughs. "You're on."

"Okay. What's your favorite country song?"

"'The Dance' by Garth Brooks."

"That's perfect for piano," I say. "Give me a sec to get the tune in my head."

I close my eyes and put my fingers on the keys. I play without playing, moving my hands to make sure I've got the song right.

I open my eyes. "Okay. It starts here. E-B-E-F#—"

"Wait," he says. "How do you know that?"

"I hear it. I hear a note and I know what it is."

"Wow. Okay. I can't do that, but I can follow along."

"We'll do it in eight-note increments," I say. "I'll play it, you play it, then we'll play it together."

And as I play the first eight notes, my mother marches over to us. "What are you doing?"

"Teaching him his favorite song," I say.

"You can't do that! Not in the middle of dinner!"

Everyone in the dining room is looking at us. So I stand up.

"Excuse me. I hate to interrupt your meals, but I'm going to spend about ten minutes teaching this man to play a beautiful song. And then I will play the song in its entirety. I think we need a little music."

Then a man in a tuxedo comes over. "I'm the manager here. What's going on?"

Chet stands. "Why is there no music this evening? I come here quite frequently, and someone usually plays while we dine."

"Our pianist cancelled. I apologize, sir, but I can't have you—"

Chet pulls the man to the side. I watch him slip the guy a Ben Franklin.

"Perhaps to set the mood," the manager says, "you could play something to soothe the crowd."

Chet looks at me.

"I know the perfect thing," I say.

So I play a little Barry Manilow.

∞

Chet gives me a hug at my car. "Thanks for an audacious evening."

I hug him back, sincerely, and he winces. "Sorry!" I say. "Did I hurt you again?"

He nods and laughs. "Are you seeing anyone?"

Uh oh. "Not really."

"Are you up for a blind date?"

I raise an eyebrow. "A blind date?"

"My...the person I'm seeing, they have a friend. I think you'd be perfect together. We can do beer and wings."

"Will you promise to wear jeans?"

He hesitates. "I promise nothing."

I laugh and kiss his cheek. "Call me. I'd love to hang out."

∞

My mother calls me as soon as I pull into traffic.

"I don't know whether to laugh or cry right now," she says.

"Laugh. Crying will ruin your makeup."

"Oh you! Randall was so embarrassed! I don't think he'll ever come here again!"

"His loss," I say. "The food is great."

"Will you just stop?" she yells. "He broke up with me!"

I cringe. Even if I think Randall is an asshole, I didn't mean to hurt my mother. "I'm sorry, Ma."

"If you think he'll let you and Chet be together, think again."

"Me and Chet?" I say. "Chet's gay."

"He…what?"

"Didn't you see him singing along to *Mandy*?"

"That's a stereotype," she says. "Not all gay men love Barry Manilow."

"But how many straight men do?"

She sighs. "Poor Chet. No wonder Randall's up his ass."

"Randall doesn't know," I say. "And don't you dare say anything. Chet needs to handle it."

"Why would he tell you something like that? You've known each other for two minutes."

"He didn't tell me," I say. "He just...he stumbled over a couple of things, and I just know. I'll find out for sure next weekend. He's gonna set me up with one of his friends."

"That sounds promising."

I shrug. "Anyway, I'm sorry Randall's gone, but I think you're better off."

"Yeah, I guess. Back to the drawing board."

It's past eleven when I get home. I wash my face, gently, brush my teeth, and throw on some sweats. My phone rings just as I sink under the covers.

Matt.

My heart starts thumping.

"Hey," I say.

"Hi," he says. "I just got your message. Is it too late?"

"No, I just got home. Thanks for returning my call. How's the head?"

"Fine. What's up?"

"Um…I have a couple questions for you, but I'd like to talk in person."

"I don't think that's a good idea," he says. "Can we just talk now?"

"Okay." I shift higher against my pillows. "First…I want to thank you."

He hesitates. "For what?"

"For being so good to me. I'd be dead without you, Matt. Literally. You saved me, and you gave me love when not even my parents did, and I've just never thanked you for that."

Matt stays quiet.

"And the reason I'm saying this is that I never realized what that might have cost you. I never thought about it, but since I've been going to therapy...I'm seeing everything differently."

"You're going to therapy?"

"Yeah. Too little, too late, I know. But I'm learning, and I'm really looking at myself, and I need to know."

"Know what?"

"Exactly why you left."

Matt sighs. "It's done, Hope. We don't need to go there. I appreciate the thanks, and I'm glad you're getting help, but it's over."

"I know," I say. "I know it's over. But I'm asking for this one last favor. I don't want to make the same mistakes. Please. Just give me honesty."

"Don't do this," he says. "I don't want to hurt you. Let's move on."

"I can't!" I scream. "I can't move on until I know what went wrong. Please tell me. I can handle it."

"You already know. I know you know."

"I can guess," I say. "Is that what you need me to do?"

"Go for it."

I sit up and push the hair from my eyes. "You couldn't be yourself with me. I was so fragile that you had to tiptoe around me, and a lot of your energy just went into making sure I was emotionally stable. And you were willing to work with me, but you wanted me to help myself, and I just refused. You wanted me to have my own thoughts and opinions, and to make a choice every once in a while, but I couldn't. All the decisions, from the mortgage down to where we ate dinner, you had to make every single one. You were exhausted." I pause. "Stop me when I say something that doesn't ring a bell."

"You're doing pretty good," he says.

"And there were other things, little things, like maybe we weren't that passionate about sex anymore, and we were way too comfortable and things were too routine…but it comes down to me. I was a mess."

Matt blows out a loud breath. "You weren't a mess."

"I was," I say. "I still am. But I'm facing it. Finally."

We sit in silence. I'm using Dr. Steinburg's trick—when you want someone to talk, you shut up.

"Part of it was me," he says. "I knew all those things about you, and I accepted them a long time ago. But it got harder and harder to deal with them. I wasn't strong enough for you."

"Don't say that," I say. "Don't make excuses for me. You did way more than you had to, and I did nothing. I gave very little. And I'm so sorry for that."

"You gave," he says. "You loved me, and I always knew it, always felt it. I never doubted you once. I don't think many men can say that about their wives."

"Thanks. That's all. I didn't mean to bring up old shit. I just wanted to make sure I'm on the right track, and that you know...I know how good you are. I know I fucked up something really good."

"Hope...I'm glad you're getting help. I'm glad that things are getting better."

"Me, too," I say. "Sweet dreams."

"Sweet dreams."

So I'm sitting here after work, in my dry-clean-only clothes, watching a demonstration of how to throw a pot. I mean, come on. Everyone's seen *Ghost*. It looks easy, right?

The wheels we have are electric, almost like a sewing machine—step on the pedal, and the wheel turns.

"Start off slow," the instructor says. "You have to be in control. But this is physics. If the wheel turns too slowly, the clay will fall."

Why is every activity I try about physics?

I get my hands nice and wet and moisten the mound of clay in front of me. Ooooh, it feels kinda cool. I like this. I rub my hands over and over the clay, just enjoying the sensation.

"All your effort is being wasted on a chunk of clay that can't feel anything," the instructor says.

I slit open one eye (I hadn't realized I'd closed them), and look down. Wow. I've fondled the hell out of the clay.

"Sorry," I say. "I've never done this before."

"You don't say?"

She moves on and I scowl at her behind her back.

Fine. No more playing around. A masterpiece is waiting to be created.

I mold the clay into a vague bowl-like shape, without the actual bowl part. Then I give a tentative tap on the pedal. The wheel spins half-heartedly and the clay doesn't move.

Right. I need to mold it as I go. I need to be bold, give the pedal a little juice.

I press down again, keeping my hands tight around the clay. The clay starts to climb above my hands, getting taller and thinner. Cool.

Except I want a bowl.

I take my foot off the pedal and the clay collapses in on itself. I wet it some more, remold it into my mound shape, and start the wheel again. This time, I keep my fingers around the top and press down, trying to get a concave depression.

"That's good," my instructor says over my shoulder, and I jump. "You'll need to go faster to get the bowl shape."

"Like this?"

"A bit more. Keep your hands around the rim. A bit more."

I give it a bit more, and my nose itches. Without thinking, I rub it, smearing watery clay over half my face, and, I don't know, there must be a real ghost in here or something, because my foot presses down all the way on the pedal and the clay whips out with a moist squelch and plasters the face of the girl sitting next to me.

My dirty hands automatically cover my mouth.

"Oh, Christ," my instructor says.

Chapter 21

"It's just the gym," Martika says for the twelfth time. "You have to exercise."

"I refuse to leave the house," I say. "The gym's a dangerous place. I could kill somebody."

"Oh come on," she says. "Stop being so dramatic. You've had a few accidents, that's all."

"I don't need an accident at the gym," I say. "I could drop a weight on your foot and crush your toe. Or maybe my socks will get tangled in the gears of the stationary bike and I'll have a mangled ankle. Or I could slip on a sweaty mat and break my leg. I'm not going."

"This new you is not an improvement."

I roll my eyes, even though she can't see me. "You only say that 'cause you can't bully me anymore."

Martika gasps. "Do you mean that?"

"Shit, Marti, I'm sorry," I say. "Of course I don't mean that. Bad joke."

"Yeah. Okay. I'll talk to you later."

"Marti—"

But she's already hung up.

I flop back on the couch. Actually…it was only sort of a joke. There's some truth to it.

I wouldn't call Martika a bully, but she's used to coaxing me into things, whether I want to do them or not. I always give in. And that's on me, but she's having a tough time with it. I'm not the Go-Along Girl anymore.

I thought that maybe I had to face my loss of Matt to find my music again. I prepared myself for that, for turning sadness and grief into self-righteous anger so that I could move on.

I did not expect to look deep within and find a serious need to change.

And even now…you'd think an internal change would be just that: internal. But it's affecting everything and everyone around me.

Figures.

Chapter 22

"You're becoming quite the YouTube sensation," Dr. Steinburg says.

I wrinkle my brow. "Huh?"

"You…didn't you know?"

"You mean the rock climbing video? Yeah, I knew that."

"That's all you've seen?" he asks.

My eyes widen. "You mean, there's more?"

He takes his tablet off the table. "This is from one of those gossip sites. Quote, 'Joe Cruz's daughter is coming out of the shadows. Dinner at the club turns into a mini concert for these lucky diners. We're not surprised she's so good with those Cruz genes, but we are surprised that no one knew about it.' End quote."

"I…how did they know it was me?"

"They're reporters," he says. "They dig. And then apparently you took a pottery class?"

"How did you know that?"

He taps on his tablet. "'Hope Cruz Nails Another One,' is the headline." He flips the screen towards me so I can see it.

"Someone videotaped that?" I shriek. "What the fuck? This is your fault. If you hadn't insisted that I find a hobby, I'd still be anonymous."

Dr. Steinburg gives me a scathing look. "Really?"

I sigh. "Fine. I take it back. But this is ridiculous."

"I'm surprised it didn't happen sooner," he says. "Have you never had to deal with it?"

I shrug. "Not really. Ever since my dad died...my mom laid low. I've never even attended a concert as an adult, at least not until a few months ago."

"I have celebrity clients, Hope," he says. "It's a complication, but it can be dealt with."

"How? On one hand, I'm trying not to hide anymore. I'm trying to admit who I am. But I don't want to be famous or followed."

"Then explain this mini concert in the restaurant," he says. "What was going through your head?"

"I didn't know someone would tape me."

Patient stare.

"I was rebelling. And the only real way I can do that is with my music. It's the only area of my life where I have complete confidence."

"Did you enjoy it?"

I nod. "Maybe too much."

"Then you'll have to decide. There are consequences to our actions. Performing will bring attention. Attention may be too much. You have to decide."

I scowl. Decisions suck.

Chapter 23

My phone rings while I'm eating lunch at my desk. When I pick it up, I see the call is from Matt's mother.

My hands start shaking. I haven't spoken to her in months, but I've missed her.

"Hello?" I say.

"Hi, Hope. It's Jan. Is this a good time?"

"Hi, Jan. Sure. What's up?"

"I've been meaning to call…I want to apologize. I should have kept in touch."

"I get it," I say. "You don't have to apologize. He's your son."

"But you've always been my daughter," she says, her voice breaking. "I shouldn't have abandoned you."

I put my forehead down on the desk. "I appreciate that."

"Someone sent me a link to a video. The one where you're playing the piano? And I took it as a sign. I just want you to know you're in my prayers."

I smile at that. "I learned Barry Manilow for you."

"I know," she says. "Anyway, I just want you to know I'm here. I know it might be weird, us having a relationship, and I wrestled with it, but…I don't care. I'm willing. So if you are…"

"Let's stay in touch," I say. "It is kinda weird, though. And I don't know how Matt will feel about it."

"He's the one that sent me the link," she says. "I guess I thought I was being loyal, but to whom? We've been a part of each other's lives for so long. I don't want to lose that."

Huh. Matt sent her the video?

"Maybe we can have lunch," I say. "I'll call you next week."

"Thank you, Hope. I miss you and I love you."

Tears sting my eyes. "I love you, too."

∞

What the hell was that?

Why would Matt send her that video? He divorced me. Why does he even care what I'm doing? I mean, he wouldn't even meet me face to face, and now he wants me to have a relationship with his mom?

Okay, I made that up. Jan didn't say that. But he started it.

I think about Jan, and Matt's dad, Jim. They took care of me. I never really let Jan in, but she knew what I was going through at home anyway. She soothed my bruises, cleaned up some of the nastier cuts, even took me to her private doctor when my dad pushed me down the stairs and broke my arm. That was the day my mother finally moved us out.

And I suddenly realize that part of my sadness is from losing them. The only loving parental figures I've ever known.

And I wonder what that says about me. How completely out of touch with my own feelings am I?

Chapter 24

Chet offers to pick me up for our group date, and then he changes his mind.

"Actually, maybe you should drive yourself. In case you want to make a fast getaway."

"That really doesn't inspire confidence in the man you've chosen," I say, and he laughs.

"I'm thinking of you," he says. "But if you want me to drive…"

"You don't even know me and you know me," I say. "I'll drive myself. See you there."

"Ciao."

I look in the mirror for the tenth time and wipe the goo from the corners of my eyes. Looking good. Got my tight jeans on, a sexy off-the-shoulder sweater with hot pink bra just in case the strap shows, and my hooker heels.

Feeling good. I know Chet's got my back, I'm just living for the moment, and I'm ready to have fun.

And then a thought occurs to me.

This will be man number three in as many months. Seems like a high ratio, I mean, a guy a month? Isn't that a lot?

On the other hand, if I average it out, say, over the last twelve years, assuming I would have started dating at sixteen…that's only one guy every 36 months. That sounds a lot more reasonable.

Okay. I'm not a slut. I'm just a girl, meeting a guy. There's no guarantee I'll even like him, let alone sleep with him. In fact, that's a promise I'm making to myself right now: I won't sleep with him. No matter who is or what he looks like or how he makes me feel. I will resist!

Maybe.

๛

I walk in The Office from its strip-mall entrance expecting a little dive (not that I've been to many dives). But this place is plush—leather booths, Tiffany lamps, mahogany paneling, and a huge bar a la Cheers, complete with spit-shined brass rails. Cool.

Chet sees me and waves. All three men in the booth scoot out to stand like the gentlemen they are.

"Beautiful," Chet says as he gives me a hug. "You look beautiful."

"Thanks. You, too," I whisper back.

"This is my better half, Clancy," and I take his hand and shake it firmly, "and this is Spencer Giles. He works with Clancy at Mayberry & Foster."

I raise an eyebrow at Spencer as he shakes my hand. "Entertainment lawyer?"

"You know our firm?"

"I'm a client."

The three of them stare at me.

"I didn't know you did anything with your music, Hope," Chet says.

"It's not for my work," I say. "My mother and I hold the rights to a valuable catalog. I usually don't say anything, but I guess you'll find out anyway…Joe Cruz. Joe Cruz is my father."

"Holy shit," Chet says. "Did my father know that?"

I give him a small smile. "I'm guessing not."

Clancy laughs. "Let's sit and get a drink. I don't work on your account, but I wish I did, 'cause I could write this bar tab off."

Spencer looks down at me, even though I'm wearing those heels of death. He must be six foot four. "I don't work on your account, either, Hope. But if this is awkward for you, I understand."

"I'm fine with it," I say. "Sit."

He slides into the booth and I sit beside him.

"Ever dated a client?"

He shakes his head. "Ever dated a lawyer?"

"Nope. But I have a couple of questions. Maybe if I ask them you can write this tab off."

Spencer laughs. "No business. I just got off work and it's eight o'clock on a Saturday night. So music runs in the family, huh?"

I nod. "Does lawyering run in yours?"

"Fourth generation," he says. "My great-grandfather was a London barrister."

"So do you actually like your job or was it just a given?"

"Both. I took some heat for going into entertainment, but it's where my contacts took me. Clancy and I roomed at Yale. He had an uncle in film, an older cousin on Broadway, and it just made sense." He shrugs.

"So you represent actors?" I ask.

"No, actually. I ended up in the software division. Mostly video game companies and associated contracts."

He pushes up his glasses with a knuckle and clears his throat. He looks kind of…embarrassed.

"Do you play video games?" I ask.

"So," Clancy says, butting in. "Here's our server. What's your pleasure?"

They all order Stella. I stick to my guns and order a Corona.

I turn back to Spencer. "So…video games?"

Then Chet leans in. "I told them the story of our first meeting," he says. "Good Lord. Not a great day for my father."

I notice Clancy sit back and scowl.

"Well, I sympathize with you there," I say. "You and I, we needed to look elsewhere for positive male role models."

"That's the fucking understatement of the century," Clancy says, and Chet sighs.

"So video games," I say again, and Chet moves to speak. I lean over the table and zip his mouth shut with my finger. "Shut it. Let the man speak."

Spencer looks like he wants to barf. "Grown men rarely play video games," he says.

"In my experience, it's the opposite," I say. "I have a few *World of Warcraft* toons. I mean, who doesn't?"

Clancy laughs out loud.

Our beers arrive, and I scoop up mine and Spencer's before he can protest. I stand. "Can you guys give us a minute? Spencer and I need to have a chat."

ഔ

I lead Spencer over to another booth and plop down. He sits across from me and takes his beer.

"I'm gonna be sort of a bitch, and I hope you take it the right way, but if you don't, fair enough."

His eyes go wide. "Okay."

"I used to be just like you, hiding who I was and what I wanted and what I liked, thinking I needed to be someone else for everyone else. But let me tell you, and this is experience talking…it doesn't work. Now maybe you don't like the look of me, or the sound of me, or hell, the smell of me. Fine. We might never see each other again. But we came here with the expectation of getting to know each other. And we can't do that if we're not honest."

He picks at the label on his beer bottle.

"If you like video games, own it. If you want a glass of wine instead of beer, order it. Fifty years from now, do you want to be drinking Stella?"

Spencer cracks a smile. "Not really."

I laugh. "Chet means well, I know. He was trying very hard to keep you from telling me about the video games you play. But if I decided I didn't like you because you enjoy a certain activity…well, I wouldn't be the right girl for you."

"I play *World of Warcraft*, too," he says. "Name a video game system, and I have it. I can blow you away at *MarioKart*."

I smile. "I'll take that challenge."

He laughs hard. "I'm sorry, Hope. I don't date much."

"Why's that?"

"My job, and…I'm not good at this. Clancy and I go to a bar, and all the women flock to him. And he's not even interested."

I take a hard look at the package in front of me. Spencer looks put together, monied, decently handsome. Not a showstopper, but hey, neither am I, nor are most people, for that matter.

"I think you look great," I say. "And you're nice, you've kept the conversation going. You have a great job and you dress well. Maybe Clancy just likes all the attention."

Spencer laughs. "Clancy definitely likes attention."

I sip my beer. "So tell me something else. Tell me what food you like to eat."

He hesitates. "Italian. I like Japanese, too. And Mexican."

"That covers most of the culinary world," I say. "Now which do you prefer?"

"Pizza," he says with a smile. "You?"

"Ugh, I hate pizza. Pizza sucks. I don't know how anyone could like pizza."

"You...pizza? Really? Who hates pizza?"

I smile. "I have no idea. I love pizza."

He blows out a breath and laughs. "I like Van Halen. And Bon Jovi. And Cheap Trick."

"Love 'em," I say. "Eddie Van Halen is one of the greats."

"That's right," he says. "You must know a lot about music. You play guitar like your dad?"

"Yep. I met Eddie once. My dad was recording and Eddie walked in, and they started jamming. I wish I appreciated it more at the time."

"How old were you?" he asks.

"Six. I still have the recording. I should go back and listen to it."

"Is it out there? Are there other copies?"

"Not that I know of," I say.

Spencer shakes his head. "That would be worth some major bucks. You should keep it in a safe."

"Thanks, Mr. Lawyer," I say with a smile. "I have a question. Do you think fame is worth it? I mean, I don't want to be famous, but I want to play my music. Do you think it's worth it?"

He clears his throat. "Do you want my professional opinion, or my personal opinion?"

"They're different?" I ask.

He nods. "Professionally, I'd tell you that of course it's worth it. The big money comes with fame. But personally...no. It's not worth it."

"Why not?"

"We represent over 640 clients in the entertainment industry. I can name maybe five who aren't completely screwed up."

"Artists tend to be that way," I say. "The question is, were they screwed up to begin with, or did the fame screw them up?"

He slugs his beer. "Doesn't matter. Fame intensifies it. Fame contributes. Fame makes it harder to deal with personal issues. I wouldn't touch it with a ten-foot pole."

I sigh. "I think I knew that. I wish it weren't the case, but it is."

"Actually…you could pull a Hannah Montana. You watched that show as a kid, right?"

"That's a television show," I say. "Not reality. In real life, how could you possibly keep your identity a secret?"

"It can be done," he says. "You just don't see it done because entertainers are fame whores. It could totally be done."

I'll chew on that another time.

"Tell me something nobody knows about you," I say.

"Hmm. I write science fiction every night before I go to bed."

"Who's your favorite author?"

"J.S. Savage. You know him?"

I nod. "I'm a sci fi nerd. You like fantasy, too?"

"Duh. *World of Warcraft? Dungeons and Dragons?*"

"Ever played *7 Wonders?*"

Spencer laughs. "We have weekly tournaments. You should come some time."

"I'd love that."

We smile at each other. I like this guy.

Chet comes over to the table, a pout on his lips. "What are you two laughing about? Come back over and join us."

Spencer stands quickly and holds out a hand to me. I smile and take it.

☙

It's after eleven, and though I've had a great night, the three beers I've had are making me yawn. Chet notices and smiles at me.

"That's our cue," he says. "Shall we call it a night?"

Clancy frowns. "The night is young! Let's go bowling!"

Spencer looks at me, and I laugh. "Bowling? I haven't been bowling since the eighth grade."

"They have Rock 'N Bowl at the Newport Striker Lanes," Clancy says. "Loud music, neon lights, and fried mac and cheese balls. It'll be awesome."

Spencer smiles. "I'm up for it if you are."

"Do you actually want to go?" I ask.

He glances at the other two men and then looks back at me. "I'd like a little more time with you."

Ahhh.

So we head over for a little Rock 'N Bowl.

My first mistake is my choice of footwear: I have no socks. But for the low, low price of $8.00 (Spencer insists on handing me a $10 bill), I can get a little pair of low-cut socks, complete with a bouncy little ball at the back of the heel, out of a vending machine. They're all sold out of white, apparently, so I can choose lime green or hot pink. I go with the pink to match my sneaky bra strap.

I'm the last to get my shoes, since the dickhead behind the counter wouldn't give them to me until I proved I had socks. The boys have already changed, and it's freaking hilarious.

Clancy pulls the clown shoes off, but he's the most casual in jeans and a button-down paisley shirt. Chet looks like a rich janitor in his khakis and Polo. And poor Spencer. Size 14 shoes—in tricolored red, green, and white—don't go so well with a navy pin-stripe suit.

But as we all laugh together about the absurdity of our footwear...I take it back. Spencer with his square-frame glasses and his perfect crew cut and his larger-than-average-but-still-sexy nose and his meek manner and his sweet shyness...the shoes fit him perfectly.

"Choose a ball, love," Clancy says. "Aim for a ten-pounder."

I choose an orange-marbled ten-pound ball, and I almost drop it on my foot. Holy crap, is it heavy. So I hunt for a nine, but they don't seem to make them, and end up with an eight. My fingers stick a bit in the holes, but at least it's light.

I notice Chet picks a twelve-pound ball, Clancy a fourteen, and Spencer a sixteen. Yes, I'm impressed. That's two gallons of milk right there.

"Do you lift weights?" I ask him as Clancy puts our names into the computer. I have to lean in real close to his ear, since the music's so loud, and I give it a good look. It's totally clean, no hair or earwax or weird crust. Excellent.

"I swim every morning," he yells back into my ear. I pray I don't have any ear funk. "You?"

I just shake my head. My lack of daily exercise is about to become apparent.

"You're up first," Clancy mouths to me.

Of course.

Okay, so my upper body strength is shit. We know that. But I have nimble fingers and excellent wrist strength and control. If I can just get my arm to swing the weight of the ball, I should be able to aim it.

I stand at the line, everyone staring at me. I know this because I turn and give them a small smile before facing forward again. Right. Clancy gave me a little demonstration, and I just have to copy him. Two steps, swing, release. Right.

I take two steps…whoops! Forgot to swing. My feet slide on the slick waxed floor, and I do a little tap dance to get my footing.

"Sorry," I say. "Gonna try that again."

I go back to the line and take a deep breath. I don't bother looking back at the guys this time, 'cause they're probably all laughing at me.

I take one step, swing my arm back, take a second step, and that front foot just keeps on sliding. In my panic, I swing the ball forward, and my chubby fingers stick, seriously delaying the release of the ball. The weight of the ball finally pulls it from my fingers, and it sails above my head. I land in a perfect split, and I watch the ball crash with a loud thunk a foot in front of the line and roll slowly into the gutter.

I look back at the boys, who are all wide-eyed.

"At least I hit the right lane," I say.

&

Yes, I also ripped my jeans. The top button tore right off when I did those splits and pinged down the lane. I think it was the middle of the second game before Chet managed to hit the button with his ball and push it into the gutter.

Spencer was gracious enough to remove his jacket and drape it around my waist as he hoisted me to my feet. He even tied the arms in a neat knot for me. Which was chivalrous. My jeans were in no danger of sliding off, but they did gape at the top, showing off my hot pink thong. And that was not something I wanted the entire bowling alley to see.

Back at the bar, Spencer walks me to my car. Sparks aren't flying, but there is something there. He is such a nice guy. And after my father…I value nice.

"I had fun," I say. "Thanks for being my blind date."

He looks at the ground and awkwardly shuffles his face. "You had fun?"

"Yeah. Didn't you?"

He finally looks at me. "Of course. Yeah. I mean, yes. I had fun."

"But?"

He blows out a breath, and I watch him gather himself. "I…can I kiss you goodnight?"

Some women would find this a turnoff—I read enough romance novels to know this. But in my twenty-eight years, no one's ever asked me. And, also for the first time in my life, I like that I have a choice.

I put my hands on his chest and go up on tiptoe. He smiles, and I notice a dimple at the left corner of his mouth. His body is shaking under my hands, and I know how much it cost him to ask me. So I soften my lips and touch them to his, and he kisses me.

His lips are plump and soft. He puts his hands on my shoulders and squeezes tight, like he doesn't want to let go. It's such a small gesture, such an affectionate rather than sexual one, that it actually makes my heart skip a beat.

He pulls me into a hug and I nuzzle into his chest.

"Can I see you again?" he asks.

I look up at him and nod. "Call me."

"This is...I hope you don't think this is weird, but...would you text me when you get home? I just want to make sure you arrive safely."

Wow. "I think that's really sweet. Of course."

We say goodnight, and I drive back home. Before I even hang up my keys, I text Spencer that I'm home safe and sound.

He insists that I don't let the bed bugs bite.

Chapter 25

Sunday brunch with my mother. I tell her about my date with Spencer, and she's clearly not happy.

"You're a client, Hope," she says. "I don't like this. That firm knows a helluva lot about us. He can find out anything he wants to know."

"It's not like we have anything to hide," I say. "Once someone knows we own the rights to Dad's work, they can pretty much extrapolate our net worth."

She presses her lips together.

"Is there something else?" I ask. "Something you're not telling me?"

"I just want you to reconsider. Business and pleasure don't mix."

"It was one date," I say. "One kiss. It's not like we're getting married."

"I won't say another word," she says. "You know where I stand."

Actually, I don't. There are over a hundred lawyers at the firm, and Spencer doesn't even work in the music industry. My mother is making a mountain out of a molehill.

"So what's on tap next?" she asks. "On the hobby front."

I sigh. "Not bowling. That's for damn sure."

She smiles. "How about something quiet? Like knitting?"

"Funny you should say that. I've actually been thinking about knitting."

"Dear God," she says. "I was joking. Grandma Helen had a knitting addiction. When you were just a baby… that was the height of her mania. Our house was covered in yarn—tissue box cozies, tea kettle cozies, butt-ugly Christmas ornaments. The woman actually knitted a cover for a fly swatter. How gross is that?"

I laugh. "I have a purpose for the knitting. Martika's pregnant."

My mother grins. "Oh, how wonderful! A baby! Benny must be thrilled."

"He's more scared shitless right now, but I think we can get him to thrilled."

"It's settled, then," she says. "You have to knit. I still have the baby blanket Grandma knitted for you."

"You do? Where is it? I'd love to have it."

"You can have it when I'm dead," she says. "I sleep with it." I raise an eyebrow and she waves a hand. "Don't say a word. It's part of my therapy."

"And how long have you been sleeping with it?" I ask.

"Since…a while."

"Why?"

She lowers her eyes and straightens the napkin in her lap. "It's supposed to be a reminder. I wrapped you up in that blanket every night, and I washed it every day. I didn't do everything wrong."

I reach across the table and wiggle my fingers. She smiles and puts her hand in mine.

"You did a lot right," I say. "You're doing a lot right. Hell, I'm gonna bury you with that blanket."

She blows out a breath. "Thank God. I'd probably haunt you without it."

Chapter 26

Benny calls me as I'm driving home from work. "Hey, are you free tonight?"

"Yeah. What's up?"

"Martika's sick as a dog, and I just got called in to work. I was hoping you could sit with her."

I make a U-turn and head in their direction. "No problem. Can I get her anything? A smoothie, or some Pepto Bismol?"

"Let me ask her." I can hear him speaking to her in soothing tones. "Ice cream. Pistachio."

"On it. I'll be there soon."

It takes me about fifteen minutes to pick up the ice cream and get to their house. Poor Martika is doubled over on the couch, rocking back and forth, a small trashcan in her hands.

"It's morning sickness," Benny says, taking the ice cream from me and putting it in the freezer. "But apparently it should be called all-day sickness."

I smile at him. "Go. I've got her."

I sit next to her and rub her back. "I brought your ice cream."

"Sounds great," she says with a moan. "If I can just get past this bout…it will help." She closes her eyes and cradles the trashcan to her chest. "Oh, God."

She sucks her bottom lip into her mouth. I can see her fighting the nausea. And then she buries her head in the trashcan and heaves.

Oh, no. The smell...I'm not good with smells. I breathe through my mouth and keep rubbing her back.

She heaves again.

I gag. Shit! I can't lose it now.

She passes me the bucket and grabs a glass of water off the end table. She swishes the water in her mouth and spits it into the trashcan.

Poor girl. Snot is running from her nose, and her eyes are red and tear-filled.

"Let me get a tissue," I say. "Do you need the bucket?"

She shakes her head and curls into a ball.

Luckily, Ben has lined the trashcan. I take the bag out and twist it shut, leaving the can for Martika, just in case.

I gag again, and my mouth floods with saliva. No, no, no, I will not throw up!

I run through the house and to the side yard, dumping the bag. Then I run back to the bathroom and grab a box of tissues. Martika is again bent over the trashcan, spewing.

"What the hell have you been eating?" I ask.

"Don't make me laugh," she says, setting the can down and taking a few tissues from my hand. "Popcorn, extra butter. It sounded good at the time. I think I'm ready for ice cream."

I laugh. "Seriously? You just threw up like six times."

"Sugar," she says. "Sugar helps."

I'm doubtful, but hey, it's not my stomach.

I take the trashcan with me to the kitchen and rinse it out in the sink. Ugh. I try not to look, but my eye catches on the mess as it swirls down the drain. Several chunks of popcorn stick to the sides of the sink.

I gag again. And then I make the colossal mistake of taking a breath through my nose. Noxious vomit wafts to my nostrils, and I gag again. I put my hands on the edge of the counter and fight it.

"I'll just take it out of the carton," Martika calls. "Hurry."

Right.

I get the small container of Ben and Jerry's out of the freezer. I pry the lid off and grab a spoon, and my stomach rolls. Christ. I'm almost to the den when I gag yet again. I turn back to the kitchen...I can make it to the sink...run, feet, run!

But I'm not fast enough. I vomit all over Martika's Ben and Jerry's.

Chapter 27

Saturday night at Spencer's for a *7 Wonders* showdown. Right on. I haven't played the game since the divorce—it was one of Matt's favorites—but I know what I'm doing.

I am the only girl, which isn't surprising. What is surprising is that all five of these guys are lawyers, all over the age of thirty-five. You'd think they'd have something more important to do.

Not that I'm judging. I could play this game all night.

"So what's your strategy?" Spencer asks as our cards are dealt.

"I go where my cards take me," I say. "You?"

He grins. "Same. But most of these guys have one way they like to win. Watch for it."

I nod.

This is a little hard-core for me. Apparently, there's no talking during the game. The first time I try to ask IP Attorney Steve to my left about his job, I get shushed. With an actual finger to my lips.

"Don't take it personally," Real Estate Attorney Taylor says. "We had to institute a no-talking rule since the great Cheating Scandal of 2013."

"I guess I'll ask about that after the game," I say, and they all laugh. And then they shut up.

As the points are being tallied at the end of the first game, Spencer gets a call. He wanders into the kitchen.

"So the cheating scandal," I say. "Sounds scandalous."

Steve laughs. "Alan and I decided we'd form a secret alliance. We had code words for the cards we wanted, hand signals for what was going down."

"And you got caught," I say. "Smooth. Who's Alan?"

"He works with Spencer," Steve says. "Couldn't get a babysitter, or he'd be here."

"I'm gonna grab a beer," I say, standing. "Anyone want anything?"

Spencer comes back in with a bottle of whiskey and a tray of high-ball glasses, his phone wedged between his shoulder and his ear. "I filed it," he says. "Fuck that. Send Dan…yes, I got a confirmation. Are you freaking kidding me?"

He sets down the bottle and slides the tray on the table. The phone falls to his hand.

"I have to bail," he says. "My fucking secretary didn't …whatever. I don't have the energy to explain. I have to run to the office."

"Dude, come on!" Steve says. "Fuck 'em. You can go in the morning."

"Can't," he says. "I shouldn't be long. An hour at most."

"But we were gonna do teams this round!" Steve cries, as though all his plans have gone to hell.

"When I get back. Hope?" Spencer nods his head to the kitchen, and I follow him in. "I'm sorry about this. I truly won't be long. Will you be okay here?"

I smile. "I'm fine. Do what you need to do. An hour's not that long."

"It would be if you were the one leaving," he says.

I blush.

He kisses my cheek, and out he goes.

The guys have poured the whiskey neat, and they're all in the process of lighting cigars.

"You want one?" Steve asks.

I hesitate. "I've never smoked."

"It's not like smoking a cigarette. You just puff on it. For the taste."

He shows me how to cut off the end and how to get it lit. I try not to inhale, but the smoke hits the back of my throat, and I cough hard, my cheeks going red and my eyes tearing.

Steve pats my back while he laughs. "I told you not to inhale."

"Right," I say. Cough, cough. I take a sip of whiskey to try to soothe the burn, but the whiskey burns more, and I double over with a coughing fit.

Everyone's laughing at me.

And suddenly the front door opens. "I'm here. Let the par-tay begin!"

"Alan," Steve says to me. He pops to his feet and shakes the guy's hand. "My partner in crime."

"Jessica got home early from her movie," he says. "I figured it was early enough to make an appearance." He notices me sitting here, puffing on my cigar. "And who is this?"

I shift the cigar to my left hand and stand. "Hope. I'm friends with Spencer. Nice to meet you."

"Likewise," he says, holding my hand too long. "I didn't know Spencer had such beautiful friends."

I raise an eyebrow. "You're married and you're hitting on me?"

"Divorced," he says. "I'm not that big a douchebag."

"And why are you divorced?"

Alan laughs. "Okay, so I am a douchebag. Pour me a whiskey, my friend."

Steve hands him Spencer's glass, and Alan takes Spencer's chair to my right and drinks deep.

"So Spencer, huh?"

"We just met a week ago, but he's nice. I like him."

Alan shakes his head. "No accounting for taste."

I look around the table. Taylor and Michael and meek little Stan are all doing statue impressions.

"Why would you talk about a friend and colleague that way?" I ask.

Alan smiles. "I was only joking. Lighten up, babe."

Babe?

I'm not sure what to do. I mean, I know what I want to do, but I don't want to leave when Spencer expects me to be here. I grit my teeth and promise to tell Alan the Asshole off at the end of the night.

"You close that deal?" Steve asks him.

He holds up two fingers. "Two, baby. Two deals this week on my biggest account. I'm putting a deposit on that new Jaguar tomorrow."

"So the old biddy agreed to sign," Steve says. "Took her long enough."

Alan lights his cigar and waves the match out. "I take my fiduciary responsibility to my clients very seriously. Very seriously."

Taylor sits back in his chair. "You mean the Spotify deal? That's the one you closed?"

"And the Horton campaign," he says, nodding. "Fucking three million dollars to play those songs at his rallies for the next three months, and there's still over a year to go until the election. Easy money, bro."

"Senator Horton paid three million dollars to use some songs at his rallies?" I say. "Whose songs?"

"Joe Cruz," he says. "Fucking tightwad estate doesn't make half of what it could. They have 'principles,'" he says, giving me air quotes.

My heart sinks to my feet, and my body starts to shake.

I knock back my whiskey and lick my lips. "Joe Cruz?"

Alan smiles. "Amazing, isn't it? You can't even get his songs on iTunes yet."

"Joe Cruz…really?" My mouth can't seem to form the words I want to say.

He pats my arm and laughs. "You must be a fan. Hey, I'll talk to the estate for you. I'm sure I can sweet-talk them into sending me a few t-shirts or something." He smiles wide at the whole table, like he's the fucking Joe Cruz superhero.

"Who…" I start to say, and then I have to clear my throat. "Who gave you permission to let Horton use those songs?"

Alan looks at me, and I lower my eyes. "What's it to you?"

"Joe…Joe Cruz is…" And then I lift my head and hold his gaze. "I'm the fucking tightwad estate."

He blinks. And then he laughs. "Yeah, right."

"I'm Hope Cruz. I want you to get…I want you to get your ass on the phone and call the Horton campaign right now. If they play even one second of one my father's songs, I'm gonna sue that fucking smile off your face."

He sets his whiskey down and plucks the cigar from his mouth. "Hey, now. Take it easy. You're Hope Cruz?"

"I meant what I said. You have thirty seconds to get on the phone."

"Your mother, she's the one I always deal with. She—"

"Would never have agreed to this," I say. "Never. And I know you need both of our signatures anyway."

Alan looks at Steve, who's frozen in place.

"Think about it for a second," Alan says. "This isn't chump change. You can make millions of dollars. Horton—"

"Senator Horton wants to legalize drugs. All drugs. I won't support that, no matter how much money it makes me, because drugs ruined my father's life. You want to laugh at my principles, go right ahead. I'll take my business elsewhere."

"You can't—"

"I can," I say, pushing to my feet. "And I'll be sure to let the managing partner know my reasons for leaving."

He stands up beside me and tries to take my arm, but I shrug him off. "Just calm down," he says. "Sit back down and let's talk about this."

I fold my arms over my chest. "Did you get my mother's permission to do this?"

"I'm a fucking great attorney," he says. "I have always looked out for your best interest."

"Answer my question."

He just stares at me until it becomes too much, and then he looks away.

"As of tonight, you're fired," I say. "I'll be sending someone to conduct a full accounting of my interests. And for the record, you were right. You are a douchebag."

∽

I almost drive straight to my mother's house, but it's after ten. She's likely asleep.

And I can't possibly sleep. I spend an hour gathering all my statements from Mayberry, all my emails, all my contracts. I'm hiring a forensic accountant first thing in the morning.

My doorbell rings. Spencer.

"Hey," he says. "Chet told me where you live."

"You could have asked me," I say.

He shrugs. "I wasn't sure you'd take my call."

I wave him in and we sit on the couch.

"Why wouldn't I take your call? You didn't do anything wrong...did you?"

He sits back. "First, I knew Alan worked on your account, but I would never have asked him about it, AND...I only invited you 'cause I knew he wouldn't be there. I had no idea he'd show up."

I nod.

"And second...I didn't work on it, exactly, but Alan did ask me to look over a contract for your estate. About a year ago."

I frown. "Why would he ask you?"

"That *Cop Killer Reloaded* deal," he says. "We also look over the video game rights."

"What?" I shriek. "You're telling me that my dad's songs are being used in that disgusting video game?"

Spencer pales. "You didn't know?"

"Of course I didn't know!" I yell. "There's no fucking way I would profit off that! No fucking way!"

He scrubs a hand through his hair and stands, pulling out his phone. "I have to call some people," he says. "I won't let Alan get away this."

"I appreciate it," I say, "but I'll handle it. You have your job to think about."

"That's why I have to report it," he says. "I can't go down with the ship."

I nod.

"Hope...I'm so sorry. Not all attorneys are like Alan."

I nod again. "I think you should go."

He sags.

I put my arms around him in a hug. "You've been great. But I need to separate myself. Completely."

This time he nods. He kisses my cheek, and I show him out.

I lean back against the closed door and sigh.

Goodbye, Man #3.

I get a phone call at one AM. I flop my arm to my nightstand, fumbling for the phone.

"Yeah what?" I mumble.

"Hey, it's Matt. Can you answer the door?"

I shove the hair out of my eyes and sit up. "You're at my door?"

"Yeah. Can you hurry? It's an emergency."

I slide my feet into some slippers and make my way to the door. "Come on!" I hear him yell.

I yank open the door and give him a glare. Matt's on my stoop with a leash in his hand, a puppy on the end of it.

"My parents' house is on fire," he says, shoving the leash in my hand. "I gotta go. Can you watch her?"

"I, uh, what? On fire?"

"I just got the call ten minutes ago. Here's some food, get her a bowl of water, take her out to pee. I'll be back as soon as I can."

"What's her name?"

"It doesn't matter—"

"I can't just call her 'Hey You.'"

He blows out a breath. "Strings."

"Strings."

"Gotta go. I'll call you."

"Don't," I say. "Just come by after ten. We'll be fine."

"Thank you." And he rushes off.

Strings. Holy crap.

He named his dog after me.

And holy, holy crap. His parents' house is on fire!

∞

Strings is the cutest little thing I've ever seen. She's a chocolate lab with light blue eyes, so small she fits in my lap. I remove the leash and carry her to the kitchen, where I fill one bowl with water and the other with food. And that is my extent of dog care-taking knowledge. I've never had a pet.

Not to mention the fact that I'm butt-ass tired.

Maybe she can sleep with me. Since it's the middle of the night, she must be tired, too.

I set her in the middle of the comforter and crawl under the covers. She bounds over to me and licks my face.

"Whoa, dog," I say. "Sleep. It's time for sleep. Not play."

I put her two feet away and lie back down.

The dog gets back up and starts nipping at my hand.

Maybe she wants to be petted.

So I pat the top of her head. "There you go. Sleep."

But she wiggles under my hand and pops to her feet. I don't really know how she's standing, as the comforter is so plush it engulfs her.

Then she yips. She bounds over to me, nips and tugs at my hair, and then bounds away as I rise. She leans forward and wags her tongue, giving me a series of annoying little yips.

"I will not play," I say. "I'm going to sleep. I suggest you do the same."

I turn over and give her my back, snuggling into my pillow.

And then she's on me again, crawling over my shoulder, her rear feet scrambling at my back, until she spills over to my face, my nose buried in her puppy butt.

This clearly isn't going to work.

I get up and close the doors to my bathroom and closet. Now she's locked in. I set her on the floor and climb back into bed.

As far as I know, she doesn't bark again.

80

I wake and stretch and glance at my clock. It's only seven on a Sunday morning, but I need to get up. Alan the Fucking Great Attorney is going down.

As I rise, a putrid scent reaches my nose. I grimace. Dear God, what is that? Did my toilet back up?

I put a bare foot on the wood floor, but the floor's all wet. Oh no! I have a sewer leak in my house!

I reach for the lamp on my nightstand and twist on the light.

My room looks like a bomb went off.

The three decorative pillows I keep on my bed have been torn to shreds, bits of cotton stuffing and goosedown feathers strewn about. My slippers have been chewed beyond all recognition. The braided rug at the foot of my bed is decidedly unbraided and has been...befouled.

Strings.

"Where are you?" I say. I step carefully, watching for any more pee or poop. "Come out here. You've been a naughty dog."

I hear a very faint, raspy cough of a bark. I follow the noise to the window. Strings is tangled in the curtains, lying on her side.

I pick her up. "Come on, you. You just cost me a lot of money, you know that?"

I carry her out to the kitchen, and then I look at her. She's limp, and her breathing is wheezy and labored.

"Oh my God, something's wrong with you. What's wrong?"

As if the dog will give me an answer.

And then she spasms, her eyes rolling back in her head. I cry out and run back to my room, cradling her to my chest.

"Hold on, hold on, hold on!" I yell, shoving my feet into my tennis shoes. I grab my purse and keys on the way out and race to my car.

കൗ

I just keep her in my lap. She's breathing, but she's working way too hard at it.

I search for emergency vets on my phone and find one five miles away. Five miles sounds close. At least it did, until I start driving.

"Hang on, sweetie, hang on," I croon as I drive. Strings gags, and vomit leaks out the side of her mouth and drips down my leg. Tears pool in my eyes and drip down my cheeks. I can barely see to drive.

I blow through a red light. I roll down my window and wave one hand out.

"Emergency!" I yell. "Outta my way! Get the fuck outta my way!"

As soon as I have the building in sight, I'm yelling.

"Help! Help! Help me! Someone help me!"

I park the car and gather Strings to my chest. I run inside, yelling all the way.

"Help! She can't breathe! Help!"

A woman rushes over to me and takes Strings. "What happened?"

"Don't know," I say, as I follow her to a back room. "I woke up this morning and she was like this."

She places Strings on a table and bends over her. "I think there's something in her throat. Did she eat something she shouldn't have?"

I'm just staring at poor Strings. Why isn't the lady doing something? Why won't she MOVE?

A different woman comes over and takes my arm.

"Your dog will be fine," she says, leading me out of the room. I look back, trying not to take my eyes off the puppy. "How about a cup of coffee?"

I nod. She physically places me in a chair, and I put my head in my hands and sob.

She brings me a styrofoam cup of coffee and sits and rubs my back.

"How long have you had her?"

I lift my head. "What?"

"What's her name? How long have you had her?"

"Oh, she…she's not mine. A friend's. A friend had an emergency in the middle of the night, and I was supposed to be watching her. I was supposed to take care of her. It's all my fault."

"It's not your fault," she says firmly. "Accidents happen." She shoves the coffee into my hands and wraps my fingers around it. "Let me go see how she's doing, and then we can tackle the paperwork."

I stand. "Can I be with her?"

"Let me see what's going on first. Just rest."

I sink back into the chair and notice the coffee in my hands. I take a deep sip, but for the first time in my life, coffee doesn't make me feel better.

Fifteen minutes later, my tears are still flowing when the lady comes back out.

"We've got the x-rays," she says. "She had some fluff in her throat, which we removed fairly easily, so she's breathing now, but…she managed to eat something, and we're going to have to do surgery."

"Surgery?" I whisper. "Oh, God, no. No!"

She puts a hand on my shoulder. "It's routine, at least in our line of work. We're getting the bloodwork done now, and we're prepping for surgery. We just need your consent."

I squeeze my eyes shut. This means I have to call Matt.

"She has to live," I say. "You have to save her. Do whatever you need to do."

"I'll print out the forms and you can sign them," she says. She goes back behind the long counter and sits at a computer.

Christ. I pat my sides, searching for my phone. But not only don't I have a phone…I have no pockets. I look down at myself. I'm wearing a see-through white tank top, no bra…and a black pair of boy-shorts underwear.

"Be right back," I say, and I rush out to my car, but I realize I don't have my keys. But the door's open, wide open, my keys dangling from the ignition, my purse in plain sight on the passenger seat.

"Thank you, God," I say as I grab my keys and purse. I go to the back and pull open the lift. All I have is an Angels blanket that Matt and I used to take to night games, but it will do. I wrap it around myself and go back inside.

The lady has everything ready for me on a clipboard.

"Do you need the owner's permission?" I ask.

"Yours is fine," she says, "as long as you agree to financial responsibility."

"Financial?"

She points to an accounting at the bottom of the first page. The total is just over $3,000.

"The costs could change," she says. "It depends on how things go. But we're usually pretty accurate."

I don't blink. She goes through each paper with me, and I sign them all and pray.

"You go home now," the lady, Colleen is her name, says. "It'll probably be the afternoon before she's out of surgery."

"Go home? How can I go home? Won't she need me?"

Colleen gives me a hug. "Strings will be fine. She's in good hands. I'll call you as soon as you can see her."

I sniffle. "You promise?"

She smiles. "I promise."

∞

So I wander back out to my car, wrapping the blanket tight around me, and I say a small prayer for myself. I think I'm going to need it.

I take a deep breath and dial Matt's number.

"Hey," he says, voice groggy. My eyes tear again. That's his sexy morning voice. "Did I oversleep?"

"No," I say. "Are your parents okay?"

I hear him shift around on his bed. "Yeah. Lost the kitchen, but the rest of the house is okay, barring some smoke and water damage."

"I'm so sorry," I say. "How awful."

"Gotta hand it to their insurance company, though," he says. "An adjuster showed up while the firemen were still there. He got them into a hotel."

Andrea Ring

"So you were saved by the insurance adjuster," I say, and he laughs.

"Yeah. Close one. How's…my dog?"

And then I burst into tears.

"Hey. What's wrong?"

"I almost killed her!" I wail.

"What?"

"She…I woke up this…sniff, sniff, morning, and she…she wasn't breathing right, so I took her to the vet, and she swallowed something. She's…having surgery."

I hear the bed squeak. "Where are you? I'm coming to you."

"I'm on my…my way home," I say, my voice laced with mucous. "Meet me there."

"Give me fifteen." And he hangs up.

I'm fucked.

Chapter 29

I was hoping to beat Matt home so I could change clothes, but that fucking five miles…

He's sitting on my front steps when I pull into the driveway. He has circles under his eyes, and the smile lines at the corners of his mouth look deeper than I remember them.

He jogs over to me as I get out. "We can take your car," he says, but I shake my head.

"I need to change. And they said she won't be awake until this afternoon. We can't see her now anyway."

"Shit," he says. "Have any beer?"

"You want a beer at nine o'clock in the morning?"

"I've only slept for two hours," he says. "It was more like a nap. We can say we're still partying."

I shake my head and open the front door. I throw the blanket on the back of the couch without thinking and head to the kitchen. I poke my head in the fridge and pull out a Corona. I pop the top and hold it out to him.

Matt is staring at me with an odd look on his face.

"Did you leave the house like that?"

"Like what?"

"Half naked?"

I look down at myself. Hell. I fold my arms over my chest. "It was an emergency."

"Tell me what happened."

"Follow me," I say. "I need some sweats."

We head to the bedroom, and the scent hits us both.

"Did you forget to take her out?" he asks.

"I…"

We reach my room and we both pause. The destruction is mind-blowing.

"I'm so sorry, Hope," Matt says. He bends down and picks something up. "I think this is a goner."

My red lace thong, chewed, is dangling from his finger. I snatch it quickly and scrunch it in my fist.

He leans forward and puts his hands on his knees. "Jesus Christ, I had no idea one puppy could do so much damage. I keep her in a cage at home."

I don't know what to say. The magnitude of the mess is just starting to hit me. My eyes sting, again, and I just concentrate on breathing.

"I'll clean up," he says. "Make yourself some coffee, and I'll clean up."

"I'll help," I say. "I already had coffee at the vet's."

"Then sit on the bed and tell me what happened. I need some cleaning stuff. At least you don't have carpet."

I get Matt the supplies he needs, pull on some sweats, then I sit on the bed and tell him what happened.

"Don't cry," he says. "It's my fault. I dumped her on you."

"About that," I say. "Why me?"

He pauses in his work. "Honestly? You're the only one I knew for sure would say yes."

I scowl at that. Some people would take it as a compliment, but not me. It only means I'm a doormat.

He finally stands and stretches. "So it looks like I'm on the hook for three or four pillows, your black flip-flops, a pair of slippers, one red lace thong, a rug, and new curtains. Anything I've missed?"

I shake my head.

"I can buy the stuff," he says. "Or would you rather do it and give me the bill?"

"I'm not letting you buy me underwear," I say. "And how would you even know what shoes to buy?"

"You're a size nine," he says. "I know your style. I could buy you shoes."

I blink. Now that I think about it, he probably could.

"I'll do it," I say.

"So…you hungry? I'll buy you breakfast." He turns to go, as though asking me is an automatic yes.

I stand up. "I don't think that's a good idea."

He turns back to me, a quizzical look on his face. "Come on. You've gotta be starving."

"I'm fine," I say. "As soon as I hear from the vet, I'll call you."

He takes a step back. "Are you sure?"

"I'm sure."

"Okay." And Matt walks out.

I know I need to deal with legal stuff, but all I can think about is the puppy I almost murdered. I tell myself that no one's really at the firm on Sunday anyway, and I give myself permission to wallow.

And something else hinky is going on. Matt named his dog after me, and then he turned to me in a moment of crisis. What the hell is that about? Could he…might he actually regret leaving me?

I shut down that line of thinking. Whatever he's up to…it doesn't matter. I've moved on. Done.

When the call from the vet comes, I find I've fallen asleep on the couch. I take the time to brush my teeth and wash my face before I call Matt.

"She's out of surgery," I say. "She's gonna make it."

"Thank God," he says. "I'll pick you up and we'll go see her."

"See you soon."

Matt is silent on the drive to the vet's. I can't read him. Is he mad at me? Just worried? Tired? Who knows. I suddenly realize that I've never been able to read him. He's always hidden his feelings from me. It's a depressing thought.

Sweet little mess-maker Strings is awake but sleepy. Matt immediately puts his face to hers and gets a few licks. He cuddles her small head and scratches behind her ears and whispers to her.

It's the sweetest thing I've ever seen. I mean, I've seen him with dogs. His parents have always had a couple. He grew up with him. I knew he was good with dogs.

Out of sight, out of mind, for me. I never considered us getting a dog. And he never asked. I wonder why. He knows I would have agreed. I always agreed.

Matt straightens and turns to me. "You wanna?" he waves at Strings.

So I walk over and put my face to hers. She nuzzles my nose with hers and gives me a lick. I laugh.

"Thank God you're okay," I say, rubbing my cheek to hers. "You're a little fighter, you are."

The vet comes in and shakes our hands. "We'd like to keep her for a couple of days," she says. "She's fine, but she's still young, and I want to keep an eye on her."

Impulsively, I throw my arms around the doctor. "Thank you," I whisper. "Thank you so so much."

She smiles and pats my back.

She explains the post-op procedures and caregiving, and we each give Strings a little more love.

"Oh," Matt says. "You didn't say what she ate."

The doctor looks at me. "Oh, I…it was tough to tell what it was."

"You don't have any idea?"

Then she laughs. "Fine. It was part of a…a tampon."

∽

"I won't ask where the hell she found a tampon," Matt says as we slide into his Jeep. "With everything she chewed, it could have been half a dozen things."

I just…don't know what to say. It had to come from the pocket of my jeans on the floor. I'm expecting my period to start any minute, and I wanted to be prepared last night. But it's no business of Matt's.

"You surprised me," he says.

"How's that?"

"I've never seen you like that. Nurturing."

"I'm nurturing."

He shakes his head. "I didn't mean it like that. You are. I just…this was different."

"How?" I say.

"You…I could never picture us having kids," he says. "I know we talked about it and stuff, but I could never really picture you as a mother.

And today…I could totally see it. I've just never experienced that side of you."

Again, I'm at a loss for words. I've never acted like a mother because I've never had the chance. I've never had a pet, never been around children…of course I've never acted like a mother. I've never BEEN a mother!

Matt pulls into the driveway and I put my hand on the door handle.

"Wait," he says. "Wait." So I turn to him. "I…thank you for taking care of Strings. You saved her life."

I nod.

"And…maybe I can come inside."

"Why?"

He blows out a breath. "Jesus, Hope, work with me here. You fucking turned me on."

"I…what?"

He shuts off the ignition and shifts to me. "You're different. You're really working on yourself, and I can see it. You turned me down for breakfast, and you loved my dog…" And he leans forward.

I stare into his eyes. Matt has the kindest eyes. My breathing speeds, and I take a deep breath, and I can smell, faintly, his coconut shampoo, and I watch his throat work, and my hands itch. They want to touch him.

I lean into him, but stop just a heartbeat out of reach.

"Hope," he whispers. "I've fucking missed you."

"I've…"

I almost say it back. *I've missed you, too, Matt.*

Except in the past three months…I haven't.

I pull away. "I'm sorry. I have to go."

And I exit the car and head inside.

Second String

The String Serial
Part Two

Andrea Ring

Dedication

To my mom, who read *First String* and said, "You did get a little serious, but it's good. Keep going."

Chapter 1

I call in sick to work and drive to my mother's. She's sipping coffee in her yoga pants, gearing up for an early-morning class.

"Did you get fired?" she asks as she pecks my cheek and moves to the kitchen.

"Why would you think I got fired?"

She pours me a cup of coffee. "It's a Monday morning and you're supposed to be at work. Was there a gas leak?"

I sigh and sip my coffee. "I called in sick. We have a huge problem with Mayberry & Foster." My mother gives me a blank stare. "Mayberry & Foster. The firm that handles Dad's music rights?"

"Oh." She goes back to her place on the couch, and I follow her. "What problem is that?"

"Did you agree to let Dad's songs be used in that video game?"

"We signed to that hero game. The one where you play along with the fake guitar with those rainbow buttons."

"Not that one," I say. "It's called *Cop Killer Reloaded*."

"*Cop Killer?*" she says with a grimace. "That game is sick. No."

"What about Senator Horton's campaign? Did you know about that?"

She swallows her coffee. "You can't get worked up about all these inquires, Hope. Our attorneys bring us the deals, and we agree or not. It's not Mayberry's fault some jackass wants the songs."

"I'm not worked up about inquires," I say. "So they brought the Horton thing to you. And you turned them down?"

"Of course I did," she says. "Don't tell me you think we should do it."

I shake my head. "It's done. I ran into one of our attorneys last night, and he didn't know who I was. He let it slip that he closed both the Spotify deal and the Horton campaign deal for us. And Dad's songs have been in that *Cop Killer* game for a year."

She pales. "That's not possible. And you and I discussed the subscription service deals, and we decided against them. I had a very pointed conversation with them about it."

"Is it possible you signed something you shouldn't have?" I ask. "I mean, I don't know how they expect to get away with this. These are three very visible deals. They couldn't expect to hide them from us forever."

"It's possible," she finally admits. "I never signed your name, though. I wouldn't do that."

I rise. "I need to hire a new attorney, just for this. And then we need someone else to represent Dad's catalog."

"I can't believe this," she says. "These are attorneys! They're supposed to follow the law."

I just laugh. "Ironic, isn't it?"

Chapter 2

I drive home after dinner. My mother and I found an attorney to sick on Mayberry, and we managed to meet with her, retain her, and get the ball rolling. I'm looking forward to a hot bubble bath and eight hours of sleep.

Several cars are parked around my house when I pull into the driveway. I step out of the car, and I notice a woman in a suit get out of hers.

"Ms. Cruz?" she calls.

I close my door. "Yes."

"Penelope Capshaw with *Entertainment Now*," she says, jogging over to me. "Can I ask you a few questions?"

I'm totally caught off guard. "Uh, I don't think—"

"Can you tell us why you visited with an attorney today?"

I rear my head back. "That's none of your business."

"Does it have to do with your father?"

I push past her and head to my door. But she follows.

"Do you have plans to release an album?"

I unlock my door and turn on her. "You're on my property. Please leave."

And I shut the door in her face.

ဆ

I lock the door tight. Then I go to every window and door, closing shades and curtains, ensuring they're all locked. This is downright creepy.

After ten minutes, I peek through the side of the front curtain. The cars are still there, and Miss Penelope seems to be doing a TV spot, with a camera on her and a microphone at her lips. Christ.

I don't know the protocol on this. Are they allowed to just stand in my front yard? In the street? Can I call the police? Should I call the police?

I decide to ignore them for the moment. If they hang out on the property, then I'll make a phone call. Otherwise, I'll probably just get more unwanted attention.

Matt, my ex-husband, calls while I'm in the bath.

"I just wanted to thank you again," he says. "The vet called me today. I can pick up Strings in the morning."

"Glad she's recovering," I say. That poor puppy, Strings. When Matt had an emergency in the middle of the night and asked me to watch her, I left her alone on the floor of my bedroom, and she managed to swallow part of a tampon that was in my jeans pocket. The vet had to cut it out of her.

"I asked the vet about the bill. She said you paid it."

I sigh. "Let it go. Strings is fine."

"I can't let $3,000 go!" he says. "It's a lot of money. Let me make payments."

I have the money and Matt doesn't. Not that I'd point this out to him.

"It's my fault," I say. "I dropped the ball. Moving on."

"When did you get so stubborn?" Matt says. "I don't remember you being this way."

"I thought you wanted me to have a little backbone," I say. "Isn't that part of the reason you left?"

He sighs. "Classic case of not knowing how good I had it. Or maybe that getting what you want never turns out how you think it will."

"My stubbornness will never affect you again," I say. "We're divorced. There's no reason for us to ever speak again."

Matt is silent.

"Matt?"

"Yeah, uh, I should go."

"Kiss Strings for me," I say.

"Will do."

And he hangs up.

Chapter 3

Dr. Steinburg listens patiently as I tell him about our problem with our attorneys at Mayberry & Foster.

But he doesn't seem that interested. He wants to know how I've been progressing personally.

"I bought a book on how to knit," I say. "My best friend's pregnant, and I thought it would be fun to knit things for the baby."

He tries to hide a smile. "While that's a great thing to do in your spare time, it's not very social."

"Three men since I've started seeing you," I say, "and three strikeouts. Being social hasn't gotten me anywhere."

"Is that how you see it?" he asks.

I shrug. "On the relationship front."

"I can name five benefits of your sociability off the top of my head," he says. "Name two."

One springs easily to mind. "I'm not really pining after Matt anymore."

He nods in agreement, waiting for me to continue.

"And I'm able to play music again."

Nod. Stare. A little more nodding.

"And…I'm owning who I am more. I mean, I can voice my opinions. And I actually went out on a blind date, without my guitar, and I had a good time. I contributed to the conversation and got to know the guy." I smile in triumph. *See, Dr. Steinburg? I'm learning.*

He smiles back.

"How's your relationship with your mother?"

"Fine," I say. "She told me that you've had her sleeping with my baby blanket. As a reminder that she didn't do everything wrong."

Nod.

"And with this legal crap we're going through…it made me realize I need to take responsibility for my own life more. She's the one who's handled my dad's estate, mostly, and I let her, because it made her feel like she was taking care of me. But the truth is…he left everything to me. An attorney had power until I turned eighteen, and then, when I did, I gave Mom the power to continue making decisions, but that was because I still couldn't face much associated with my dad. It's long past time I faced it."

"He left everything to you? Everything?"

I nod. "I hated him for that, because I know a part of my mom resented it. I mean, how could she not?"

"Your mother never told me this," Dr. Steinburg says. "I strongly feel that if it had bothered her, she would have said something to me."

I shrug. "Who knows what goes on in her head? It's one of the few things Matt actually fought with me about."

"How so?"

"He thought I should give Mom their house. Sign the deed over to her, I mean. And it's not that I didn't want her to have it—I certainly don't want it—but I just couldn't face all the legal stuff. And I was pretty sure she wouldn't take it."

"She's living there now, right?"

I nod.

"I'm not going to try to persuade you one way or the other," he says, "but you realize this creates a difficult power dynamic between you two?"

I nod again. "I know. She's at my mercy. If I decided to screw her over, I could. I could evict her from the house, or stop paying her monthly royalties—"

"Wait. Your mother is completely dependent upon you for her finances?"

"I'm sure she has money saved," I say. "She makes, like, $50,000 a month."

Dr. Steinburg frowns. "And you're okay with that?"

My eyes sting. "My dad set things up this way because my mom was a bigger mess than I was. He didn't want me to have to rely on her."

"And he knew you'd take care of her," he finishes.

I nod.

"You know, your mother is not a mess anymore. She's stable, and she's capable. It's your choice, but I think you should think about separating your finances. I would say the same to any parent whose adult child were dependent on them. You cannot have an equal relationship with that kind of concentrated power."

I nod again.

"Just think about it."

Chapter 4

Martika invites me over for dinner. As soon as I walk in the door, she waves me over to her computer.

"Take a look at this," she says.

I'm looking at the *Cupid's Lair* website, and a profile of…me.

"What did you do?" I say.

"I created a profile for you," she says. "Read it. Tell me what you think."

"Martika."

"Just read it."

So I read aloud: "Single and sweet musician/writer looking for that special loyal guy to share music, memories, and passionate nights. I enjoy baseball, rock climbing, playing guitar, and cooking dinner for my man. I prefer boxers to briefs, open my presents Christmas morning, and hate rude people. I'm looking for someone active, fit, intelligent, and well-read. Cowboys, especially, should contact me."

She laughs, and I raise an eyebrow at her. "Seriously?"

"You can tweak it," she says. "That was just off the top of my head."

I close her laptop with a click. "No way. I'm not writing some ridiculous singles ad."

She opens the computer back up, totally unfazed. "Something like 10,000 couples a day get married from this site," she says. "Those are great odds."

"You actually believe that?"

"Ben and I met online," she says. "You know that."

"But you were both in the military," I say. "Neither of you had many options when you were deployed."

"You can't dismiss this," she says. "Tons of people meet this way. And it's totally secret. You can just browse your matches, and no one knows. If none of them interests you, then fine. No harm, no foul."

"With my luck, I won't get any matches," I say.

She nudges me. "Come on. Just tweak the ad and hit send. It'll give you matches right away, based on the questionnaire I filled out. Let's just see."

"I'm not contacting any of them," I say.

"Fine."

We work on my blurb for over an hour. What a waste of time. Martika reads the final product:

"Musician/writer looking for loyalty, honesty, and trust. I love to play my guitar, cook for my friends, and take care of my family. What you look like, how much money you make—not important. I want to be with a nice guy, be treated well, and give the same to him."

I nod once. Sounds good to me.

Martika sighs. "It's you. And it's honest. Let's just hope the lack of marketing pizazz doesn't hurt you."

I roll my eyes.

If a guy is looking for pizazz…yeah. Probably best to look elsewhere.

৪৩

I hit send.

The computer churns. And returns 75 matches.

Martika squeals. "See? I told you!"

Huh. I start scrolling through them.

"Wait. Stop! That guy is gorgeous."

"It says he's Mormon and that faith is important to him," I point out. "I'm not gonna try to convert a sexy Mormon."

"What would you convert him to?"

"Nothing," I say. "That's the point. It's important to him. Why would I waste his time?"

"Because he's hot."

"Why would he even show up in my search?" I ask. "Isn't religion an important factor?"

"Oh," she says. "I put that you're Catholic. Maybe that's why."

"My parents were Catholic," I say. "Not me."

"You were baptized," she says. "You had your First Communion."

"Stop hassling me," I say. "I don't practice, and you know it."

"Why is that?"

I glare at her. "I refuse to be like him. My dad actually carried rosary beads in his pocket every day of his life. What a fucking hypocrite."

Martika looks at me. "I'm sensing some hostility."

I laugh. "You think?"

"You know…religion and spirituality, they're personal. There are plenty of people from every religion who are hypocrites or jerks or outright murderers. That has nothing to do with your personal faith."

"Can we please table this discussion? We're supposed to be looking for hot guys."

"I thought you wanted a nice guy, not a hot guy."

I sigh, and we go back to scrolling.

"How about him?" Martika says. "Fourth-generation almond farmer. I didn't know almond farms were a thing. He looks fit. And farmers are hard workers. You like almonds."

"He's two hours away," I say. "Next."

We scroll past mustache guy, dirty guy, lives-with-his-mother guy.

"Here's an interesting one," she says. "'Divorced with three kids. Looking for an equal partner, someone independent, fun, and drama-free. I want to grow old with someone and share the important things.'"

I look at the picture. Distinguished, in a nice suit, bold emerald tie. Hair going silver, but in that hot Sean Connery way.

"Says he's 45," I say. "Do you think that's too old? And I want kids of my own. He already has some."

Martika looks at me. "You're interested."

I shrug. "I like the equal partner thing. And maybe he's pretty set in his life since he's older. I like the idea of not having to coddle someone."

"He's in Newport Beach," she says. "Message him. You have nothing to lose."

She's right. I have nothing to lose. So I type a brief message and send it.

Chapter 5

I meet with Mr. Alec Chang at his office in the Orange City Centre. I didn't tell him who I was, or give him any details when I made the appointment. I was afraid someone in his office would let it slip to the press.

Paranoid is me.

But I'm impressed that I get a cappuccino before I can even sit, and that I'm treated well by his staff despite being fairly young. I appreciate being taken seriously.

"Ms. Russell," he says when I enter his office. He shakes my hand firmly and waves me to a seat. "It's nice to meet you."

"You, too," I say. "Thank you for seeing me on such short notice."

"May I ask how you found me?" he says as we both sit. "If it was a referral, I'd like to thank the person in question."

"My new attorney recommended you. Alice Wills? I seem to be ass-deep in legal drama at the moment."

Mr. Chang frowns. "That doesn't sound good. I went to school with Alice. She's a good friend, and a great attorney. What can I do for you?"

"I inherited quite a bit from my father, but his entire estate went to me. My mother didn't receive anything. And I'd like to remedy that."

He takes out a legal pad and starts making notes. "Can you detail your father's estate for me?"

I shuffle through the papers in my hand and hold out the trust paperwork my father created.

"It's all here. Basically, there are three real properties, two in LA and one here in Orange County. There are 27 guitars, all valued over ten grand a piece. There's controlling interest in Plucked Strings Studios, a recording facility, also in LA. And then there's my father's music rights."

His eyes are glued to the trust. Then he raises them to me. "Joe Cruz is your father?"

I nod.

He sits back in his chair. "And what would you like your mother to have?"

"The Orange County home, for sure," I say. "Beyond that…maybe you can give me some advice. I mean, when she goes, it will all revert back to me anyway. But right now, I basically control her life, and I want her to control her own life. I don't want her to have to take care of too much, but at the same time, I want her income to be significant. So I was thinking of maybe dividing the music rights between us."

We go over all the numbers, how much income each asset brings in, how much each costs to maintain.

And then I tell him about our current legal battle.

"You need to have that resolved before we reallocate any of the assets involved," he says. "And I'd like to crunch the numbers some more and give you options. But we can give your mom her house right away."

I nod. "That's the most important piece."

"I can do that paperwork today," he says. "And the rest...how about we meet again next Thursday. We can talk over lunch at Modern Kitchen."

"You're gonna make me get dressed up, huh?"

He laughs. "I doubt the daughter of Joe Cruz has to do anything she doesn't want to do."

I shake my head. "I'm not a celebrity, Mr. Chang. And I don't wield my money that way. Being a Cruz is nothing but a burden."

His eyes soften. "Hope, I apologize. That was out of line."

"No, don't," I say. "I'm overly sensitive to it. I'm blessed, and I try not to take it for granted, but everything I have was given to me by a man I despised. He was gifted and successful, but he treated his family like dirt. I should have done this a long time ago, but I hate talking about it. I hate looking at his signature. I hate knowing I owe him."

I can't believe I just admitted all that. To a virtual stranger.

He leans forward. "My parents were Chinese immigrants. Never got a hug or a kiss from them my entire life. When I got into law school, Penn, they said, you should have gone to Harvard. When I passed the bar, they said, how many questions did you miss? When I bought my first home, they said, why doesn't it have a pool? And when I divorced my wife for being an alcoholic, they said, what did you do to drive her to drink? They owned a restaurant in China Town in LA, ran it for twenty years, but lived a very modest life. And when they passed away, to my astonishment, they left me over two million dollars in cash. I used it to start my own practice, and to put in a pool."

I smile at him. "We all have trials. I'm sorry. I didn't mean to dump on you."

"You didn't," he says. "Sometimes it's good to know we're not alone."

I nod and rise. "So Thursday. Modern Kitchen. Anything else?"

"I'll call you if there is."

He rises and shows me out.

∞

After work, I throw a potato into the oven and start a chicken stir fry. Don't judge. Potatoes go with everything.

I think about Alec, about being completely successful and feeling like it's never good enough. I didn't get that, exactly, from my parents—I was just ignored. An A on a test meant nothing to them, as they were too wrapped up in their own lives—or too stoned—to care. Maybe it amounts to the same thing.

And then I think about how similar our positions are. We both profited off of our parents. The difference is, Alec used his money to be even more successful. I haven't done that. I give a healthy amount to charity, sure, and I bought my home, but I only used enough money for a down payment. I make the monthly payments with my own salary. I've never really dipped into the estate and done something significant for me.

So…if I did decide to do something, just for me…what would that be?

Chapter 6

I met Sarah through this guy Sam, the first guy I dated after my divorce. Sam and I no longer talk, but Sarah's become a good friend. We go shopping, or have lunch, and I'm teaching her to cook. And in return, Sarah has promised to get me comfortable around kids.

She's a first grade teacher. She knows a thing or two about them.

I take a personal day at work, and I meet her in her classroom before school starts. She gives me a big hug.

"Can't believe I finally got you in here," she says. "You ready for this?"

"I have to be ready?"

She laughs and goes to her desk. She hands me a large cup of coffee and a cinnamon roll. "Here. You'll need the caffeine and the sugar."

She goes over the basic structure of the day as we eat, and then the bell rings.

"Follow me," she says. "The kids line up outside, and we lead them in."

Her students are lined up in a jagged row. They're so small and cute! Sarah marches to the head of the line while I hang back.

"Everyone ready?" she says. "Daniel, we don't pick our nose. Lily, hands to yourself. Onward!"

Whoa. Sweet Sarah has morphed into a drill sergeant. Martika would love her.

She waves me to the front of the room while everyone gets settled.

"Friends, this is Ms. Russell. She's going to help us out today. While I'm taking roll, let's get your math workbooks out. You know what to do."

A little girl with red pigtails and a face full of freckles raises her hand. "Someone stole my pencil."

"What should Josephine do, friends?" Sarah asks.

"Ask her neighbor," half the class intones.

"Or?"

Several kids raise their hands. Sarah points to a girl with glasses. "Reagan?"

"She can take one from the cabinet, but her table gots to lose a point."

"That's right," Sarah says. "It's Josephine's choice."

Wow. That seems harsh. Especially if someone stole her pencil.

Josephine starts asking the other kids at her table for a loaner. I sneakily move to the cabinet in question and pull out a pencil. When I think no one's looking, I stoop next to Josephine's desk.

"Oh my gosh, look! I found your pencil!"

Josephine looks at me. "Nope. My pencil had little hearts on it."

I look at the pencil closely. "I think you're mistaken. This is definitely Josephine's pencil." I give her a wink, but the kid doesn't catch on.

"No. My pencil—"

"Was yellow," I say. And then I lower my voice and lean into her ear. "Take the pencil. Then you won't lose a point."

Understanding dawns. She takes the pencil with a smile, and I stand up. Sarah's glaring at me, but she's working to hide a smile.

I smile back.

∞

The kids are learning to borrow in subtraction. Seems like a basic concept, but the workbook has me totally lost. It's telling the kids to draw blocks—42 of them!—and visually remove 17 to see how many are left over.

Sarah looks over my shoulder. I'm helping Ethan, a cute little blonde who can't pronounce his Rs. Actually, Ethan is helping me.

"You group by tens," he tells me. "No, the extra two don't matter yet. Now take one of the tens, and subtract the seven. How much do you get?"

"Three," I say, and Ethan grins.

"Good one. So how many tens are left?"

"Three," I say, but Ethan shakes his head.

"We already subtracted the first ten. It was seventeen, not seven, remember?"

"Right," I say. "I forgot. So there are two tens left."

"Now count the ones," he says. "Three plus two is…"

"Uh…five?" I say.

"So two tens plus five is…"

I smile. "You tell me."

"I already know," he says. "You do it."

Sarah laughs, and I glare at her behind Ethan's back. "Twenty-five."

"Yes!" he cries, pumping a fist in the air. "You got it."

I swipe a hand over my brow. "Phew."

ଛେ

The day ends with art, thank God. I thought I'd done okay in first grade, but times have changed. The whole day I've felt like an idiot.

Winter break is coming, so we're making snowflakes. Sarah demonstrates how to fold a piece of paper in fourths, and then how to cut out shapes in the paper so that when you unfold it, you get a snowflake.

This looks like fun. So I grab my own piece of paper and fold it. I pull up a small plastic blue chair next to smarty-pants Ethan, and Sarah hands me a pair of scissors.

Snowflakes are round, right? So I go around the edges of my square paper and round them all off. I notice my mistake too late, and I now have four little pieces of paper instead of one.

Ethan looks at me and laughs. "You cut the folds," he says. "Didn't you listen to Miss Klein's instructions?"

"Of course I did," I say. "I wanted four tiny snowflakes instead of one big one."

"But that's not following directions."

"This is art, isn't it?" I say back. "Isn't the artist free to create?"

Sarah goes to the front of the room. "Friends, is Ms. Russell allowed to make four tiny snowflakes instead one large one?"

"No!" the class screams. Sheesh.

"And why not? Madison?"

"'Cause she gots to follow directions."

Sarah smiles. "That's right. What should Ms. Russell do? Daniel."

"Get a new paper," he says. "And she should lose recess for not listening."

My eyes go wide. "Gee, thanks, Daniel."

The class laughs.

So I get another piece of paper.

When everyone seems to be done with this step, Sarah has the kids get the glue from their desks, and she sets out bowls of glitter among them.

"Remember, you don't need a lot of glue," she says. "Just a thin layer. The more glue you put, the longer it will take to dry." She comes over to me. "Let's go around and help them with the glue. And after they sprinkle glitter, help them tip the excess back into the bowls."

I wander around. Some kids are meticulous, putting dots of glue and little pinches of glitter on top. Some squeeze the bottles for all they're worth and use their fingers to smear the glue. Daniel has managed to squeeze out half his bottle, and glue covers both of his hands and the tip of snotty nose.

"Need some help with that?" I ask.

He shakes his head. "I got it."

Then he takes the bowl and dumps the entire thing on his snowflake.

"Whoa, there," I say. I take the bowl from him and set it down. "Why don't you wash your hands, and I'll get the glitter?"

He goes to the sink, and I try to gingerly pick up his creation without messing it up. But the glue has made it all soggy and floppy. I finally get it flat in my hands and move it over the bowl.

"You done yet?" Daniel asks. I look down at him, and he's still covered in glue.

"Not yet. Almost."

I start to tip the snowflake in, and without warning, another kid grabs the bowl. The glitter slides off onto the top of the desk. I sigh. And then I feel a tap on my leg.

"You done yet?" Daniel asks again. "Hey. You done?" He puts both hands on my legs.

And I take a step back to get away from his gluey hands, but I back into little Liam's chair, and I trip. It's like slow motion. I feel myself fall. I try to keep Daniel's snowflake safe, but the edge of it sticks to my hair and is ripped from my hands, I tumble backwards right onto poor Liam, and I reach a hand out to catch myself, and my hand ends up smack dab on Liam's snowflake.

And I keep on tumbling backwards.

My head hits the corner of a desk at the next table over and I'm out.

Chapter 7

An EMT leans over me and pulls my eyelids up.

"Can you speak?" he asks.

I lick my lips. "Yeah. I'm okay."

"Don't try to sit up," he says. He cradles my head and examines the back, parting my hair along the scalp. "This is pretty deep. You need stitches."

"Stitches?" I whisper. "I'm bleeding?"

He takes some gauze out of his medical kit and holds it to my head. "Who's the teacher here?"

I can't see Sarah, but I can hear her voice behind me. "I am."

"Let's get the kids outside," he says. "They don't need to see this."

Sarah gathers the kids, and I hear the door open. The EMT starts cleaning my cut.

"Do you feel dizzy?"

"A bit."

"Do you feel nauseated?"

I grimace. "If I think about the stitches."

He laughs. "Like I said, don't move. I've stabilized your neck. It's just a precaution."

I gulp. "You think I broke my neck?"

"I don't know," he says honestly. "The 911 call said you were unconscious. That was over seven minutes ago, and you weren't awake until I roused you."

I can't process this. Seven minutes…I don't remember being unconscious at all.

And I have a neck brace on? Oh my God, I've lost seven minutes of my life!

A sneaky tear leaks from my eye. "I've had five concussions," I say. "Is that important for you to know?"

He stops working on my head and looks at me. "Five? Were any recent?"

"No."

"How?"

My throat is tight. "Rough childhood."

His eyes soften. "We'll take care of you. The guys are bringing a stretcher in. Just hang in there. And if you feel like you need to vomit, let me know."

෨

Sarah is holding my hand in a little emergency room cubicle when my mother bursts in.

"Hope!" she yells. She throws her body over mine and hugs tight.

I pat her back. "I'm fine, Ma. Everything's fine."

"Fine? You're in a hospital! What happened?"

"I fell and hit my head. School is a dangerous place."

"School?" she cries. "What were you doing in school?"

I sigh. "You haven't met Sarah. Sarah, this is my mom, Rosalyn. Sarah's a first grade teacher. I was helping out."

Sarah gives my mother a tentative smile.

"Do you have a concussion?"

"Yes," I say, "but it's mild. No bleeding in the brain. Just a few stitches."

"How many?"

"Thirty-two."

"Thirty-two," she whispers. "Where?"

I point to my head, and my mother leans in for a look.

"They shaved half your hair off!"

I look at the ceiling. "It was that, or bleed all over myself. Stop it, okay? I'm fine."

She takes out her phone. "Can you sit up a bit?"

"You are not taking pictures."

"This will make a fabulous Snapchat story," she says. "People love this shit."

Sarah looks at me. I roll my eyes.

"Sarah, dear," my mother says as she snaps a final photo, "could you go to Hope's house and pack her a bag?"

"Of course," Sarah says, but I jump in.

"I'm not staying with you, Ma. I only need a babysitter for one night. Why don't you come stay at my house?"

"You have all those guitars in your spare bedroom," she says. "They creep me out."

I sigh. "Sarah, you don't have to."

"It's the least I can do," she says. "I almost killed you."

"Thanks," I say with a smile. "I have a travel bag that's already stocked, in the bathroom cabinet. Just some sweats and underwear would be great." She fishes my keys out of my purse. My mother gives Sarah her address, Sarah plants a smack on my forehead, and she leaves.

"How soon can you get out of here?" my mother asks, pulling up a chair.

"They're getting the release paperwork done now. Shouldn't be too long. What time is it?"

"Close to midnight. My phone died, or I would have gotten your message sooner. Are you in pain?" She takes my hand and squeezes tight, and then she looks down. "What is all over your hands?"

"Glue," I say. "And glitter."

"It's in your hair, too. Why?"

I just sigh.

I get through the night with my mother and settle back at home. Day two of a concussion...sucks. I've been through this enough to know. My head feels like one of those punchball balloons, while it's being punched.

But I refuse to take pain meds. Nope. No drugs for me.

I prop my laptop on my knees and check my email. Huh. Someone from the *Cupid's Lair* website messaged me. I click on the link, and it takes me to my dashboard on the site. The message is from Nick Martelli, the divorced father of three I contacted with Martika.

Hope, thanks for getting in touch. I admit, I haven't had much luck on this site, and I'm thinking my profile is to blame—I have more baggage than Samsonite (ha,ha). Reading your profile struck a chord with me. I think you went the honesty route, too, and that's important to me. Not to get too heavy too early, but I'm not playing around. I want to find a serious relationship, and it sounds like you're looking for that, too.

I have a few deal breakers, so I might as well get them out there. No drugs, no heavy drinking, no felonies. I have three kids, ages 10, 13, and 16, and while I won't involve them with my "dates" until I develop a commitment, I want a partner who will be a good role model. I share custody and have them with me every other week. They are my highest priority.

Boy, I've got you running for the hills, don't I? Seriously, though, I'm a pretty good guy. I run my own software company, I play golf and tennis, and I love going to concerts and movies. I also love to travel, but I haven't done much traveling since my divorce (three years ago). I need a traveling buddy.

Tell me about yourself and what you're looking for. I'm looking forward to getting to know you better.

Nick

Huh.

Brutal honesty is good, if a little awkward. But that's what dating is—awkward.

I kind of like this whole setup. I can get to know a guy without any pressure. No uncomfortable eye contact, no wondering if he's going to kiss me, no worries about my makeup or my breath. Maybe Martika knew what she was doing.

Nick, thanks for the reply. I love that you have a sense of humor about things while still taking this whole thing seriously.

No drugs, I only drink socially and quit when I get sleepy (which is way before I get drunk), no run-ins with the law. Sounds like we're good there.

I admit, I was hesitant to contact you because of the age difference, but I feel like a bit of an old soul. I was with my childhood sweetheart for 17 years (10 married), and we divorced a year ago. No kids. Three teens are a bit intimidating, but I'm open to it. As an only child, I've always wanted a large family.

I play tennis, never tried golf, love concerts and travel. Since my divorce, I've been getting adventurous and have been trying new hobbies. I play several instruments, and my music is important to me. This past year has been a process of discovery. I didn't realize how little I knew myself as an individual, a person outside of my marriage.

My idea of a great relationship would be one where we can both be individuals, but being a couple makes us stronger. Where we communicate openly and often, give and receive support, and where we are each other's greatest champions.

Does the age difference give you pause? What are you looking for?

Hope

I agonize over the message for an hour, then I finally hit send.

My phone rings, a number I don't recognize.

"Hello?"

"Uh, hi. Is this Glitter Girl?" a deep voice asks.

"Glitter Girl?" I ask. "I think you have the wrong number."

He laughs. "Is this Hope?"

I hesitate. "Yes."

"My name is Noah. I'm the EMT that treated you when you hit your head yesterday. I wanted to see if you're okay."

"You had those gorgeous eyelashes," I blurt out without thinking. "I'd kill for lashes like yours."

Noah laughs again. "Eyelashes...okay, I'll take it. At least you remember me."

I laugh, too. "Sorry. I have a raging headache and no ability to filter right now. But I appreciate the follow-up call. This is a first."

"This isn't exactly a professional call," he says. "And if you're in pain, I should let you go. Rest. Maybe I can call you in a few days."

"For what?" I ask.

"Well...I was talking with your friend, Sarah. The teacher? She gave me your number."

I blink through the pain and try to figure this out. "And?"

"And...I thought maybe if you want, I can take you out some time."

"Oh." I was about to tell him about my pain level, the slight nausea, the throbbing behind my left ear.

But that's not why he called.

"Uh...it's Noah, right?"

"Yes. Good memory. Especially for someone with a head injury."

I laugh. "I'm open to that. Except, yeah, I need a few days. Maybe you can text me next week?"

"I'll do that," he says, and there's an erotic promise in his voice. It makes me shiver. "I'm sorry I called so soon. Patience isn't my strong suit. So get back to healing, and we'll talk soon."

"Okay," I say. "And thanks for calling."

"Later, Glitter Girl."

I laugh. "Later, Noah."

I just stare at my phone. How weird was that?

And the phone rings again, startling me. It's my attorney, Alec Chang.

Butterflies unexpectedly tumble in my stomach.

"Mr. Chang," I say. "How are you?"

"I'm well, Hope. And please, call me Alec. I'm just following up on the paperwork I had messengered to you. Did everything look alright?"

"I haven't looked at it yet," I admit. "Actually, I had an accident yesterday. Thirty-two stitches in my head and seven hours in the ER. I probably won't get to it until tomorrow."

"Are you alright?" he asks, concern in his voice. "What happened?"

"I'm fine," I say. "I tripped and hit my head. Stupid, really. But I can't take pain meds, so it'll be a slow recovery."

"Is there anything I can do?" he asks. "I can have my assistant run some errands if you need it."

I smile. "I really appreciate that, but I'm fine. I don't know if I can make Thursday, though. Let me see how I feel."

"You recover and don't worry about the meeting. I'll follow up and see how you're doing. Just get better soon."

"Thanks, Alec. Take care."

"You, too, Hope. I mean that. Take care of yourself."

Double huh.

There was something in Alec's voice, a genuine concern for me. Hmmm. Gonna chalk it up to great customer service for the legacy of the Cruz dynasty.

All this communication has me exhausted. I snuggle into my pillow and sleep.

Chapter 9

Martika rouses me just after six. She gets a fresh bag of ice for me and lays it on the top of my head.

"Lift your feet," she says, and as I do, she sits down where my feet were and settles them on her lap. She rubs my toes, and I sigh in contentment.

"Thanks," I say. "This is the first time I've really been sick since the divorce. I didn't realize how awful it is to be alone and in pain."

"Nurse Martika to the rescue," she says. "It's a good thing I'm over the morning sickness. Can you imagine the two of us, rocking back and forth on the couch, moaning in unison?"

I smile. "Matt and I both had food poisoning once. It was awful. We were in that one-bedroom apartment, one bathroom, and I was hurling in the sink while he was shitting his brains out. Then we'd switch. Ugh."

"Ah, marriage," she says. "How's the legal crap coming?"

"Fine," I say. "Guess what? That divorced guy Nick responded back to me on *Cupid's Lair.*"

Martika smiles. "And?"

"And then the EMT that came to my rescue called me and asked me on a date."

She laughs. "That's awesome. Was he good-looking?"

"Very. And then…I kind of have a small little thing for my estate lawyer."

She raises an eyebrow. "Don't tell me he asked you out, too."

I smile. "No. But there's something there. He was very concerned when I told him about my accident."

She shakes her head. "Three men. Wow. Are you gonna date them all at once?"

"Of course not," I say. "I mean, only one officially asked me out. It's just kind of nice to have options."

"I don't know," she says. "Too many options in love is not a good thing. You're gonna start comparing them, feeling guilty if you kiss one and not the other…"

I laugh. "I haven't even gone on a date with any of them. I can't count my chickens before they hatch."

"They're cocks, not chickens," she says.

We both laugh.

The doorbell rings. Martika answers it and comes back to the couch carrying a huge bouquet of wildflowers and a gift basket.

"Man number three has struck," she says. "They're from Alec Chang & Associates."

She sets them on the coffee table, and I pull out the card.

Hope, here's to a speedy recovery. Let me know if there's anything I can do. Alec

"How sweet," I say. I dive into the basket. There are apples, Band-Aids, chocolate, a bottle of wine (*Better than pain meds!* a handwritten note attached to the neck says), a heatable neck wrap, an eye mask, fluffy socks, and a box of fortune cookies.

"Holy crap," Martika says. "I want stitches. What's with the fortune cookies?"

"His parents owned a Chinese restaurant," I say. "It's a nod to the story he told me."

"I thought he bought this basket off the Internet," she says. "You mean, he put it together himself?"

"Looks like it," I say. I show her the note on the wine bottle. "I told him I can't take pain meds."

She smiles. "I think you're right. There's something there."

⌘

Martika tucks me in bed. I've got my fluffy socks on and the microwaved wrap around my neck. She leaves, and I know I need to sleep, but this headache is making sleep impossible.

So I go back to *Cupid's Lair*. Nick has sent me a new message.

Dear Hope,

It's weird, isn't it, getting out of a long relationship? When I first moved out, I was at a loss. I had an entire apartment to decorate all by myself, and I had no idea what I was doing. I basically set up one bookcase to look exactly like a bookcase we'd had in our living room, and then I thought, what am I doing? I don't HAVE to put pictures of Vanessa on this shelf, and pictures of Caleb on another. I can do anything I want! So I mixed all the pictures up. Silly, I know, but it was a freeing moment for me. So I know how you feel.

What am I looking for? My ideal partner would be someone I have shared interests with, and someone who is content if I have to work late on a Friday night. Because I own my own biz, yes, I work a lot. But I also have more freedom, too. I can meet you for lunch, or take off work to watch my son play soccer, but you might have to have dinner with friends and meet me after for drinks. I'm pretty good at balancing (now, I wasn't always this good), and I keep my commitments. I guess I'm saying that I'd like a partner who understands all that.

As far as the physical…if your profile picture is accurate, all I can say is WOW. No worries there. I'm not necessarily looking for someone under thirty, but I'm open. As I said, I haven't had a lot of luck, but it's not because I've been overly picky, I don't think. A lot of the women I've met are looking for someone to take care of them. I want to take care of my partner in an equal way, but if…sigh. I'm not a sugar daddy, and that's what my profile projects, apparently. Let's leave it at that.

Tell me about your perfect date.

Nick

So I open a new message and type.

Nick, I had a moment similar to yours with the bookcase, but for me, it was my fridge. I was used to having Tabasco sauce and IPA beer stocked at all times. I bought those things after the divorce, only out of habit, and when I finally figured out how nice it would be to have a Corona in my fridge…there wasn't any room. I dumped all the IPAs down the sink, and suddenly my fridge was half empty. I think that sums up divorce nicely. :)

My perfect partner helps. If I'm cooking dinner, which I love to do, I'd love it if he came into the kitchen and kept me company rather than watching TV. If I come home from the store and have a ton of bags, if my partner is there and not busy, I'd like him to help bring the bags in. He'd have to be okay with me playing guitar. He'd give me time to spend with friends and not make me feel guilty about it.

Physical appearance is not particularly important to me, but I liked your picture right away. So no worries. :)

My perfect date is spent at home, actually. Just the two of us, music, cooking a meal, sharing stories, being silly, being intimate. I enjoy going out, but since you asked for my perfect date…there it is.

I'd love to meet for coffee. Let me know what your perfect date is and if you're interested.

Hope

I yawn. I almost shut my laptop, but I suddenly see three dots pop up under my message. Nick is typing right now!

So I wait…

Can you do coffee in the morning before work? I don't even know if you have a 9-5 job, but there's a great place halfway between us—The Grinder on 10th St? I have a 9:00, but if we meet at 7, that gives us two hours. The rest of my day is booked, and I'd rather not wait two days to meet you. Nick

Whoa. A seven AM date…that's a new one. I can push through the pain, but my hair…fuck it. If he's gonna test me with an early-morning date, I can test him with a shaved head.

Yes, I have a 9-5, but I have this week off. I'll see you there at 7. Good night, Nick.

Chapter 10

The pain this morning has backed off a bit, but my stitches have started to itch. Nick will probably think I have lice, the way I keep scratching at it.

It's December and freezing, so I don't have a lot of choice as far as wardrobe goes. Jeans, tight sweater, knee-high stiletto boots. My purple wool swing coat. Hair in a ponytail to hide that half of it's gone.

It's five after seven when I pull into the parking lot. There's already a line, and I notice Nick right away, near the front. He's in a black suit, polished back shoes, shiny cobalt blue tie. Mmm. He looks good.

Recognition hits him as the door swings closed behind me. He smiles wide, and I make my way over to him.

"So glad you could make it," he says, giving me a kiss on the cheek. "I was worried I'd scare you off with the early date."

"Not remotely," I say with a smile. "I love a man who's up and around early."

He grins. "Then you're gonna love me."

The line moves forward, and it's our turn. "What's your pleasure?" he asks me.

"Tall coffee black," I say. "No room for cream."

"Same," he says to the girl. "Anything to eat?"

"No, thank you."

We get our coffees and get settled at a table.

"Are you sure you're not hungry?" he says.

I tell him about my accident, and that my stomach's off. He winces in sympathy.

"I can't believe you came to meet me this morning," he says. "You should be in bed."

"I'd rather be here." Nick smiles, and his teeth are straight and white. "Tell me about your kids."

He ducks his head. "Caleb is 13, into soccer and basketball. Lucy is 10, a girly-girl, very social and bubbly and always wanting to be in the spotlight. And Vanessa is 16 going on 26. Bright, sweet…but she takes too much on herself. Especially since the divorce. I'd love to be able to get her to loosen up."

I smile. "She sounds like me. My parents divorced when I was 14, and I think I took everything too seriously. Maybe still do."

"I'm trying not to put too much responsibility on her," he says, "but she takes it anyway. I wish she had more fun."

"Is it necessary for her to be more responsible?" I ask. "I mean, is your ex-wife pulling her weight?"

He laughs. "Maybe not in the way I'd like, but yes."

"Then I think you have to let your daughter do what she needs to do. I mean, give her opportunities to be a kid, but don't make her feel bad for taking things seriously. It's a good problem to have. I think most parents of teens are trying to get their kids to be more responsible, not less."

He smiles. "True. They're great kids. I really have nothing to complain about. What about you?"

"You mean kids?" I ask, and he nods. "I don't have any, but I would like to have a few. Are you open to having more?"

"With the right woman." He holds my gaze.

"Is that a line, or are you serious?"

Nick laughs. "I'm serious. But it would have to happen soon. I don't think I want babies after 50."

I smile. "Fair enough."

"So tell me about your job."

I fiddle with the rim of my coffee cup. "I'm a technical writer. Beyond that, I'm financially independent. No sugar daddy needed."

He smiles. "Did you win the lottery?"

I shake my head. "My dad passed away and left me his estate."

"What did he do?"

"Music," I say.

"Would I know him?"

I nod.

Nick reaches across the table and takes my hand. "Don't tell me yet. Let's get to know each other without the other stuff."

Huh. "Okay. What about the rest of your family? Are your parents around?"

He nods. "They live two streets over from me. I grew up in Newport. Two brothers live in Orange County, too, and we're close. They're younger than me, and their kids are younger, but we still get along."

I sigh and prop my chin in my hand. "I love that. You are very lucky. I'm an only child, and the little extended family I do have...we don't talk."

"I'm sorry," he says. "That must be hard."

I shrug. "It's not all bad. I have my mom, and we're close. Although..."

"What?"

I cringe. "She's only seven years older than you."

Nick laughs. "How do you think she'd feel about that?"

"Honestly...I'm not sure. I never can tell with her."

"Does she live nearby?" he asks.

I nod. "Same city, five minutes apart. But she'll be supportive, I think. She just wants me to be happy."

We chat for another hour nonstop. Nick is interesting and funny and intelligent. He's a bit on the stuffy side, but I don't mind that.

Suddenly his phone beeps. He takes it out and pushes a few buttons. "That's my alarm. I have five minutes before I need to leave."

"You set an alarm?" I ask.

"I didn't want to be rude and constantly check my phone. This way I know how much time I have to ask you out again."

I smile. "You want to ask me out?"

He nods. "Are you busy tomorrow night?"

I pretend to think about it. "I think tomorrow night works."

"Are you comfortable with me picking you up? Or would you rather meet me somewhere?"

"You can pick me up," I say. "I've never had that. A real date."

I told Nick my dating history, but he still seems surprised. "Okay, then. How's six?"

I give him my address, and he walks me to my car.

I pause, fiddling with my keys.

"Thanks for the coffee," I say. "I had a good time."

"Me, too." He gives me a warm hug, and then a kiss on the cheek. But I don't let him go.

He pulls back, just enough to look in my eyes, and my brain goes fuzzy. His eyes are a copper hazel, with flecks of orange. He blinks.

"Hope," he whispers, and I push up on my toes and our lips meet.

The kiss is tender, soft. And then I open my eyes and find him staring at me, and I deepen the kiss. Nick responds. I drop my keys and put my arms around him, and I feel his hands flatten against my back and squeeze.

"That was unexpected," he whispers against my lips.

I pull back an inch. "Too much?"

"God, no," he says, kissing me again, and suddenly we're sucking face like two teenagers. We both break out in a laugh, and Nick hugs me to his chest.

"I'm looking forward to tomorrow night," I say.

Nick grins. "Me, too."

Chapter 11

I get home close to ten, and there's Matt, in blazer and jeans—his teaching clothes—waiting for me on the front steps. He jumps to his feet and rushes to my door as I pull in the driveway.

"What are you doing?" he says. "You shouldn't be driving!"

"Who told you?" I ask, shrugging him off as he tries to take my arm and help me out of the car.

"Benny. Why didn't you call me?"

I sigh. "Matt, I appreciate the concern, but I'm fine. Why would I call you?"

He follows me to the front door. "You've had five concussions that we know about, and probably lots more that we don't. You need to take care of yourself."

I open the door, and Matt follows me in.

"I'm fine," I repeat. "What are you doing here?"

He glances around, like he's not quite sure himself. "Benny said you were unconscious for ten minutes." As if that explains his presence.

"Seven."

"Seven minutes, Hope! Jesus! Get out of those boots and lie down. I'll rub your head."

Tears sting my eyes. "We're divorced," I say, my voice all croaky. "You divorced me! Why are you doing this?"

"You were hurt, and I wasn't there!" he screams. "Do you know how much that kills me?"

I swallow hard. "I'm sorry you feel guilty, but this is on you. This was your decision. You're not my husband anymore. You don't get to ride in and save me."

He stares at me helplessly.

"And frankly, I don't need your sword and shield anymore. I'm doing okay on my own."

"Don't say that," he says. "We both know you've never done well on your own."

I fold my arms over my chest. "Thanks. Thanks for reminding me that I'm grateful you left."

"Shit, I didn't mean it like that."

"That's exactly how you meant it," I say. "And you're right. I relied on you, and you let me down, and I had to figure out how to stand on my own two feet. You're not upset that I got hurt. You're upset that I don't need you anymore."

He clenches his hands into fists. "That's not true. I know I left, but I still care about you."

A tear slides down my cheek. "You don't have that right. I mean, you do, but you'll have to care about me from afar. I can't do this, Matt."

"Do what?"

"This! I'm moving on. I'm trying to get on with my life. But I can't do that if you keep showing up!"

He fights to hide a smile. "So you still care about me, too."

I throw my hands up. "Of course I do! I always will. But now we've dated other people, slept with other people…we can't go back."

His eyes narrow. "You've slept with other people?"

"Don't you dare," I say. "You cheated on me with a fucking grad student. At least I waited until the ink was dry on our divorce papers."

He looks away.

"You've been acting really strange," I say, "and I know communication has never been your strong suit, but why don't you just come clean. What do you want from me?"

He sighs. "Jesus, Hope."

"If I can yell at you, and I can stand here and listen to you yell at me, you can certainly be honest."

He stamps his foot, like a two-year-old having a temper tantrum. "I don't know what I want, okay? I just know that…"

I wait patiently.

"I miss you."

"Is it me you miss, or do you miss my cooking? My laundry skills? My amazing back rubs?"

He smiles. "And your music. The house is fucking empty without it."

I force myself not to smile back. "Are you dating anyone now?"

"No," he says.

"I am. And I'm not gonna screw it up for someone who doesn't know what he wants."

He shoves his hands into his front pockets. "And what if I figure it out? What I want?"

I shrug. "We don't always get what we want."

Chapter 12

I open the door to software-mogul Nick in jeans and a navy v-neck sweater. He gives me a single red rose and a tight hug.

"You look beautiful," he says.

I blush. "Thanks. Let me put this in some water, and we can go."

"Nice home," he says as he follows me to the kitchen. "Did you pick the colors?"

I laugh. Every wall is a different color, and yes, I picked them all. "I did. I like bright."

"I noticed that with the purple coat."

I find a vase and fill it with water. "What's your house like?"

"White," he says. "I don't have much patience for decorating. But this is…interesting. It's homey and artistic at the same time."

"My ex wouldn't let me paint our house," I say. "Not the way I wanted to. He was worried about resale value."

Nick smiles. "I'm guessing you're not worried."

I give a mock pout. "Are you saying that no one would like this house the way I decorated it?"

He holds up his hands. "Not at all. I meant that you must feel settled. Like you won't be moving any time soon."

Rose watered, I pick up my purse. "That's true. I love this house."

He takes my hand and leads me to his car, a Maserati. He holds the door open for me and helps me in.

"So where are we going?" I ask as we drive.

"You'll see."

We chat on the drive, and fifteen minutes later, we pull up to the beach in Laguna. Nick pulls out three blankets and a basket from his trunk, and we walk down to the sand. He lays out one of the blankets, and we both sit.

He rummages in the basket and pulls out two Coronas and a bottle opener. He flips the tops and hands me one.

"You remembered the Corona?" I ask.

He smiles. "I hope you were serious with that story. And yesterday you told me about your love of Italian food, so I brought spaghetti."

I smile. "That was thoughtful. Thank you."

We eat and we drink. Nick tucks a blanket around me as the chilly December wind picks up. I have a nice two-beer buzz going when he pulls me down beside him and points to the sky.

"Do you know the constellations?" he asks.

"Most of them," I say. "I took astronomy in college, thinking it would be about the moon and the stars. Turned into a math nightmare, but some of it stuck. There's Orion and his belt…the Pleiades…the Big Dipper."

He turns on his side toward me. "You constantly surprise me."

I flip to my side and face him. "Don't know why. You don't know me yet."

Nick smiles. "I know. I guess I just had this preconceived notion about 28-year-olds. And you don't fit any of them."

"Is that supposed to be a compliment?" I ask.

He laughs. "Tell me you don't have a few preconceived notions about a 45-year-old father."

I smile. "You're right. I have wondered."

"About what?"

"Sex," I whisper. "What does your body look like, feel like? Will you be teaching me things, or will you struggle to keep up?"

Nick laughs again. "Fuck. That's not what I expected you to say."

"Well?"

"If there's something you want to know," he says, "ask."

"Okay. How's your stamina?"

He wriggles a little closer to me. "I run five miles every morning. Never had a complaint."

I grin. "Is the hair on the rest of your body going gray, too?"

He smiles. "You'll have to figure that one out yourself."

"And how long does a 45-year-old man usually date his…dates, before he sleeps with them?"

"A 45-year-old man knows how to read his date," he says. "He waits for the proper time. Could be one date, could be ten."

"So he's not waiting for marriage," I say.

Nick's eyes go wide. "Are you?"

"No."

He laughs. "What do 28-year-old women want? How do they decide that the time is right?"

I prop myself on one elbow and look down at him. "I don't have a lot of data to go on. But I want to wait until I'm completely comfortable. I want the sex to be amazing."

Nick props himself up, too. "What do you need to be comfortable?"

"I need to feel like I can share anything, even the bad stuff, and still be accepted."

His eyes soften. "What kind of bad stuff?"

I shake my head. "I don't want to ruin this moment. I'm sure you haven't had a perfect life, either."

"I was a pothead in high school," he says, and I laugh. "I was lucky I graduated."

"I appreciate the honesty," I say, "but that's not what I meant."

Nick slips his hand in mine and squeezes. "You can tell me, Hope. I won't think less of you or judge."

His eyes are so sincere. His voice…so soft. But I don't want to be pitied. There's plenty of time for that.

"Soon," I say. "It's just about how I grew up, not about anything particularly bad I did myself. Someday I'll share."

He nods. "So what are you doing tomorrow besides playing hooky?"

I smile. "Actually, I'm meeting my mom for lunch. I have a surprise for her."

Nick raises an eyebrow.

"I'm finally signing over the deed to her house to her. It was my dad's house, but they lived there their entire marriage, and it should have been hers all along, but she signed an iron-clad prenup. I should have done it a long time ago."

"Have you consulted an attorney?" he asks. "There could be tax implications."

I frown. "Yes, *Dad*, I have an attorney."

Nick groans, and I flop backwards.

"I shouldn't have said that," I say. "Sorry."

"No," he says, "I overstepped. I apologize."

"No, you didn't," I say. "You were just giving advice. I should be able to take advice." I sit up and look out at the waves.

Nick sits up, too. "This is a problem, isn't it?"

I turn and look at him. "Maybe. But only if you see me as young and incompetent, and only if I see you as wise and all-knowing. And you have to accept that I will make mistakes, and I have to accept that you have life experience to share."

He shoves a hand through his hair. "I can't deny that I feel a little bit...wiser."

"And I feel a little bit young. But I can fight it if you can."

Nick takes my hand. "I'm willing to try."

I lean forward. "Did you feel that I was young and incompetent when I kissed you?"

He drops my hand and places his hands on my cheeks. "Do it again," he whispers.

Our mouths meet, and his tongue slips between my lips. His hands slide into my hair, and I crush my chest to his, and then the tips of his fingers dig into my wound. I wince and gasp, pulling back.

"Oh, shit, did I hurt you?" He grabs my arm tenderly, concern crinkling at the corners of his eyes.

I breathe through the pain. "It's okay. No harm done."

"That's a lie," he says. He gets to his feet and pulls me up beside him. "Let's get you home."

He packs up and drives me home, walking me to my door and even taking my keys and unlocking the house for me.

"Thank you, Nick," I say at the door. "Thank you for such a thoughtful date."

"I'd really like to see you again," he says. "Maybe this weekend?"

My head is pounding. "I'd like that. Call me tomorrow."

He gives me a sweet kiss and a wave, and I shut the door.

Christ.

I go to the bathroom, and my stomach churns. I flip on the light and try to look at my wound, but it's in exactly the wrong place. I touch a finger to it, and it comes away tacky with blood. So I get a clean cloth and hold it on my head. I kick off my shoes and curl up in bed. As soon as the pain lessens, I'll get out of these sandy jeans.

Instead, I fall asleep.

∞

I wake to the doorbell. That had never happened to me in my life, until a month ago when Matt's parents' house was on fire, and he needed a late-night babysitter for his dog. And now. That's twice. What's with the midnight emergencies?

But as I swing my legs off the side of the bed, I realize it's light out, completely light out. My clock says 9:30. Crap.

I push to my feet, and the room spins. Whoa. I grab the edge of my dresser for support. Guess I got up too fast. So I keep a hand on the furniture, and the wall, and gingerly walk to the door.

The doorbell rings again.

"Who is it?" I yell when I finally have the door in sight.

"Alec Chang," a voice calls.

"I'm coming." But to get to the door, I have to cross the open space to the foyer, without any support. My vision blurs.

"Hope?"

"Coming," I say again, but I know my voice is barely louder than a whisper. I have to get to the door.

Suddenly the knob is in my hands. I don't remember walking this far. I twist it, but the door won't open.

"Hope?"

"I can't…Alec, I can't…"

"Open the door, Hope. Can you open the door?"

Apparently I can. Because I'm suddenly staring at Alec from inches away, and he's holding me up.

"It's okay," he says as I slide to the floor. "Hold on. I've got you…"

Chapter 13

I wake up two days later and a pint of blood lighter. Well, I was a pint of blood lighter, until they gave me that transfusion.

Apparently I tore open some of the stitches, the deep ones, and I bled all night long. I was lucky that Alec arrived when he did.

And though, as a rule, I don't take pain meds...the nurses give it to me without asking. I sleep better than I've slept in weeks.

My mother insists on keeping me at her house. After going it alone the first go-round, I'm grateful. Even if the house stinks of Tahitian vanilla and her weird Patchouli incense.

It's been three days since I got out of the hospital, and my mother's barely let me pee by myself. I feel pretty good this morning, so I get up, place a plastic shower cap over my head, and take a shower.

God, does the hot water feel good.

I get back to my room and throw my towel on the bed. My mother actually put my clothes away in her dresser drawers, as though I'd moved in. I open the top drawer. Weird, this is so weird. Feels like I'm back in high school. Now, where did she put my underwear?

I close the drawer, bend down, and open the bottom one. Bingo.

And the bedroom door creaks open.

"She'll be so glad to see you," my mother says, and then she gasps.

I turn at the intrusion, my Captain America thong dangling from my fingers, and there is my mother and Alec.

I duck down behind the bed. "Ma!"

"Sorry, sorry," she says, a laugh in her voice. "I thought you were in bed."

"You thought wrong!" I yell.

"I'll just make us some tea," she says, closing the door.

Shit. I slide to my butt and stifle a giggle. Alec Chang just got a great view of both my ass and my boobs.

And me, in a shower cap.

So much for my little crush.

∽

Okay, so I dally. I dilly. I try to put off the inevitable, but my mother finally yells at me.

"Hope, come on, how long does it take to get dressed?"

So I steel my spine and exit the room.

"Hey, Alec," I say. "Ma, can you give us a minute?"

She huffs, but she stands and goes to her room.

Alec stands, too. "Hope, I am so sorry. I didn't see anything, I swear."

"Liar."

"You can't prove otherwise," he says. "But, damn."

I laugh. "Guess there's not much I can do about it. I could ask you to strip. A little tit for tat."

His mouth quirks up in a grin. "You have to buy me dinner first."

"The gentleman always pays."

"Tonight," he says. "Let me make you dinner." He takes my arm and guides me to the couch. "I'm serious."

"Isn't that against the ethics code? Dating a client?" I ask.

"I quit," he says. "I can pass your stuff to one of my associates."

I shake my head. "Why?"

"Honestly? I don't know. I haven't stopped thinking about you since we met. You told that story about your dad, and I just…I felt something. I haven't felt something in a long time."

"I felt it too," I say. "I told my best friend that there was something there."

"Are you going back home today?"

I nod. "Although I'm not looking forward to the cleanup."

"It's done," he says. "I got a cleaning crew in there."

"Thank you," I say, my eyes stinging a bit. "It's been weighing on me. I can't believe you thought of that."

"I saw the carnage," he says. "You bled all over the floor. I thought you'd been stabbed."

"Shit."

We smile at one another.

"So I can come over tonight and cook for you?" he asks.

"You cook, huh?"

"Family biz."

I smile. "Then it's a date."

My mother comes out with my phone pressed to her ear.

"You can't fire her! She's been in the hospital! Of course we have a doctor's note! Fine. You'll be hearing from my attorney!"

I stand. "They fired me?"

She waves a hand. "It won't stick. What an asshole your boss is." And then my phone rings, and she answers it without asking me. "Who is this? Nick? Nick who? This is Hope's mother. She's been in the hospital. Yes, she tore some stitches and almost bled to death. Why didn't she call you? She was at death's door! Why don't you call her in a few days?"

I wince.

"Who's Nick?" she demands.

"A friend," I say. "Although I don't know if he'll want to be my friend anymore after that."

She tosses my phone at me. "You need new friends."

I look at Alec. She's right.

Alec shows up on time for dinner, but instead of groceries, he's carrying take-out bags.

"I hope you don't mind," he says. "My last appointment ran late, and I'm out of energy. Rain check on the homemade meal?"

I take a bag from him. "No problem. What are we eating?"

"The best macaroni and cheese in the world," he says.

I raise an eyebrow. "No way. From Haven Gastropub?"

"You know it?"

I grin. "Know it? It's my favorite restaurant!"

Alec shakes his head as we move to the kitchen and open the bags. "I can't believe that. I eat there at least twice a week. It's a five-minute walk from my house."

I grab us each a beer. "You live in Old Towne Orange? I love that area."

"Me, too," he says as we sit and dig in. "I've always loved the architecture, particularly the Arts and Crafts style. Before my divorce, we lived in Irvine, land of the tract home. I wanted a house with some character."

"I almost bought there after my divorce," I say, "but I decided to stay close to my mom."

"So family's important to you?"

I nod. "As you know, I didn't have a great family growing up. But my ex's family was pretty solid. I know we can't all be born to the perfect family, but I want my kids to be."

"I have a huge family," he says. "My dad was the only boy of eight kids, and my aunts all relied on him and looked up to him. And now they're intent on taking care of me."

"Are they all local?"

Alec nods. "LA, but the two-hour drive doesn't deter them. If I never wanted to do another load of laundry or take another trip to the grocery store, I'd be set."

I laugh. "I can't imagine that." And then my eyes sting and I blink.

"What's wrong?"

I shake my head. "It's silly."

"I don't mind silly."

I force myself to smile. "I just realized…I've never had that. Family I could totally rely on no matter what. I mean, I have my best friend, and she's amazing, and my mom's okay now, but…ugh. Ignore me. I'm fine."

"It's okay to share what you're feeling," he says.

"But I sound pitiful."

"You sound like you've been through some tough things, and you're trying to find your way out. There's nothing wrong with that."

"Thanks," I say, giving him a genuine smile.

Alec smiles back. "So do you play guitar like your dad?"

"I wouldn't say I play like my dad, but I play."

"My parents forced clarinet lessons on me. Seven years. You can imagine my dating life in high school."

"High school girls are stupid. I can appreciate a clarinet player."

Alec shudders. "I still have nightmares about it."

I laugh. "I have a clarinet. Will you play something?"

He gapes at me. "You own a clarinet? Do you know how to play it?"

"Not really," I say. "A little bit. I like the way it sounds."

He shakes his head. "Too bad we didn't meet when I was sixteen. You would have been all over me."

ॐ

We spend five hours lingering over dinner, laughing and talking. But as it nears midnight, I physically wince as my pain meds wear off and my stitches throb.

"You okay?" Alex asks.

I nod slowly. "Just my head. I think I better get to bed."

He glances at his watch. "Shit. I've kept you up way too late."

Alec pulls me to my feet and gives me a hug. "Thanks for the company. You...this was fun."

"It was," I say. "Thanks for dinner."

We pause awkwardly. I want to kiss him, but my head is screaming at me.

Alec senses this, I think. He kisses my cheek, and I walk him to the door.

"When you have a free night," I say, "let me know. I'd like to do this again."

Alec nods. "Me, too."

Chapter 15

I didn't fall asleep until close to dawn, and by the time I woke up, even though I was starving, I didn't have the energy to make anything. I plowed my way through an apple, some carrot sticks, and two bowls of cereal.

But my body is used to starch and fat. Sad but true. So when Alec calls and asks if I'm up for dinner again tonight, I start drooling.

He asks me what I feel like eating, and I hem and haw. I'm trying to think of something Chinese that sounds good to my empty stomach, but the only thing that flashes through my brain is CHEESEBURGER.

He laughs. "I can do a mean cheeseburger."

So we're sitting on my back patio, the burgers on the grill, sipping hot chocolate. Hey, it's cold outside, and coffee's been burning a hole in my belly lately. Chocolate sounded perfect, and Alec graciously agreed to appease me.

"Do you need another blanket?" he asks as he notices me shiver.

I shake my head.

"Are you sure? We can move inside."

"I'm not cold, Alec," I say.

"But you're shaking. I can see it from here."

I laugh. "That's because you're here. And you make me nervous."

He rears back. "I'm sorry. I didn't mean to—"

"It's not anything you're doing," I say. "Well, it is. You're nice and smart and thoughtful. And you rescued me. And we have a ton of things in common. And I keep thinking about you walking into my room, and I wasn't wearing anything apart from that stupid cap, which we won't mention. 'Cause when I think about it, my hair is perfect and long and brushed, and I look beautiful, and you just cross the room and take me."

Alec just stares at me.

"So that's why I'm shaking. I want to touch you so badly I have to sit on my hands to keep myself from mauling you."

He smiles and lowers his eyes to his mug. "I was raised in a very Christian household, did I tell you that?"

"No."

"I met my ex-wife at church. She was my first."

"And how many have there been since?" I ask.

He shakes his head. "None."

"That was me," I say. "Married my first everything. But I've dated since. I get it."

"I don't have reservations," he says. "I mean, I'm not saving myself. I just haven't met anyone."

"Are you nervous?"

"Not with you." And then he laughs. "That's not entirely true. My wife wasn't very adventurous. I think I'm way behind the curve."

I sit back in my chair and sip my hot chocolate. "Is there something you've always wanted to try but never have?"

Alec ducks his head. "It's embarrassing. But in the interest of honesty…I've never given nor received oral sex."

I blink. "That sucks."

We both laugh.

"How's your head?" he asks.

"I'm riding the codeine," I say, "and I never thought I'd say that. This is the last day I'll take it, though."

Alec holds out a hand, and I slip mine in his, and he pulls me to my feet.

My shivers intensify. The look in his eyes…he's thinking about going down on me. And boy, do I want him to.

We're just holding hands and staring into each other's eyes. Neither of us makes a move.

"I'm going to kiss you," he whispers, but he still doesn't move.

I just nod lamely.

His fingers start to caress mine. He brings my hand to his mouth and kisses my palm. Then he slides my middle finger into his mouth and sucks on it.

Wah. I never knew that felt so good. I close my eyes, and I feel the suction of his lips, the tickling graze of his tongue, his warm mouth...

He reaches with his other hand for my cheek. He trails his fingers down the side of my face and traces my lips. I open them, and he puts his thumb in my mouth.

I suck. I lick. And his eyelids lower, and he shifts his stance, but still, he doesn't move closer.

I shudder, and my clit tingles.

And suddenly, he's on me. Alec's entire body is pressed to mine, and he welds his lips to mine, and our tongues dance. He cradles my cheeks in his hands as he worships my mouth.

"God, you taste good," he says as he trails his lips down to my neck and sucks the tender skin at my throat.

"Take me to the bedroom," I say.

We stumble all the way there, our mouths locked.

Alec lifts me by the waist and sets me on the edge of my bed. He slides my jeans and underwear off and tosses them to the floor. Then he pushes both my shirt and bra up and puts his lips around my nipple.

"Ahh," I say, cradling his head to my chest. He gives me the edge of his teeth, scraping them gently across the swollen flesh.

His fingers find my clit. He rubs it in circles while mercilessly biting my nipple. My thighs tremble and I start to pant.

He pushes me backward and pulls my ass to the very edge of the mattress.

"Guide me," he says, and then his mouth is on me.

"Lick my clit," I say. "A little to the left."

He laughs against me, and his tongue goes flat, and he licks upward, pulling on my clit with a long, steady swipe. And again. Another slow lick. Fuck, he's killing me!

"Faster," I say, and he speeds up. He traces a finger through my folds as he licks, and then he slides his index finger inside me and presses his thumb to my perineum. He rubs that delicious space above my ass while he pumps his finger, and his tongue flicks, and I'm seeing stars.

"Oh, God, I'm close," I say. "So close. There. Don't stop."

And suddenly my orgasm hits, and I cry out, and he continues to rub and pump his finger, and then he puts his lips around my clit and sucks on it.

Another orgasm hits, right on the heels of the first. I scream, and he sucks, and I try to move, but he has my legs pinned, and all I can do is ride the pleasure.

And then I laugh. Alec lifts his head with a grin, and I just laugh.

"Did you come?" he asks.

Ha.

I hold up two fingers. "Twice. I can't believe it. I've never done that."

He frowns. "Only twice?"

I sit up on my elbows. "Only twice? Twice is amazing!"

"I read where that technique can produce five orgasms, minimum," he says, shaking his head. "I must have done it wrong."

I nod my head. "I think you're right. You really should do it again. Give it a little more effort this time."

He looks at me suspiciously, and then he laughs. "So that was good for you?"

I tug him up to me and he crawls up on the bed, wrapping his arms around me.

"I want to return the favor so badly," I say. "I just don't think I can yet."

Alec kisses my nose and looks down at me. "I wouldn't let you. Heal first. It'll give me something to look forward to."

"Thank you," I say. "I…"

"You what?" he asks.

I sigh. "I just think you're really special. I feel lucky that we met."

He pulls me onto his chest and rubs a hand up and down my arm. "Me, too, Hope. Me, too."

ഔ

We forgot about the burgers. Charred little hockey pucks, they were.

We ate them anyway.

I don't exactly blow Nick off, but I tell him what happened, that I'm recovering, and that I just can't deal with a relationship right now. He has the nerve to argue with me, saying I should have called him. Maybe I should have. Decent guy, I guess, if a little overwrought, but it just didn't happen.

Now I have Alec.

Okay, so we've been dating a week, and Christmas is in two days. I got presents from him just for being a klutz, so even though we haven't discussed it, I know we're exchanging presents. I just have to figure out what to get him.

So Martika and I are shopping.

"How about a tie?" she says. "Lawyers always need ties."

"I don't want to get him something he needs," I say. "He can buy a tie. I want to get him something he'd never buy for himself."

"Have you slept with him yet?"

I shake my head. "It's weird. I want to sleep him, maybe more than I've ever wanted to sleep with anyone. But I love the fact that we haven't. I haven't even seen his body yet. I just feel all gooey when I'm with him."

Martika laughs. "It's only been a week. You can't expect that feeling to last."

"I know. After Matt, God knows I know. But I'm enjoying it."

"You should," she says, bumping her shoulder into mine. "How about sex toys? That could spice things up."

"Were you listening?" I say with a laugh. "We're hot. We don't need any more spice."

"You could go the tame route," she says. "Massage oil, maybe a book of erotica to read aloud, a butt plug."

I stare at her. "On what planet is a butt plug tame?"

She grins. "Whoops. Guess I just shared a little too much. Benny always—"

"Stop. Don't tell me."

Martika laughs. "How about the *Kama Sutra*? You could try out a different position every night."

I smile. "That's…intriguing."

"Ah. I found something you like. Let's go to that sex shop on Tustin Avenue. You probably don't even know all the possibilities." She takes my arm and steers me in the direction of our car.

"I don't know," I say. "I've never been to one of those places. Maybe I can just browse on the Internet."

She stops and looks at me. "You've never been to a sex shop?"

I shake my head, and she smiles.

"Excellent. A virgin."

ဢ

Bed Knobs and Broomsticks is a store I've passed a hundred times and never knew existed. In the center of a run-down strip mall, it looks like it's vacant—the windows are blacked out, and the neon lettering of the sign is broken, just the first B flickering on and off with a loud hum.

"I think they're closed," I say, but Martika just drags me by the arm with a roll of her eyes.

She opens the door and insists I go in first. Right.

Holy Mary Mother of Joseph.

The place is packed. I look back to the parking lot, not that I can see it through the blackened windows, and I swear there were only two cars in the lot. Where did everyone park?

A young girl with a nose piercing bounces over to us. "Welcome!" she says, handing us each a flyer. "Christmas sale. Two-for-one on all dildos, the pony play accessories are 50% off, and crotchless panties are buy one get two free. Lots of other deals. Let me know if you need any help."

"Oooh," Martika says. "Crotchless panties. Thanks!"

I smile weakly, and the girl moves on.

"What's pony play?" I whisper to Martika.

She grins. "Nothing you'd be interested in. Unless you want to prance around like a horse while Alec pulls on your pony tail and whips your ass with a crop."

My eyes widen. "That's a thing?"

"Don't you watch porn?"

I giggle. "Apparently I've been watching the wrong kind."

"Let's look at the lingerie," she says, and I follow her. "That's pretty tame."

Except nothing in this store is tame.

I wander over to a rack of corsets. I've never worn a corset. Except none of these have cups for your boobs, just cut-outs, so you're hanging in the wind. Some are leather, some shiny vinyl, one is a kind of tapestry print with silk ribbons that tie up the back. It's rather gorgeous, like something you'd see in a historical movie. Well, maybe a Victorian-era porn. Do they make those?

I check the price. Holy crap. It's $256.

"What do you think?" Martika is holding up a red vinyl body suit, two holes cut out for the nipples. And it's crotchless.

"I think it looks hot," I say. "I mean, like you'd sweat a lot."

She shrugs. "Sex makes you sweat anyway. If you're doing it right."

"Good point."

She sighs and puts it back on the rack. "I can't justify $500. Not even for great sex."

"Five hundred dollars?" I gulp.

"It's an investment in the relationship," she says. "That's how you have to look at these prices."

Apparently.

We find the crotchless panties, $32 each. But today you get three for that price.

Crotchless panties really defeat the purpose of panties at all. I almost dismiss them. But then I think, what if I were wearing a pair with a skirt? What if we went out to dinner, and I slid Alec's hand between my thighs, under the table? That could be fun.

I gravitate to the white, thinking that's what Alec would like. But white doesn't look good on me. You'd think being half Hispanic that my skin would be darker, but nope. I got my Mom's skin. I can tan, but I don't like to. Mom's skin, Dad's dark hair and eyes.

I look great in black. But black's so boring.

I choose a lacy hot pink.

"Pick two," I tell Martika. "My treat." She squeals and picks a shiny black vinyl and a red mesh pair.

Then we wander over to the toys.

Yikes. Half of this stuff...I have no idea what it's for. I'm completely embarrassed to be in here.

Martika feels none of that. She marches over to a display and grabs a giant red dildo.

"This sucker's heavy."

I lean into her ear. "Wouldn't that hurt? How the hell does that fit inside you?"

"Women's bodies are amazing, aren't they? If you can expel a baby, certainly you can accommodate this guy."

I cringe. "But why would you want to?"

She laughs and puts it back. "I forgot. Tame. Oh! How about this?" She picks up a box and flips it over. "A couples' massager."

It looks like a two-pronged clip. The picture on the box shows one end of the clip inserted into the woman, and the other end rests on her clit. Both ends vibrate.

"How is it for couples?" I ask.

She points to the last picture. "You use it during sex. The guy slips right in above this prong, and he gets the vibrations, too. Sounds fun."

I stare at the picture. "Wouldn't it hurt?"

She hands me the box and picks up the massager on display. "Feel it. It's wrapped in that rubbery silicone. If you lube it up, I don't think you'd feel it at all."

I continue to read the box. It suggests that a woman could wear the massager all day long, with no one the wiser. There's even a phone app you can download to discreetly change the vibration settings.

I imagine that, wearing the massager while I go about my day. I wonder how many women do this kind of thing and I never noticed.

"What do you think?" Martika asks.

"It's interesting," I say, "but it's a little early in the relationship."

"Get it for you," she says. "Do you even have a vibrator?"

My cheeks burn. "No."

"What color? I'm buying it for you for Christmas. Use it alone, and when you're ready, you can share it with Alec."

"Martika."

"Hope."

I stare at her. I kind of want it. Just to see.

"I'll buy it," I say. I choose the purple one, of course. "Now, let's focus. I need to find something for Alec."

I choose some massage oil that smells like margaritas and tastes like lime. Supposedly. I also choose some lubricant, a book of erotica, and a book on fellatio. I think I'm pretty well versed, but since Alec has never experienced it, it can't hurt me to brush up on my technique.

We wait in a twenty-minute line, and when we finally get to the register, I'm dying. Every time the door opens, I expect to see someone I know and be caught. I just want to pay and get out.

"Oooh, you chose the couples' massager," the girl says loudly with a grin. "It's awesome. You're gonna love it."

"Great," I mumble. And then to my horror, she starts opening the package.

"There are no returns on these," she says. "I mean, how gross would that be, right?" She takes the purple clip out of the box. "Have you used one before?"

I shake my head.

"It comes with about ten minutes of charge, just enough so we can prove it works. Be sure to plug it in as soon as you get home. Once charged, it should be good to go for a few hours. Now, this is the end you stick inside your vagina. It comes with ten different speeds, and ten different pulses. Here, hold on to it, and I'll show you."

I can't believe this. At least ten people are waiting behind me, listening to this entire exchange. Martika has to take my hand and place it on the insertable end.

"Touch this button once to turn it on. Press it to change the pulse. This is the continuous vibrate...and this is the cha-cha-cha...the sine wave...the—"

"I get it," I say, snatching my hand back.

"Obviously, you can't press the buttons while it's inside you, so that's why they have a phone app. Do you want me to demonstrate it?"

"No. I can figure it out."

"Great! So we know it works. Here's a sheet for tips on keeping your toys clean. I'll just put it in your bag. You know, it works great for a man, too. Slip this end in his anus, and rest the other at the base of his penis. He'll love it."

Martika is snickering next to me. I finally get to pay, and we get the hell outta there.

And as we step into the sunlight outside, she bursts out laughing.

"Your face," she says. "You should have seen your face."

I glare at her. And then I burst out laughing, too.

Chapter 17

Alec has an older sister who is married with two young kids. According to Alec, she did everything right—graduated top of her class at Berkeley, spent five years at Ernst & Young, married a nice church-going Chinese boy who is now a thoracic surgeon—and yet it still wasn't good enough for his parents. When they passed away, she quit her job, got a tattoo, and became a stay-at-home mom and part-time graphic artist. She still has to hide the tattoo from her in-laws, but her husband loves her anyway.

Alec also has a large extended family, and they always get together on Christmas Eve. He asked me to join them, and though my stomach's in knots, I accepted.

"So tell me what to expect," I say as he drives us to his aunt's house in Pasadena.

"There will be at least sixty people there, I told you that, I think," he says, and I nod. "Don't let it overwhelm you. My aunts will be very accommodating and doting. Guests are important to them. They'll ply you with food and drink, so just thank them and take what they offer, and if you've had enough or if there's something you don't like, just pass it to me."

I smile at him. "Thanks."

He smiles back. "It's just a bunch of us sitting around catching up. But my aunts always insist on singing Christmas carols. My sister will dutifully play the piano, bitching under her breath the entire time."

I laugh. "I love Christmas carols. I can do that. I can even play if she doesn't want to."

He glances at me. "I thought you just played guitar."

"Guitar, piano, bass...I played the harmonica for a while, but I like to sing more. You know I've messed around with the clarinet. And I can do some drums."

"You're a one-woman band. How come you haven't played for me yet?"

"Because it's only been a week. Maybe I'll play for you tonight."

He grins. "So are you gonna tell me what's in the bag?" He points to the large Macy's bag at my feet.

"Gifts. I brought gifts for the kids, and one for your aunt. You said she collects antiques, right?"

Alec reaches a hand out and squeezes my thigh. "That was really thoughtful. You didn't have to do that."

"I wanted to. But I admit, I'm nervous."

"Don't be. They'll love you."

∽

Auntie Ju-Ju greets us warmly with hugs and bows.

"You are lovely!" she says, taking my hand and patting it. "So lovely."

"What a beautiful home," I say, and I mean it. It's an historical Victorian, with oriental rugs, velvet settees, and Ming Dynasty vases. I only know this because I got a mini introduction to antiques when I went shopping for her gift.

"Oh," she says, waving a dramatic hand. "Such junk. Everything old. Like me!"

I laugh. I know she's only around 60, and if it weren't for her graying hair, she'd look like she's in her forties.

Alec leads me to the parlor-turned-family room, where a couple is sitting on the couch, two kids at their feet.

"Jane," he says, and the woman looks up and smiles. She pops to her feet and gives Alec a hug.

"Thank God," she says. "Someone normal. Sort of." She pokes him in the stomach with a smile. "Auntie Betty is driving me crazy."

"I want you to meet Hope," he says, turning to me and taking my hand. "Hope, this Jane, and this is her husband Ernie, and their kids, Ryan and Faith."

I shake Jane's hand, then Ernie's. "It's nice to meet you."

She raises her arms to the ceiling. "Hallelujah! You chose a white girl. Us Chinese, we're crazy."

I just stare at her, and Alec sighs.

Jane laughs. "I'm kidding. Sort of. Alec's ex-wife was fresh off the boat and madder than a hatter. Buy American. That's the advice, isn't it?"

"Uh…" I have no idea what to say to that.

Jane links her arm through mine. "I'm kidding. Sort of. Ignore me. Ernie's been in surgery for forty-eight hours, and I've been stuck with the kids. It's made me loopy. Let's get you a drink."

She starts to lead me away, and I look back at Alec.

He smiles. "She's kidding. Lighten up, Jane. I actually want Hope to speak to me tomorrow."

Jane just laughs.

�∽

Jane pours us each a glass of champagne, and we wind through groups of people, her giving me quick introductions, me remembering none of them. We finally settle on a bench in the perfectly manicured English garden out back, and Jane gives me a long look.

"So how long have you and Ernie been married?" I ask.

"Twelve years. Took me ten before I appreciated him, but now, I'm hooked."

"I want that trick," I say. "Isn't it usually the other way around?"

She smiles ruefully. "I was an asshole as a teenager. My head was so far up my father's ass I couldn't see straight. He barked, and I jumped. I picked Ernie for him. Then I had to grow up and figure out what was good for me. I'm blessed that Ernie was that thing."

"That is lucky," I say, and she nods.

"How did you and Alec meet?" she asks.

"I needed an estate attorney, and he was referred to me by a colleague."

"Oooh," she says, a wicked gleam in her eye. "Dating the client. Nice."

I smile. "We just connected. I've only known him a couple of weeks, but it feels like longer."

Jane swallows some champagne and leans back against the bench. "Did he tell you about his marriage?"

"A bit," I say.

"He deserves someone nice. Someone with her shit together. I swear, he'd be ruling the world by now if she hadn't held him back."

"It was that bad, huh?"

She nods. "I won't spill details, but…yeah. He twisted himself in knots trying to please her, trying to fix her. But enough about that. Do you babysit?"

I laugh. "Never have. Are you trying to recruit me?"

"Absolutely," she says. "I'm giving Ernie a ski trip for Christmas. We desperately need some alone time. Maybe you could help Alec out."

I raise an eyebrow. "Alec is keeping the kids?"

"Yep. Four days. The guy's a saint. I give him a hard time, but honestly...he's a great guy, Hope. His crazy family not withstanding."

I smile. "I think his family's pretty great. No complaints."

Jane laughs. "Wait until you meet Uncle Harold, Betty's husband."

"Alec said we'll probably sing carols later. And that you have to play the piano?"

She rolls her eyes. "That's why I'm on my fourth glass of champagne. It's painful."

"I can play if you don't want to."

She eyes me. "You play?"

I nod.

She stands up. "Excellent. Let's go take a test run."

80

We sit side-by-side at the grand piano. It must be over a hundred years old, but it's polished to perfection, and the ivory keys show no signs of chipping. Either it doesn't get a lot of use, or Auntie Ju-Ju is meticulous.

"Let's start easy," she says. "*Silent Night.*"

That's one of my favorites. I close my eyes, set the tune in my head, adding a few flourishes here and there just to show off, and then I play. I get lost in the music. At some point, Jane slips off the bench, but I finish the song.

And suddenly the entire house seems to burst into applause.

I open my eyes and turn around. The room is crammed with people, and they're all applauding.

"*The First Noel*" someone yells.

Tears sting my eyes. I don't know why.

Then Alec sits beside me. "Do you know it? *The First Noel?*"

My throat is too tight to speak, so I nod. I set the tune…and I play.

Alec's pitchy voice, low, is in my ear. It makes me smile.

And then the entire room is singing. I join in.

For two hours, I sing and I play.

ଓ

Most of the family has left by the time Auntie Ju-Ju, Auntie Betty, and Uncle Harold insist on one last drink. I suddenly remember my gift, and Alec grabs it from the foyer and sets it in Auntie Ju-Ju's lap.

"For me?" she says. "Oh no, oh no. Not for me!"

"Alec told me you love antiques," I say. "I went to the antique mall in Old Towne Orange, and the clerk helped me pick this out. She said you'd love it."

She tears open the paper and carefully opens the box. Nestled inside a bunch of packing peanuts is an Ansonia mantle clock, circa 1897.

Alec and Harold both gasp. Auntie Betty looks away. Ju-Ju just looks speechless.

"She didn't know," Alec says, but Auntie Ju-Ju waves him off.

"Shush, you! Beautiful! My, my. I never had such beauty in my home before! Ansonia is old and expensive. Very expensive." She rummages in her pocket and pulls out a penny, holding it out to me. I look at Alec, and he nods his head. So I take the penny.

"I put it here, above the fireplace," Ju-Ju declares, placing the clock front and center. "Where all can see."

Alec is fighting a smile. I don't get it.

"What?"

"Alec, you a good boy," Ju-Ju says, "so shut up. Now. Let's drink."

∾

As soon as we get in the car, I turn to Alec. "What was with the clock?"

He smiles. "A clock is just about the worst gift you can give to the Chinese," he says. "The word for clock sounds like the word for death. You basically told her her time was short and she was going to die."

My mouth hangs open.

Alec laughs. "But she didn't care. She loved it. And she loved you, or she would never have put that clock out."

"You're telling me I just insulted the matriarch of your family?"

"Pretty much."

My eyeballs burn, and I blink hard.

"Hey. Are you crying?"

I stare out the passenger window. "No."

"Hope, it's fine. You didn't know, and she's lived here for thirty years. You gave her a beautiful gift, and that's exactly how she took it."

I try to nod, just to see if it will make me feel better. It doesn't.

"What was with the penny?" I finally manage.

"She was buying the gift from you, so that it wasn't a gift anymore. That way, she wasn't subject to the death implications."

"I'm sorry," I say. "Insulting her was the last thing on my mind."

Alec pulls up to a stoplight and looks at me. "Hope, everyone knows that. You have nothing to feel bad about."

"Uncle Harold wouldn't even say goodbye to me. I guess that's why."

"He's a fruitcake, and he's not even Chinese," Alec says. "He's Jewish. And I'm sure Auntie Betty has lots of stories about Harold trying to fit into our family and failing."

I sniff. "Would you ask her?"

We both laugh.

"You know," he says, "this is kind of a turn-on."

"Me insulting your family?"

He shakes his head. "You crying. I mean, not the actual crying, but you so upset because you care that much about my family."

I finally look at him. "My crying doesn't bother you?"

"I don't want you to feel bad," he says, "but no. Why would your crying bother me? That's like saying your laughter bothers me. It's a part of you."

∞

Alec drops me off at my mom's so I can wake up with her Christmas morning. He gives me a long kiss, his fingers entwining with mine and holding tight.

And when he tries to leave, I won't let go of his hand.

So we sit on the front step, my head on his shoulder, and we talk. And when it's two AM, I finally let him go home.

New Year's Day, I have coffee and watch the Rose Parade with my mother and then brunch with Martika and Benny. Martika's finally starting to show, just a bit in her lower tummy, enough that she can't button the top of her jeans. And she's a healthy eater normally, but the baby has other ideas. I'm in awe as I watch her plow through an omelet larger than her plate, an entire side of hash browns, and eight pieces of bacon.

I'll give her a pass on the bacon.

And then I head to Alec's. A date with his niece and nephew.

We haven't seen each other since Christmas Eve, even though we've talked every day. I woke up Christmas morning with the flu, and Alec was working overtime so that he could take four days off to watch the kids, and then Martika and Benny and I and a few others had bought tickets months ago to a New Year's Eve Rolling Stones concert. I was perfectly ready to give up my ticket, but Alec had poker night planned with his friends, so I went.

I still have Alec's presents in my car. But I'm thinking that today, with the kids about, wouldn't be the appropriate time to give them to him.

He has a gorgeous home in Old Towne Orange, close to his office and about five miles from me. It's a craftsman-style bungalow, meticulous in every detail. It's one of those houses that you drive by and itch to see the inside.

Four-year-old Faith opens the door when I knock.

"Uncle!" she yells. "She's here!"

I step inside and crouch down. "Hi, Faith. It's nice to see you again." I notice Alec and Ryan enter the room.

"Take your shoes off," she says, sticking a finger in her ear. "They go there." She points to a shoe rack next to the door.

"Right," I say. "Thanks for the tip." She smiles as I stand, and I slip my flats off and put them in a shoe cubby. Faith is staring at my feet.

"Your toes are purple," she says.

I wiggle them. "Yep. Would you like purple toes?"

"Daddy has a purple toe," she says. "I dropped a soup on it."

"You dropped a soup?"

She nods, and Alec laughs. He comes to me and gives me a hug.

"A can of soup," he says. "You dropped a can of soup on his toe."

"That's what I said," Faith says.

I cringe. "Ouch."

"Let me take your coat," Alec says, easing it off my shoulders. He also takes my purse and hangs them both on the hall tree. Then he claps his hands together. "So. I'm fixing lunch, and then I thought we'd go to the park. Any objections?"

Six-year-old Ryan pumps a fist in the air. "The park. Yes!"

"Will you push me on the swing?" I ask.

Alec grins and leans in my ear. "That sounds like foreplay."

"What's foreplay?" Faith asks, and my eyes go wide.

"I said four days," Alec lies, ruffling her hair. "Come on. The sooner you eat, the sooner we get to play."

Alec has made peanut butter and jelly sandwiches. The kids have impeccable manners. I notice they both place their napkins in their laps, although neither one of them uses the napkin. Ryan wipes his mouth on his sleeve between bites, and Faith doesn't seem to notice the peanut butter on her nose or the jelly on her chin.

"Let me give you a tour while the kids eat," Alec says. He takes my hand and leads me around. "Guest bath. And this is my office. Three bedrooms total, so I pilfered one for work. This is the spare bedroom—never had any use until now. And this is the master."

I walk into Alec's bedroom. He has a mission-style bedroom suite, which fits the house.

A plush black velvet comforter tops the bed. Everything's neat and tidy and perfectly in place.

"Do you actually live like this, or did you clean up for me?" I ask.

He laughs. "A bit of both. I'm generally neat, but not this neat."

"Do you have a maid?"

He nods. "Once a week. I could do it myself, but I just don't have time."

"Same here," I say. And then I laugh. "Actually, now that I don't have a job, I do have the time."

"Have you thought about it?" he asks. "Suing them?"

"I'm not gonna do that," I say. "I'm taking it as a sign. I've wanted to pursue my music for a long time, and now I don't have an excuse not to."

"I can't wait to hear you play the guitar," he says. "If you're better at that than you are at the piano...wow."

"There are a million talented musicians out there," I say. "I'm not that special."

Alec grips my arms. "Don't say that. Don't create obstacles for yourself. You're amazing. A-mazing. Believe in yourself."

I lean forward and take his mouth with mine. Alec sighs into the kiss and puts his arms around me. I run my hands down his back, feeling the strained muscles, and then I grip his ass tight.

He laughs. "God, I can't believe we have to wait four days."

My erect nipples are rubbing against my bra, and my underwear's now uncomfortably damp.

"Me, either."

₮

The park. I haven't been to the park since I was a kid.

As soon as we hit the grass, the kids run ahead of us to the jungle gym. Alec wraps an arm around my waist and sighs.

"I love this," he says. "I don't do this enough."

"Relax, you mean?"

He nods. "I run, and I get to the gym most days, but I don't really get outside and just enjoy the day."

"I started taking walks after my divorce," I say. "I'd get up early, before the sun was even up, and there's a smell to the air. You can predict the weather based on that smell. And you realize how loud the day is when you get up early. No gardeners blowing leaves, no cars honking. Sometimes I miss silence."

We settle on a bench near the play area where we can keep an eye on the kids.

"What's your perfect life?" Alec asks. "Describe for me a day in that life."

I smile. "An early-morning walk with my husband. Doesn't have to be long, maybe twenty or thirty minutes, but just some time to connect in that silence. Coffee, news, maybe splitting a bagel. And then the kids get up, all of them, lots of them, and I help dress them and brush teeth and sing songs, and I get tight hugs and sloppy kisses from the whole lot, even the teenagers...then work. Writing songs. Recording. Whatever I need to do. Laundry, I'd imagine. Then homework and watching the kids play sports and music and acting in plays, and kissing boo-boos and telling them that yes, that Sophie is a mean bitch and you have my permission to ignore her...and a loud family dinner, all of us, together. Then bath time and story time and snuggles...then a beer with my husband, a bath together, a couple hours of making love and touching and whispers...and then sleep. Glorious sleep."

Alec looks away, and I frown.

"Did I say something wrong?"

He turns back to me, and his eyes are shiny. "You just described my perfect life."

∞

We get the kids down for bed. Only took four readings of *Goodnight Moon* and five repetitions of the theme song to *Mickey Mouse's Clubhouse*.

We settle on the couch with coffee, and Alec pulls a present from the side of the couch.

"I know it's late, but Merry Christmas," he says.

"I have your presents in the car, but I want you to wait to open them."

"Why?" he asks.

"We need to be alone."

Alec grins. "I can wait. But you have to open this now."

I slide the gold ribbon off the small package and tear off the wrapping. I lift the lid of the box.

Inside is a business card.

I pick it up. *Joseph Kirshner - Producer, Lockstep Records.*

"Look on the back," he says. So I flip the card over.

January 18, 10 AM, my office is written in block letters.

I look up. "You know Joseph Kirshner?"

"We were frat brothers at Penn," Alec says. "He wants to meet with you."

"Lockstep Records," I say, the card trembling in my hand. "You believe in me that much?"

"More," he says. "But this is the best I could do."

"Alec…to call in a favor, from a friend…"

"I didn't call in any favor," he says. "I showed him your video from that restaurant, and the one my sister took of you playing at Christmas. He requested the meeting. I didn't have anything to do with it."

I launch myself at him, peppering his face with kisses, and Alec laughs.

"Do you think we can make out?" I ask. "Just a little bit?"

He grins. "I thought you'd never ask."

I spent all four days with Alec and Ryan and Faith. I fell in love with them. All of them.

There it is. I love Alec Chang.

It's been on the tip of my tongue to tell him. Every time he laughs, every time he frowns, every time he touches me...I want to shout it!

But I'm waiting for tonight. Finally...we'll be alone.

Alec doesn't finish with work his first day back to the office until after eight. He comes in my door dragging, his fingers clawing at the tie around his neck.

"Rough day?" I ask as I take his coat and jacket.

"Not rough, but long," he says. "Come here."

I nestle into him and give him a kiss. "Do you need a drink?"

"I probably shouldn't if my goal is to be wide-awake, but yes."

I pour us each a glass of wine. "Nerves?"

He shakes his head. "My cock has been hard since lunch just thinking about tonight. I swear everything took twice as long because I couldn't concentrate."

I laugh. Then I push his presents, sitting on the kitchen counter, toward him. "These might help."

He opens the massage oil and lube and grins. He opens the erotica and gulps. And then he gets to the last present.

I wrapped the couple's massager. Of course I charged it first and set up the app on my phone.

He stares at the box, and I can see it shaking in his hands.

"Interesting, don't you think?"

He looks up at me, his lips split in a smile. "Have you tried this?"

"Not with a partner."

"Are we…using this tonight?"

I shake my head. "Not tonight. First I'm gonna take care of you. And then you're gonna fuck me. And then we're gonna make love until we fall asleep."

෨

I tell Alec to sit on the bed and watch. Then I stand in front of him.

I slowly unbutton my blouse, one button at a time. Alec watches me with hooded gaze, his eyes focused on my fingers.

I hold the shirt closed and slide it off my shoulders. He smiles.

And then I let the shirt drop. I'm not wearing a bra, and my 34 D cups spill into the cool air. Alec starts to rise, but I push him gently back down.

I turn my back to him and slide the skirt from my waist. I bend all the way forward and step out of the skirt. I look over my shoulder, and Alec's lips are parted, his breath coming faster.

I straighten up and face him. "Now you," I say.

His fingers go to the buttons on his own shirt, but I shake my head.

"Stop. Let me."

I move to him and work on the buttons. I watch his throat work as he swallows.

"Hope, you're so beautiful. I feel like I've waited a lifetime for this."

I grin. "It gets better."

He shakes his head. "I don't think it does."

I slide his shirt off and get a good look at him for the first time. He's perfectly toned, lean, and there's not a hair on his chest. I run my hands over the smooth skin. I can't believe this is mine. All mine.

I unbuckle his belt, undo his pants, and run my fingers over his stomach. The muscles contract, and he catches his breath.

Then I slide his pants and boxers down in one swift motion. His cock springs out and nearly slaps me in the face.

He steps out of his pants and laughs. "I think I need to lie down. My legs won't hold me up."

I get a great view of his smooth, tight ass as he climbs on the bed. I follow him up and lie down across his chest. He pulls me in and kisses me.

I melt into him, my tits pressed against his hard nipples, his tongue swirling against mine. I nibble at his lips, and my hands roam, until I've got one wrapped tight around his cock. It's so smooth, hardened velvet, and it swells in my hand.

"I'm not gonna last if you do that," he says. "I've been ready to come since breakfast."

I laugh and slide down between his legs. "You don't have to last. Don't worry about how long it takes, and don't hold back. Just go with it."

Alec leans back into the pillows. "You want directions?"

I slide my hand down his cock and grip the base tight, giving it a squeeze. "If you want it to be good, hell yes."

He laughs, and I open my mouth and take him in. The laugh turns to a gasp.

I run my tongue along the rim of the head and then down the length of his cock. I get it all nice and slicked up, and then I concentrate on the head, sucking on it gently in a pulsing rhythm.

His cock hardens some more. I didn't think that was possible.

Then I pump my mouth over him, up and down. I manage to get about three quarters of it down my throat with every stroke, and I use my hand to rub the bottom, twisting it on every upstroke. Alec's hips start to buck along with me.

I have a free hand, so I swirl my finger in my saliva and rub it around the rim of his ass.

Alec groans. "Fuck, Hope. Oh my God. Harder."

I suck harder. I grip harder. I taste that sweet salty bit of pre-come as Alec climbs, and I flick my tongue on the spot where the head of his cock meets the shaft. Alec twitches, and I laugh against him.

"I'm close," he says. "Faster."

I bob my head faster, loving every minute of this, every moan and twitch and gasp making my nipples harder, my pussy wetter, until Alec shoves a hand in my hair and grips tight.

"Yes, Hope. Yes! Oh, God!" And he unloads a mouthful, and I swallow it all eagerly, and I lick and suck until he calms done and his balls loosen.

I finally lift my head, and Alec lifts his. "Kiss me," he says.

I lie on top of him and ravish his mouth. He flips me over onto my back and locks his lips around my nipple. I hold his head to my chest. I can already feel his cock growing hard again against my thigh.

I'm on the pill, and Alec knows this. Nothing to be awkward about now.

"You said I'm gonna fuck you first, right?" he asks, his hands still caressing my thighs.

I nod.

"On all fours."

I grin. I climb to my knees and thrust my ass in the air. One of his hands massages it, squeezing and rubbing, while the other rubs his cock over my pussy lips.

And then he's inside me.

He pumps his hips, and I thrust backward to meet him. He reaches forward and finds my clit with his fingers, rubbing in circles while he fucks me.

"Alec," I breathe. I pull a pillow under my chest and hold it tight. Alec speeds up, pumping into me hard and fast, so hard I have to fight to catch my breath.

"Don't stop," I say. "Yes."

My ass slaps hard against his groin. I feel his cock to the tips of my toes. My entire body tingles, and my arms shake.

"Go, Hope," he says, bending forward to kiss the small of my back. "Let go."

I reach a hand between us and place it on top of his. We both rub my clit, and my orgasm bursts, and I cry out, my pussy muscles clamping down hard on him.

Alec groans. And then he pumps into me twice, hard, and collapses against my back.

My knees give out, and my cheek buries itself in the pillow. Alec licks my ass and gives it a sweet kiss.

"I can't move," I say, and we both laugh.

He falls down beside me, and we stare into each other's eyes.

"I never thought I'd have this," he says. "It doesn't seem real."

"I know," I say. "I feel the same way."

"Hope." And then he places his hands on my cheeks. "I'm in love with you."

I flip to my back and sigh. "Damn it!"

Alec sits up in alarm. "Damn it?"

"I wanted to say it first!" I turn back to him, and he laughs. I run the back of my fingers over his forehead, down his cheek, over his lips. "Alec, I love you."

And then we kiss. And explore. And discover.

We love.

Chapter 20

Dr. Steinburg gives me a hug when I enter his office. I have a goofy grin on my face, and he smiles at me.

"I know my hugs are golden, but I'm sensing something else is at work here."

I flop back on the couch. "I'm in love."

He chuckles. "Wow."

"I know," I say. "It's been about a month, but I found him. He's everything I want."

"Tell me."

"He's an attorney," I say. "He has a loud, messy international family, which is interesting. He's Chinese, and none of his Chinese aunts— seven of them—married someone from their own culture. His dad's family were missionaries, and they grew up in Indonesia, South Africa, different parts of Asia, so they married men from all over the place. His parents passed away, but he's still close with the rest of the family, most of whom immigrated here. He has grandparents in Beijing."

"You've met the family?" he asks.

"At Christmas. I made a major cultural faux pas, but they were gracious about it. I loved them."

"That's a challenge in itself," he says. "Meeting the family. And to have cultural differences, doubly so."

"I still have a lot to learn, I think, about their culture, but Alec was born here. He's not that different from me."

Dr. Steinburg nods. "Tell me more."

"He's kind," I say. "Intelligent. Sexy. And he's comfortable with my feelings. I cried when I accidentally insulted his aunt, and it didn't bother him at all."

"And how does he feel about your music?"

"Completely supportive," I say. "And he kept his niece and nephew overnight for four days when his sister went on a trip, and he's amazing with them. He wants a family, just like me."

"He sounds wonderful," Dr. Steinburg says. "And have you told him about your childhood?"

"He knows who my dad is and how he treated us. I haven't given explicit details, though."

"And have you come across anything that would give you pause? I don't want you to pick at the relationship, but I also don't want you to ignore any warning signs."

"He does work a lot," I say. "He runs his own firm, so he has to, but it's nothing abnormal or unhealthy. He's really neat. I mean, I'm not a dirtbag, but I'm not as neat as he is. And he's pretty serious, but I like that."

"You mentioned that his dad's family were missionaries," he says. "Is he religious?"

I nod. "That's how he was raised, but he doesn't go to church much. Just holidays, mostly."

"And you're okay raising your children with his faith?"

I shrug. "I haven't thought about it."

"A month is a little early, perhaps, but I'm sensing you're all in. If this moves fast, you'll need to have that discussion."

I nod.

"How does your mother feel about him?"

I sigh. "She met him briefly, but that was before we started dating. I think she's avoiding getting to know him. She's still peeved at me that I gave her the house."

Dr. Steinburg nods again. Since Mom sees him every week, he probably knows more about her thoughts on the matter than I do.

"I'm gonna try to pin her down this weekend," I say.

"Does Alec know about our sessions?" he asks.

"No."

"Does he know you have brain damage?"

"No."

"Does he know you can't have children biologically?"

I shift on the couch. "I can have children biologically."

"Does he know you shouldn't?"

"I don't know that," I say. "You don't know that. No one does."

Dr. Steinburg stares at me. I stare back.

"Why do you think you cannot acknowledge that you live with a heart defect?"

"I acknowledge it," I say. "It was corrected before I turned one, and it hasn't affected me since."

"And when was the last time you saw your cardiologist?"

"I go annually," I say. "Last March, I think. I've never had a problem."

"Hope." Dr. Steinburg leans forward and throws his legal pad on the table between us. "Stop this. Talk to me. I know you're not this obtuse."

I press my lips together. "My mother had no right to talk to you about this. I'm not discussing it."

"Ignoring it won't make it go away," he says. "I've done some research, and based on what your mother has said—"

"My mother doesn't know what she's talking about!" I yell. "She hasn't gone to the doctor with me since I was 14! I can have children!"

"At what cost?" he asks softly.

Tears well in my eyes, and I choke on a sob. "Do you...do you know what's it like? I had a shitty childhood, and that's putting it mildly. I have visible lesions in my brain...brain damage so bad that I...I had to learn how to write my name again when I was 10. And now...I'm living. Trying to live. And you want me to face the possibility that I...my adulthood will be as shitty as my childhood? That my aortic valve is going to leak...I'll have open heart surgery, and a mechanical valve, and...I can't. I can't think about it. I don't want to think about it."

Dr. Steinburg gets up and sits next to me on the couch. He puts his arms around me, and I sob into his chest.

He doesn't speak.

And the only reason I can think of for that is that he has nothing comforting to say.

Chapter 21

I spend my days polishing the songs I want to play for Joseph Kirshner. I choose the ones that best represent me and the kind of album I'd like to produce. Bluesy, a little bit folksy, stripped down and raw. Kind of like Tori Amos with a guitar instead of a piano.

Alec finally has an early evening available, and I set up dinner with Martika and Benny. They haven't met him yet, and I'm dying for them all to meet. I just hope Martika doesn't embarrass me too much.

I get home after running some errands, and start a load of laundry. My doorbell rings.

I yank it open, and there's Matt.

"Hey," he says. "Happy New Year."

I hang on the edge of the door, blocking his entrance. "Happy New Year."

He holds out a postcard. "This came in the mail for you. Guess they didn't update your address."

I stare at the appointment reminder card for my cardiologist. Why the fuck do these things pop up all at once?

"Thanks."

"How's the head?" he asks.

"Fine."

"I came to see you in the hospital," he says. "Did your Mom tell you?"

I blink. "No."

He smiles. "Figures. So no complications?"

I shake my head. I can't seem to tear my eyes away from the postcard.

"You okay?" he asks.

"I'm seeing someone." I finally lift my eyes to his. "He's great, and I love him, but I haven't told him about this."

Matt swallows hard. "You love him?"

I nod.

Matt looks away across the yard and shoves his hands in his pockets. "If he loves you, too, it won't make a difference."

"How do I say it? How do I tell him I might not...might not be able to have kids?"

Matt's eyes turn glassy, and he blinks hard. "You just say it. If he can't handle it, it's better to know now, right?"

I shake my head. "I can't handle it. How can I expect him to?"

Matt puts his arms around me. I don't hug him back, but I do bury my head in his chest and concentrate on breathing.

"If he can't handle it, fuck him," Matt says. "Stand up for yourself, Hope. Nothing is more important than your life."

He kisses my forehead and goes back to his car. I watch him until he's out of sight.

Matt gave up his ability to have kids for me. When he was just 24 years old, he got a vasectomy, insisting that my life was the most important thing. He said he was happy to adopt.

Except not a lot of agencies are willing to adopt kids out to a mother with a congenital heart defect and brain damage.

And now…I'm resigning Alec to the same sentence.

℘

We arrive at Martika and Benny's right on time. Martika hugs me and kisses my cheek, and then she pounces on Alec. "Welcome to the family!" she declares.

Family. Ha.

But Alec's all smiles.

Martika plies us with drinks, pours lemonade for herself, and we settle on the couch.

"Hope tells me you're expecting," Alec says. "When's the due date?"

"May fifth," Martika says, rubbing her belly. "We just found out yesterday we're having a boy."

I slosh my beer on my knee as I sit up too fast. "You are? You didn't tell me!"

"Congratulations!" Alec says, and he and Ben tap beer bottles.

"I knew I was seeing you tonight," Martika says. "Can you believe it? Benny gets the soccer goalie he's always wanted."

Acid burns in my throat. I feel like I might throw up.

Alec puts a hand on my knee. "You play soccer?" he asks Ben.

Benny nods. "Grew up with it. Played in college. There's a league down by Orange Coast College. The guys are intense. You play?"

Alec laughs. "Not since high school, but it sounds like fun."

"You should come out some time," Benny says. "You play any other sports?"

I excuse myself and go to the bathroom. I lock the door and lean on the counter, breathing deep.

"Hope?" Martika calls through the door. "You okay?"

I shake my head, not that she can see.

"Hope?"

I open the door. "I'm fine. I'm so happy for you. You know that, right?"

She takes my hand. "What's wrong?"

Then Alec and Benny come up behind her.

"There should be a law against this," Ben says. "Female powwows in the bathroom."

Martika ignores him. "Talk to me, Hope."

I raise my eyes to Alec. He suddenly catches on that something's wrong, and I see the concern in his eyes.

"I have a heart defect," I say. "It doesn't really affect me now, but my doctor says I'm looking at a valve replacement in the next ten years. I can have kids, I mean, I can get pregnant, but she thinks it would strain my heart too much."

Nobody moves.

"I'm sorry I didn't tell you," I say. "I didn't want to face it. But I've been incredibly selfish. I made you fall in love with me, and now you have to choose, me or kids. And that's so unfair. I'm not worth it."

Martika drops my hand and looks back at Ben. They both hightail it to the kitchen.

Alec turns and follows them. "Thanks for having us," he says to them. "I'm gonna take Hope home. I'll have her call you tomorrow."

He comes back to me, carrying my purse. I follow him to the car.

ଚ୬

It's a silent drive. I feel numb. There are so many things I know I need to say, but I can't make my mouth open.

We get to my house, and Alec turns off his car and moves to open his door.

"You don't have to come in," I say. "I understand."

"What do you understand?" he asks.

"Why you have to go."

He opens his door. "Come on. Let's talk inside."

I sigh and follow him to the door.

We stand awkwardly in the foyer.

"It must be really hard to see Martika having a baby," he says.

"It wasn't before," I say. "I mean…I'm genuinely happy for her. But over the past couple of days, my heart condition was brought up, twice, and I'd forgotten about it. I hadn't thought about it in so long. And now it's all I can think about. I didn't mean to hide it from you, but there it was, in my mind, and I was feeling guilty for not telling you, and then I saw Martika, and—"

"Hope."

"What?"

"Take a breath." He moves to me and rubs his hands down my arms. "We went so fast. If you think about it, we haven't even been together two months."

"But if you had known from the beginning—"

"But I didn't," he says. "We can't go back. We can only deal with now."

I nod. "So…what are you thinking?"

"I'm not thinking," he says. "I'm feeling. I'm feeling protective."

I move away from him. "I don't want you to stay because you feel like you have to rescue me. I've been there in my last marriage, and all it does is create resentment."

"I'm a big boy," he says. "I take responsibility for my choices. I'd never blame you."

"You say that now, but what happens when you wake up one day, and you're forty, and we don't have kids, and I disgust you."

Alec frowns. "I knew you were self-deprecating, but I didn't know you hated yourself."

I have nothing to say to that.

"Tons of people can't have kids," he says. "Lots of them find love."

"But you want kids of your own," I say. "I know you do."

"Why are you pushing me away?" he asks.

"You're ignoring the other piece," I say. "I might die young. I have a 50% chance of developing Alzheimer's before I'm 50 because my dad knocked me around so much as a kid. Save yourself."

"Jesus!" he explodes. "The medical issues, we can deal with them. There are advances all the time. But your attitude is pissing me off!"

"I don't want to drag you down!" I scream back. "You don't deserve that!"

"I want you!" he says. "You! Hope Cruz, with all her neuroses, all her quirks, all her talent, even with her broken heart. I just want you!"

Tears spill from my eyes, and Alec takes me in his arms.

"You're a messy crier, you know that?"

A laugh bubbles out of my throat.

"I wouldn't have told you I love you if I didn't mean it," he says. "I meant it. I'm not going anywhere."

He kisses me. I gasp against his lips, trying to catch my breath, but there's no give in him. Alec kisses me hard and scoops me into his arms.

"Now I'm gonna show you," he says as he carries me to the bedroom.

Chapter 22

Lockstep Records is in the heart of LA, in a towering glass building. I ride the elevator to the thirtieth floor, where I spill into a waiting room that looks like it belongs in a law office. Except for the records and posters all over the walls. Can't picture those at Alec Chang & Associates.

Can't picture the goth girl behind the desk there, either. She's friendly, but the bullring through her nose is a little bit scary.

I don't know what I expected of Joseph Kirshner, but since he's friends with Alec, I guess I expected sedate. Professional. But he comes bounding into the waiting room in a red leather jacket and backwards ball cap, shooting a rubber band at someone behind him in the hallway.

"Bastard!" he yells with a laugh. "I'll get you next time!"

∙

The meeting doesn't go the way I expected it to, either.

Joseph insists on regaling me with stories of Alec in college, and while they're funny...I thought we were going to talk about music.

"He just sat there," Joseph says. "His skinny little hairless white legs dangling in the Jacuzzi, and that girl, rubbing her tits all over those legs...I think three of us banged her while he sat there."

Okay. That's one story I didn't need to hear.

"Anyway, you and Lockstep, it's a no-brainer. I have three songs looking for an artist, and they're poised to go to the top forty. Can you do pop?"

"Uh, what?"

"Pop music. You're a little old, but Carly Rae Jepsen pulled it off. With a little makeup and Botox, I think it'll work."

"You want me to get Botox?"

He rummages through the mess on his desk, and finds some sheet music. "Play this."

I take the music and look it over. "You want me to play right now?"

"That's what I said, didn't I?"

I take a deep breath. *Calm, Hope, calm.*

I take my guitar out of its case and set it on my lap.

I can see that the song is intended to be played fast. But it shouldn't be.

I slow it down and strip it down. I play it how I want to hear it.

Twenty seconds in, Joseph waves at me to stop. "Huh."

"Huh what?"

"Try this one. It's a ballad."

I examine the song, and again, it's all wrong. It needs a little tempo. I only manage the introduction before Joseph interrupts again. "What is this?"

I raise an eyebrow. "What do you mean?"

"Alec didn't tell me you can actually play. I thought you just copied stuff off YouTube."

"You think the daughter of Joe Cruz doesn't know how to actually play?" I ask.

He bursts out with a laugh. "What?"

"I thought Alec told you—"

"He didn't tell me you were the fucking progeny of Joe Cruz! That asshole!"

I bristle at that, but I get his point.

Joseph takes off his hat and throws it across the room. "I'm sorry, Hope. I had no idea. The fact that you're interested in Lockstep representing you...I'm honored. How many contracts have you been offered?"

I almost say none. But then I catch myself.

"I'm looking at all my options at this point," I say. "I haven't made any decisions. Obviously, Lockstep is high on my list."

"Fucking-A, we are," he says. "Let me get with the higher-ups. I'll fast-track it, and I promise you, our offer will be worth waiting for. Can you hold off on a decision until we can meet again? Say, next Monday?"

I hesitate. "That's over a week. But yes. I think I can wait until then."

"Great."

I put my guitar away, and he takes my arm and walks me out.

"I'll have a car pick you up at your house. Say Monday morning at 11? We can do lunch, I'll introduce you around. We'll make a day of it."

I nod and shake his hand. "Sounds great."

ๅ

I don't know whether to laugh or be pissed. Assuming the terms of the contract are decent, I'm about to be signed to Lockstep Records—all because of my father.

And God love Alec. He didn't even tell Joseph Kirshner who I was. I love him even more for that.

I get to Alec's house around eight, and I find him sitting in a corner of the couch, the room dark.

"Hey, babe," I say. "Why are you sitting in the dark?"

He laughs, but there's an edge to it. "I hadn't even noticed."

"Did something happen?"

He heaves himself to his feet and flips on a light. "You could say that."

"You're scaring me," I say. "Does it have to do with us?"

He steers me to the couch, and we both sit.

"I have to go to China."

"Okay."

"And I don't know when I'll be back."

I stare at him, and he looks away.

"That's all you're gonna tell me?" I ask.

He sighs. "That's all I know."

"Does it have to do with your grandparents?"

He stands. "I have a red eye. I'm leaving tonight."

I stand up in front of him. "You're not even gonna tell me why?"

He doesn't say anything.

"Are we talking a few days? A week? A month?" I ask.

"I don't know. Maybe a month," he finally says.

"Are you breaking up with me?" My heart is rattling in my chest, and my stomach flip-flops.

"No, but I…I don't expect you to wait."

"I thought we were stronger than this," I say. "I thought…I love you. I thought you loved me."

"That's not the issue," he says.

"Then what is the issue?" I say. "Give me something. I'll wait for you, Alec. Whatever the reason."

He blows out a loud breath. "I have to pack. I'll call you. As soon as I know more."

"So that's it."

Silence.

"Damn you." I clutch my purse to my chest and run to my car.

Chapter 23

Three days, and I don't hear from Alec.

I was so angry with him for shutting me out. So angry, that I almost broke up with him over text.

And then I was hurt—didn't I mean something important to him?

And then I was disappointed in how he handled things. I thought we had a pretty good line of communication going. I thought he was close to perfect, but he broke the love spell I had going and made me look at him without the false veneer.

And then…Martika gets a hold of me.

"This is contrary to everything you know about the guy," she tells me as I cook away my sorrow over a bubbling pot of chili. "I can't believe he'd just leave with no explanation. That doesn't sound like him."

"I guess we don't really know him," I say. "Two months isn't that long. That's the lesson here."

She shakes her head. "Sure, you don't know every little detail, but you said the L-word. He doesn't seem like the kind of guy that just tells you he loves you to get in your pants and then leaves."

"He had already gotten in my pants," I say. "He didn't have to tell me he loved me."

"Proves my point. Maybe he's a lawyer for the Chinese mafia," she says. "Maybe he's running for his life, and doesn't want to suck you in."

"The Chinese mafia?"

"That's a thing," she says. "Maybe he's a spy."

"Martika," I say, "this is not fiction. This is real life."

"Which can be stranger than fiction. Maybe he has a wife and family over in China."

I roll my eyes. "He does not have a wife in China. He has an ex-wife who…"

Martika looks at me. "Who what?"

"Maybe it has to do with her," I say. "Alec's sister said she was a mess and that she was Chinese, I mean, born in China. Maybe she went back after the divorce."

"Why don't you call Alec's sister? Maybe she knows what's going on."

"I already thought of that," I say, "but I have no way to contact her. I don't have her number. All I know is where Alec's aunt lives, and I'm not even sure I could find it again."

Martika sighs. "It's kind of weird showing up to the aunt's. And if he didn't tell you what was going on, I doubt he'd tell her. Maybe the sister, but not the aunt."

I nod. That was my feeling, too.

I dish us up two bowls of chili and plop a scoop of sour cream on each. Martika covers the top of hers with cheese, and we sit on the couch to eat.

"My vote is that you hang in there," she says, cheese dangling from her chin. "Alec's a good guy. There's a rational explanation for all of this."

"I want to believe that," I say. "But if it were something simple, like rescuing his ex-wife, or his grandparents got sick, why wouldn't he just tell me? All evidence points to either something illegal or, more likely, something wrong with our relationship. I'm just too dumb to figure out what that is."

"Have you tried calling him yet?" she asks.

I shake my head as I blow on my spoon. "I was afraid I'd say something I'd regret."

"So what are you saying?"

I shrug. "He didn't want me to have to wait. He said he'd get in touch, but he hasn't. Maybe I shouldn't wait."

"It's only been three days," she says. "Or is there something else you're not telling me?"

I pause with my spoon halfway to my mouth. "What are you talking about?"

She shrugs. "I thought you didn't have a single doubt about Alec, especially after he accepted your illness. But you seem to have a lot of doubts. That doesn't have to do with…someone else, does it?"

"Someone else?" I say. "Like who? Nick?"

"I was thinking about Matt."

I laugh. "This has nothing to do with Matt. Nothing."

"Okay, okay," she says. "Just checking."

Then I narrow my eyes at her. "How do you know Matt's been sniffing around?"

"He has? I didn't know that. I just know...he and Ben still hang out, you know that, and he's been really confused, and I just don't want his confusion to spill over on you."

I stir my chili. "It wasn't. I mean, with Alec, it was easy to fight off. Without Alec..." I shrug.

"Alec is still in the picture until he isn't," she says. "If and when he's out...this is a conversation we can have, but Matt broke your heart, Hope. I loved him like a brother, but I'll never look at him the same way again."

I nod. "But that's not really fair to him. I wasn't a saint, Martika. No, I didn't cheat, but I refused to look at all my issues and get help. I'm not saying I want to be with Matt, but he's a good guy, too. He gave up a lot to be with me, and he gave everything he had. It's not his fault I needed more."

"He could have done the honorable thing and just left," she says. "He didn't have to go the douche route and cheat."

"Maybe I went the douche route by keeping my head buried in the sand," I say. "It takes two to end a marriage."

Martika sets her empty bowl on the table, and then grabs my hand. "You learned something. You're working on yourself. And you found love again. Don't throw that away. Not yet."

Chapter 24

Lockstep Records wants me bad.

Or maybe they court all their artists this way. Who knows.

I get picked up in a limo with Joseph Kirshner waiting inside. Champagne, caviar (yuck!), and a bouquet of fifty red roses are lavished on me, and that's only in the first five minutes.

I meet the head of the label, two other producers, and am given a private tour of their recording studios. I get to watch at least three platinum artists recording, and meet several others. They gush about Joseph and what a genius he is, and Joseph seems to agree.

I care about none of it. I want to know if I can make the music I love, and what the terms of the contract are. That's it.

It's late by the time Joseph and I hit the limo for the ride back to Orange County. He finally pulls a bulky manila folder from under his seat and hands it to me. Whoa. It must be 100 pages long.

The freaking contract was here the whole time???

"There are some really special things we're doing just for you," Joseph says. "We understand that you don't have a following yet, and we want to make sure you hit it big, fast."

"I'm familiar with contracts," I say. "What special things did you do?"

"We're all in, Hope," he says. "I think we've shown you that. We're prepared to take all the costs right on our shoulders."

"That's kind of the point," I say. "After all, if I wanted to pay the costs myself, I'd just record and release on my own."

Joseph laughs. "Exactly. But we've thought of everything. Merchandising, touring, publishing…we'll take care of it all."

I flip through the contract. I know exactly which clauses interest me.

"So you want to pay me 50% of net on merchandising and ticket sales. So the costs come off the top, and I get 50% of what's left over. But you don't have to get my approval on costs."

He waves a hand. "You're an artist. You want to create. You don't want to have to stop every thirty seconds to sign approval for this t-shirt or that key chain. We know what we're doing."

"Right." I flip to the next clause. "And you want all my publishing rights. For life."

"That's standard."

"I thought I was special."

Joseph laughs again. "Not much gets over on you, does it?"

I smile. "Not much. You want to own my website, too?"

"Don't tell me you want to maintain it yourself," he says. "That costs time and money.

The only thing you have to worry about is the music."

I flip again. "A twelve-month deal to start, with options to renew, and ten commercially-acceptable masters in that period. I want 'commercially-acceptable' stricken."

"Again, Hope, that's standard. We want to make sure the masters are the highest quality."

I give him my best stink eye. "No, you just want control. You can dick me around and keep me in the contract even after the first year is up, all under the guise of 'these tracks aren't 'commercially acceptable.'"

He smiles. "Every contract is open for negotiation. Why don't you take a couple of weeks to read it, and we can meet again?"

ജ

I know enough about the ugly side of the music business to know that this contract sucks.

And there's no way I want to work with Joseph Kirshner, frat boy douchebag extraordinaire.

As soon as I get home, I throw the contract in the trash.

Chapter 25

Nine days, and no contact from Alec. To be fair, I haven't contacted him, either.

So I gather my courage, and as I'm lying in bed, I send him a text.

I miss you. I don't know what you're doing or why you've been so secretive, but it's killing me. I wish you would let me in so I could give you support. I'm here, waiting, ready to offer whatever I can give.

Love, Hope

I fall asleep, my phone in my hand.

And when I wake in the morning, I have a reply.

Hope, my life is about to change, and I won't drag you in with me. I love you, but this is more than I can ask of anyone, especially you. Take care of yourself. Don't wait.

Alec

My heart drops to my feet.

With shaking hands, I dial.

"Hey. I've just been thinking about you. I know I wasn't completely honest, and I know I held some things back, too many things, and I have so much to work on, still, but I…I need you."

He hangs up on me.

Ten minutes later, my doorbell rings. I swipe my eyes and open it.

Matt.

I open the door wide, and he walks in.

Strung Out

The String Serial
Part Three

Andrea Ring

Dedication

To Julie, who has become not only a
supporter and a helping hand, but also a friend.

Chapter 1

I don't know why I called my ex-husband. I don't know what I expected from him.

I didn't expect him to show up.

Matt walks in the house with the grace of an athlete and the bulk of a badass. He stops two feet in front of me, and we lock gazes.

"Why did you call me?" he says, and there's not a hint of curiosity in his voice. I can tell he doesn't really care about the why. He just wants an excuse to make a move.

I edge around him and grip the back of the couch for support. "You already know."

He shakes his head. "You need a Scrabble opponent?"

I crack a smile. "I beat you 99% of the time. What fun would that be?"

"So you wanted a little fun?" His eyes seem to darken as he focuses on me and thinks about the fun.

I swallow hard. I didn't think this through.

"We haven't had fun together in a very long time," I say.

"I can fix that," he says, shifting his stance. My eyes dart down to the bulge in his jeans and quickly back up to his face. Is it my imagination, or is the bulge suddenly…bulgier?

"Why are you here?" I ask.

"You called me," he says. "You said you needed me."

I did.

My boyfriend Alec had just texted me all the way from China, telling me not to wait for him. He basically dumped me. And in that moment, with all the pain I felt, I did. I called Matt. I told him I needed him.

"I don't know what I want," I whisper.

Matt laughs. "Join the club."

"So where does that leave us?" I ask.

Matt takes a step toward me. "Are you still seeing that guy? The one you said you loved?"

I shake my head.

"Do you still love him?"

I nod.

"Fuck it," Matt says, and he crosses over to me and crushes his lips to mine.

I close my eyes. I take a deep breath, and Matt's scent—sweet sweat, his aftershave, that funny Irish soap he's used since he was a kid—fills my lungs. Matt. It's so familiar, yet at the same time, I'm a completely different person now than I was when we were married. The last time I kissed him, he was the only man I'd ever been with. The only man I'd ever loved. Now...he's not even the one occupying the most space in my heart.

Tears prick my eyes. My body is responding as though Matt is my one and only. Every cell in my body relaxes as our tongues caress and his hands rub my back. But my heart…it's torn.

I pull back, breathing hard. "Do you think this is a good idea?"

He buries his mouth just below my ear. "We both need it," he says. "Just to see."

"See what?"

He groans against my neck. "Why are you overanalyzing this?"

"Are you going to fuck me and leave?" I ask, and I force myself not to inject even a hint of disapproval in the question. It's just an honest question.

He straightens up and looks me in the eye. "Yes. Because neither of us knows what we want."

I nod. This is true.

Matt takes the nod as an invitation. Before I can blink, my jeans are around my ankles, and I'm draped forward over the arm of the couch, and Matt is fucking me hard. It feels so right, so comfortable, but the tears still spill down my cheeks, and my breath hitches in my throat, and I want to say something, something important, but the words won't come.

But I come. I come in one long, loud scream, and Matt, always the quiet one, groans softly, and then he leans forward and places a tender kiss on my shoulder blade.

"I fucking love you, Hope," he whispers.

My tears speed up, but I force myself not to let him see.

I hear the zipper as Matt fastens his jeans.

I hear the front door close as he leaves.

And I wonder what the fuck I just did.

Chapter 2

Martika hands me a Bloody Mary and pours a glass of straight tomato juice for her pregnant self.

"Since when do you drink tomato juice?" I ask her as I sip.

She shrugs. "My taste buds have a mind of their own. Or my stomach does. I don't even recognize myself right now. I took my bra off last night, and you know what I saw? Little yellow dots on the inside of the cups. I was totally puzzled. Why were there stains on the inside of my bra?"

I raise an eyebrow. "Did you figure it out?"

She nods. "I looked at my nipples, and there was some yellow crust on them. What the hell? So I kind of picked it off, and yellow stuff oozed out."

I laugh. "Serious?"

She laughs, too. "Completely freaked me out. I mean, I knew I was going to breastfeed, and that meant stuff coming out of my nipples, but actually seeing it? Crazy."

I sigh and take a huge swallow of my drink. "I'm never gonna experience that, and I'm starting to think that's not such a bad thing."

Martika sits beside me on the couch and puts a hand on my thigh. "If it'll help, I'll tell you all the awful things about pregnancy. You'll pity me."

I lay my head on her shoulder and sigh again. "So what are you and Benny doing today?"

"Working on the baby's room," she says. "He's freaked out about the baby smelling paint fumes, so he wants to get the painting done today. He read some article that said the fumes need three months to dissipate."

I lift my head and smile. "You're so lucky. He's gonna be a great father."

She rolls her eyes. "Not that I disagree, but the master sergeant in him has kicked in. He's making lists. He hired some safety guru to come in and baby-proof the house."

"I didn't know that was an actual job," I say.

She nods. "A thousand bucks for something we can do ourselves for a hundred. And he's researching bottles and nipples. Some of the cheap brands apparently have cancer-causing chemicals in the latex. Not to mention that babies can be allergic to latex."

I smile. "This is kind of perfect. Since I saw you unearth a Skittle from your couch cushions last week and pop it into your mouth, I'm thinking you'll balance each other out."

Martika laughs. "Yep. The five-second rule is one I live by. Unless there's sugar involved. Then it's more like a five-month rule. So what does your mom have planned today?"

According to my mother's therapy, we spend Sundays together. My mother usually dictates the activity.

"Yoga," I say. "She's been trying to get me to go for years. I agreed with the stipulation that I get a cheeseburger afterward."

"That explains the Bloody Mary," she says. "Need another?"

୨୦

So mid-morning yoga at The Enlightened Soul. My mother made me buy a mat, one of those squishy things that's not actually comfortable on a hard floor, and I tried it out last night. I spent two hours brushing all the dirt off the bottom (and I thought my house was clean!). Apparently, every little hair and speck of dust sticks to these damn things.

My mat is purple with swirly yellow flowers all over it—yay! But when I meet my mother in the parking lot, she looks at my mat and grimaces.

"What did you buy?" she asks.

"Isn't it purdy?" I say. "And it was on sale."

"That's because no one who actually does yoga would buy it," she says. "It doesn't even have any grip marks. It's like a slip 'n slide."

I grit my teeth. "Do you have to criticize every little thing? Why didn't you tell me I needed a mat with grip marks?"

She starts to walk toward the studio entrance, and I'm forced to follow. "I didn't know they made them without them. Why didn't you buy one here, like I told you to?"

"Because they're $54 here," I say. "I'm not spending $54 for one hour of my life."

"So you're already assuming you won't be back," she says. "Honestly, Hope, you need to have a better attitude." She pulls on the door and holds it open for me. I ignore her and walk in.

Gah. It's like a hundred degrees in here. I can feel the sweat oozing from my armpits already.

My mother grabs my arm as she marches to the middle of the room and forcibly positions me to her right.

"Shoes and socks against that wall. Then we meditate until we start," she says.

"Um...can't I keep my socks on?" I ask.

"No."

She rolls out her plain blue mat, strips off her shoes and socks, and deposits them against the wall. Then she sits on her mat in the lotus position. Her eyes close and the wrinkles of disapproval around her mouth relax.

Fine. I roll out my mat and take off my shoes. My socks...good Lord, I didn't know I'd have to be barefoot. I haven't actually painted my toes in a month. Chipped bits of Purple Orchid polish dot my toenails, which also look a bit long. Christ. I try to hide my toes by curling them and limp to the wall to deposit my shoes. Then I run back and sit down.

My knee pops. I grab my left ankle and drag it up tight against my inner right thigh. Yow. That actually hurts.

Now my right ankle. *Owwie, owwie, owwie!* I cry in my head as I get into position. How can anyone relax while their thighs are screaming at them? The toenail on my big toe digs into my calf and draws blood.

"Welcome, friends," the instructor says. "Rosalyn, I see you've brought someone. Finally. You must be Hope?"

I smile at her. "Yep. I'm Hope. Hello."

"Have you done any yoga before?" she asks.

"No," I say. "This is my first time."

Someone behind me snickers.

"I'm sure Rosalyn told you, but this an advanced class, so just do what you're comfortable with. If there's a pose you're having trouble with, don't push it. Just do what you can."

I nod. "I will, thanks."

"Okay," she says. "Let's start by getting on all fours, breathing deep, relaxing our neck, and drop to a Downward Dog."

"Did she say dog?" I ask a little too loudly.

"Don't talk," my mother whispers. "Just do it."

I try to copy what everyone around me is doing. But of course, when I drop my head, I can't see shit. Plus, the blood rushes to my head and makes me dizzy. I spend the first twenty minutes with my neck craned at awkward angles, trying to open up my hips (whatever that means), and sliding into a cobra. Which is kind of fun, I admit. I can slither. But my arms aren't strong enough to hold a plank position and lower myself down. I thud to the mat ungracefully before every slither.

"Now lift your leg up," the instructor says, "then curl it back, open up the hips, make room for your neck, make sure it's relaxed..."

My leg flails up. My arms shake. I try to curl my leg back, and I topple over to my left and crash into my mother.

"Ooph," she says from underneath me.

The instructor rushes over to us and helps me roll off Mom. "Are you hurt?" she asks.

"My leg just got a little excited," I say. "We're fine."

"Speak for yourself," my mother says. "I'm bleeding."

We both look at Mom. She has a cut on her cheek.

"How'd you do that?" I ask.

She glares at me. "Your toenail."

∞

I slide into the booth across from my mother. The cut on her cheek has at least stopped bleeding.

"Her beginning classes are quite good," my mother says after we order lunch. "You need strength training. Your arms are like rubber bands."

"I'm not going back there," I say. "It was humiliating."

"It's not my fault you don't exercise," she says.

"It's your fault I tried a handstand," I say. "I can't do a push-up. What made you think I could do a handstand?"

"You have to try to succeed," she says. "Yes, you'll fail a million times. But the million and first, you won't. That's the point."

"Poor Howard," I say, referring to the man on my right in the yoga class. "I hope the swelling goes down quickly."

"It's not Howard's first yoga accident," she says. "He'll be fine. But maybe you should bring him a bottle of scotch next Sunday. As a peace offering."

"I'm not going back," I repeat.

Mom just smiles. "We'll see."

Chapter 3

Dr. Steinburg's office is colder than usual. Or maybe it's just that my body has the permanent shakes since that night with Matt.

"So how goes the love?" my therapist asks me as I take my regular seat. My eyes sting, but I'm determined not to cry.

"Well...Alec had some emergency and had to go to China for an indeterminate amount of time. So he told me not to wait for him."

Dr. Steinburg raises an eyebrow. "Did he say why he left?"

"No," I say. "Just that his life was about to change, and he couldn't put me through that, so that's it."

"Are you alright, Hope?" he asks.

I shake my head. "Not really. And I'm so not alright that I slept with Matt."

He shifts in his chair. "Are you seeing him?"

"No. He's been showing up, and saying he's confused, and I've been fighting him off. But when Alec told me to get lost...I instigated it. I called Matt."

"And what were you hoping to get out of that call?" he asks.

I shrug. "Company. Commiseration. Empathy. I just didn't want to be alone."

"But you could have called Martika," he says. "Or your mother."

I nod. I could have.

Should have.

"And how did you and Matt leave things?"

"The same," I say. "We both acknowledged we don't know what we want. It was a moment of weakness."

Dr. Steinburg nods. "Weakness, yes, but also immaturity. You ran back to the familiar without thinking about the consequences."

"Probably," I say. I don't really want to discuss it.

Dr. Steinburg reads me perfectly and changes the subject. "What's going on with your music?"

"I had a meeting with Lockstep Records," I say. "But they're jerks. I've been writing some new songs, and I was thinking about just starting my own thing. Maybe using a fake name."

"What's wrong with your real name?"

I glare at him. "You already know."

"So you're choosing the most difficult path just because you don't want to give your dead father the satisfaction of knowing his name opened doors?"

"I can do it on my own," I say. "And I can be anyone I want to be."

"Besides your name," he says, "and besides your father, what's so awful about being Hope Cruz Russell?"

"Nothing," I say. "I mean, it's not that."

"Isn't it?"

My eyes find my lap. I can't make myself look up. "I want to live long enough to grow old with someone. I want to have confidence. I want to take advantage of every minute I have left and make my mark on the world. That's..."

I finally raise my eyes. Dr. Steinburg is staring at me patiently.

"That's the one thing my dad taught me. He grabbed life by the balls. He didn't let anything stand in his way. He told the world to listen up or fuck off."

"So what is stopping you from doing the same?" he asks.

I sigh. "I'm just not that kind of person. I'm quiet and shy, and I have trouble with crowds, and I just think that maybe if I created a new persona, it would be easier."

"You know, the only way to change our inner selves is through our behavior. Oh, you'll hear all this crap about positive thinking and imagining yourself doing what you want to do, but imagining gets us nowhere. You want to be outgoing? Then be outgoing. You want the world to listen up? Then you have to tell them to listen up. And then your actions will change your emotions. They will change your thinking. You will become that which you do. We are our actions."

"You make it sound easy," I say.

"Easy? No. But it is quite simple. I kind of like this idea, now that I think on it. Choose a stage name. Be that stage name. See how it goes."

I laugh. "You think I should do it?"

Dr. Steinburg nods. "Really think about the person you want to be, the inner person. And I'm not talking about fame. I'm talking about confidence, grace, poise, passion. Then do the things that such a person would do. I look forward to meeting the person you become."

∞

I get home and open my laptop.

I already know who I want to be. I just need to be her.

I order six wigs and ten new pairs of sunglasses off Amazon. I buy a leather biker jacket with a gold zipper. I buy a white pair of leather creepers that I've always wanted but was too much of a pussy to buy. I buy a knee-high pair of purple combat boots. Who knows how I'll wear all this stuff, but I like it. It feels like me.

The new me.

Lady Strings.

Here I am.

Chapter 4

It's open-mike night at The Ugly Mug in Old Towne Orange, and you have to sign up in advance to play. I liked the idea of that—I'm committed. If I'd just had to show up, I might have chickened out.

Or maybe not. I like the playing music part. It's the "act like a rock star" part I'm not so good at.

Martika and Benny are coming tonight to offer some support. According to Martika, they'll be the crowd exciters. No musician wants to play to a sedate crowd, and Martika knows how to be loud.

So I've got on my platinum blonde bob wig, oversized black sunglasses ala Jackie O, a tight black top that shows off my boobs under my leather jacket, and my purple combat boots. I look ready, even if I don't feel ready.

I get one song, more if the audience responds. Fingers crossed that they respond.

The place is packed when I enter, but I spot Marti and Ben right away. They snagged the front-and-center table. Typical. So I check in with the staff and then squat down next to Martika.

"What do you think?" I whisper to her.

She glances down at me and leans away. "If you're playing tonight, I hope you go first. 'Cause once Lady Strings comes on, she's not leaving the stage."

I cock my head. "She's that good, huh?" I can't keep the laughter out of my voice, and Martika's mouth drops open.

"Hope?"

I nod.

Martika squeals and throws her arm around my shoulder, squeezing my neck tight. "Oh my God, you look incredible! I didn't know it was you!"

"Shhh," I say. "That's the point."

She releases me with a smile. "Knock 'em dead, kid."

Benny smiles and gives me a thumbs up.

I stand up and lean against the wall near the back. There aren't any open seats anyway, and this way I get a good view of the crowd and can gauge their reactions.

The first musician to come on is a greasy guy, mid-twenties, with hair down to his butt and a Ron Jeremy mustache. He looks like a transplant from the seventies.

And that's pretty much what he is, as he sings "Hot Blooded" by Foreigner, butchering every note. The audience cringes every time he goes into the chorus. But he's enthusiastic, I'll give him that. He's strutting his stuff, bending over the mike stand and closing his eyes as he sings the high notes. He looks the part.

He gets tepid applause at the end, and lots of cheers from a table in the middle. He grins to his buddies, and sits on a girl's lap.

Next up is a college girl in a floral sundress. Hello, it's the beginning of February. She sings a Fall Out Boy song, has a decent voice, but is wobbly with nerves. Seems like she lost a bet or took up a challenge from her sorority sisters. Either way, she gets some genuine applause and some cheers of encouragement, but not enough to warrant an encore.

My turn.

I pull a stool up to the microphone and adjust the stand. I get a few whistles, and a "Yeah, Baby!" from the frat boys at the back. I grin.

"My name is Lady Strings, and I'm thrilled to be here tonight. Sing along if you know this one."

Martika gives a loud "Whooo!" Ben gives a "Yeah!"

Then I tap the flat of my hand on the guitar four times and play a stripped-down version of Britney Spears' "Hit Me Baby One More Time."

It takes the first verse before people recognize the song. Everyone's staring at me slightly open-mouthed, and I see the moment when that recognition hits—people lean in to their neighbors, whisper, I get a few hoots, and toes start tapping.

By the second verse, everyone's singing with me, and Martika gets to her feet and starts clapping in rhythm over her head.

Ben joins her.

And then, I don't know, maybe the people behind them just can't see me anymore and want a better view, but they stand up. The sorority girls get to their feet giggling, belting out the lyrics. The frat boys move closer to them. I crook my finger at the girl in the floral sundress, and she mouths, "Me?" and I nod, and she comes to stand next to me, and we sing together.

And when I finish, the place goes wild. People are stamping their feet and cheering, and the applause shakes the rafters. I laugh and stand up for a bow.

"You're really great," Sundress Girl says. I slip my sunglasses down just enough to show my eyes, and I give her a wink.

"Another one!" Martika yells. "We want more!"

I look up at the manager of the coffeehouse and cock my head. He nods at me, so I sit back down on the stool.

"Wow, thank you," I say. "Thank you so much. Okay. Let's do another."

So I play "Personal Jesus" by Depeche Mode. Even the younger kids in the crowd know this song. Martika leads the way, clapping hard as a substitute for drums. The crowd joins in, and we rock.

I follow that with one of my original songs, and end with "The Scientist" by Coldplay.

After, I'm mobbed, and I give out all the USB sticks I'd brought with six of my songs on each. Martika drags out her iPad, and gets people to sign up for my exclusive mailing list. I book the next four Wednesday nights at The Ugly Mug.

When I finish my free latte and stand to leave with Martika and Benny, my eyes go to the door. I see the back of Matt as he slips out without a word.

Chapter 5

"This is becoming a habit," I say as I exit my car and spy Matt on my front steps. "Maybe I should put out a lounge chair for you."

He stands. "I saw you tonight."

I don't say anything.

"Why are you wearing a wig?"

"You don't like me as a blonde?" I ask.

Matt shakes his head. "It's fine. It's just not you."

"Maybe you don't know me," I say. I head past him to the door, and Matt pulls on my arm.

"Are you afraid to be you?"

"I'm not afraid of anything, Matt," I say. "I'm just trying to play my music without my dad involved."

He takes his hand away and stuffs it in his pocket. "People will find out eventually. Isn't it exhausting, trying to be somebody you're not?"

"It was one performance," I say, "at a little nothing coffee shop. I'm not in danger of exhausting myself over one performance."

"What's wrong with Hope Russell?" he says. "You don't have to do this."

"You found plenty wrong with Hope Russell, if memory serves," I say.

Matt growls in frustration. "It wasn't about you, okay? The whole thing was about me. I was the failure! I was the one who couldn't help you! Do you know what that's like? Waking up every day and feeling like you're worthless?"

I just stare at him. Yep, I know something about that.

"I fucked that grad student not because I loved her, not even because I liked her. I just needed to feel like I was good at something. She looked up to me in the department, and she thought I was successful, and...I just needed that feeling."

"I'm so sorry," I say. I bow my head. "I'm sorry I didn't give you that. I never thought of you as a failure."

"Christ, don't apologize!" he screams. "I'm the fuck-up."

"You are," I say. "But I'm still sorry."

Matt huffs a breath and smiles. "You're the only thing that's ever mattered to me. Your health, your happiness...that's all I ever wanted."

"I'm healthy now. And happy. At least, happier than I've ever been."

He flinches at that. "Really? You're happier than when we were married?"

"With myself," I say. "My state of mind. Looking back...I thought I was happy at the time, but now that I'm facing stuff and being honest with myself...we were going through the motions, Matt.

I didn't even know what love and sacrifice meant. Happiness was the absence of conflict. And that's not real happiness."

"You're right," he says. "We weren't happy. But that doesn't mean things couldn't be different."

"I'm not ready," I say. "I'm not ready to jump into that comfortable place. What if nothing changes?"

"We won't know that unless we try."

I scuff my boot over the concrete. "Maybe we could try being friends."

Matt grins. "With benefits?"

I shake my head. "No benefits. Just friends."

The smile slips from his lips, but he nods. "I'd like that."

He moves to stand in front of me. My body trembles at the closeness as he leans into me. And then he plants a very soft, sweet kiss on my cheek.

"I was proud of you tonight," he whispers. And then he walks to his car.

Chapter 6

My mother and I meet with Alice Wills, our new attorney who's looking into the shady dealings of our former attorneys who handled the music rights for my dad's catalog. Alice waves us each to a seat and takes the great big leather chair behind her desk.

"So," she says. "Looks like Mayberry & Foster did indeed close the Spotify deal, the *Cop Killer Reloaded* video game deal, and the one with the senator's campaign. I have the contracts here." She hands us each a stack of papers.

I immediately flip to the signature pages.

"That's my signature," I say, "but I absolutely did not sign these."

"I know," she says. "They're forged. I have a handwriting expert who can pick out the little details. But we also just received the accounting report, and everything's on the up and up. Even though you didn't sign these contracts, the monies are in your escrow account at the firm. And they've accumulated a nice bit of interest."

"Are you saying that we need to suck it up because they didn't steal any money?" my mother shrieks.

"No," Alice says patiently. "What I'm saying is that we have to prove damages. You don't have any financial damages, so we then look at damage to the estate's reputation. Obviously…it's a gray area."

"Doesn't look gray to me," Mom says. "That video game promotes violence. We don't condone that."

Alice nods. "Yes…but the jury's not going to look at your background, Mrs. Cruz. It is your husband's character that will be on trial. It's common knowledge that he died of a drug overdose and that he was arrested for assault on numerous occasions. Is there something in his past that would indicate he'd be against these things today?"

"Just because he was an ass doesn't mean he'd want to profit off all his bad behavior," Mom says stubbornly.

"But Mayberry & Foster will make exactly that case," Alice says. "Look, they did something that is absolutely wrong and illegal. And we'll make them pay for that. But I don't want this case to go to trial. Besides dragging you two through the mud, a jury trial is just plain unpredictable. We can probably fill the jury with people sympathetic to your stance on the video game, and even Senator Horton's legalize-all-drugs campaign. But the subscription service deal is dicey. People are starting to believe that information should be widely available and even free. People want to hear Joe Cruz's music, and right now, they can't unless they buy it the old fashioned way or steal it."

"It isn't even about the specific deals, is it?" I ask. "It's the fact that they forged our signatures and profited off of something they had no right to."

"That's exactly what we'll focus on as we negotiate a settlement," Alice says. "But in a jury trial, they'll try to obscure their guilt using any means possible."

"I want those attorneys fired," Mom says. "That's non-negotiable. I want them disbarred."

"That's really what this is about," I say. "You know we don't need some huge amount of money. Whatever we get will go to charity. We just want justice."

Alice closes the file in front of her and grins. "Justice is what I do."

ℴ

I sit down with my laptop after dinner, and my hands itch. I want to write a letter to the editor of the LA Times, telling the world about my scumbag lawyers. I want to rip them apart on Yelp. Or post a picture of the douchebag attorney Alan with a mustache and horns and a one-inch dick hanging out of his pants.

But I can't. I can't say a word about any of it, or they can turn around and sue me.

A text distracts me. Chet, the son of one of my mother's ex-boyfriends. *Come have a beer with us.*

I smile and answer back. *Where?*

Gino's. We're at the bar. Huuuurrrrry!!!

Ahh. It's kind of nice for someone to want my company that much.

I exchange my wool pants for jeans, my heels for the creepers. Throw on the leather jacket and some shiny green eyeshadow.

Chet is leaning on the arm of Clancy, his better half, who's gesticulating to a group of men leaning on the bar. I hug Chet from behind and kiss his shoulder. "I've missed you," I say.

He turns around and smiles, bestowing my cheek with a kiss. "Ditto. I thought a night of debauchery with us was preferable to a night of moping at home alone. What are you wearing?"

I spin around. "You like? It's my new look."

"I like," Clancy says, pulling me into a hug. "But your poor hair."

I shrug and run a hand over the back of my head, which still bears the scar of an unfortunate head injury. "Nothing to be done unless I want to shave it all," I say.

"Excellent," Clancy says. "I have an electric razor at home. If you pay me in tequila, I'll do it."

I laugh. "I'm not shaving my head. And if I were, I wouldn't let a drunk lawyer do it."

Clancy holds out his hand and spreads his fingers. "Look at me. Not a shake. I'm solid as a rock."

Chet waves a hand. "Clancy has no idea what he's doing, it's true. But this is a good idea. Why don't you cut your hair?"

Those words sound foreign to me. "Cut my hair? No way. I've always had it long."

Chet lifts my hair up off my neck and kind of tucks the ends under. "Cute. It'd be so cute! And you can dye it. Maybe pink?"

"Lavender," Clancy says. "That lavender gray that's so popular right now. Damn, that would be hot."

I laugh again. "I just bought a bunch of wigs. I think those are a safer bet."

"I saw the video," Chet says. "The bob was great, but the blonde washed you out."

"Gee, thanks," I say.

He smiles. "If you're wearing wigs, then who cares what your real hair looks like? Live a little!"

"I'll think about it," I say. "Now buy me a drink."

"Ooh, the lady's feisty tonight," Clancy says. He pulls on the shirt of the guy standing next to him. "Logan, you're into feisty ladies."

Logan turns and gives me a smile. He reminds me of the Marlboro man—tall, beefy, rugged. Not classically handsome, but definitely sexy and all male.

I hold out my hand. "I'm Hope."

"Hope," he says, shaking my hand firmly. "Logan. Clancy and I are neighbors."

"Ah," I say. "What do you do, Logan?"

"He's a firefighter," Chet whispers loudly. Then he giggles.

I laugh. "Looks like he's good at lighting the fires. I wonder how good he is at quenching them."

Chet and Logan laugh, and Clancy rolls his eyes. "That's the best line you can come up with? 'He's good at lighting fires?'"

"You've got a better one?" I challenge.

Clancy smiles. "I bet he has the longest hose here. And if you want him to put out the fire, just stop, drop, and roll."

We all laugh, and then I look at Logan. "You heard those before?"

Logan grins. "My favorite is, wanna slide down my pole?"

I roll my eyes. "That's never actually worked, has it?"

"I don't know," he says. "But it looks promising so far."

Chet puts an arm around my shoulder. "I'm sorry, Logan, but Hope's off limits. She wants an actual commitment."

"Doesn't mean I can't flirt," I say.

"Fine," Chet says, "but no sex!"

"What are you, my mother?"

Chet looks at me, dead-pan. "Funny."

"I can have sex if I want," I say, "but I need a few drinks first."

Logan signals the bartender.

෨

My only excuse is that…let's face it. I have no excuse. I'm at the bar with a bunch of horny men and I'm wasted.

But at least I know I'm wasted. That has to count for something.

We all climb in a cab and head to Clancy's. But as we pass a drugstore, Clancy orders the cab driver to stop and wait. Five minutes later, he's back in the car, his purchase tucked under his shirt. Despite Chet's ribbing, Clancy won't tell us what he bought.

Inside his apartment, I start to sweat. "Is it hot in here?"

Logan puts his hands on my waist. "With you in here, it is."

I laugh. That's like the funniest thing I've ever heard.

I unzip my jacket and throw it on the couch. The men all gape at me. "What?"

"Oh, dear," Chet says, shaking his head. "I'm not being a very good friend tonight, am I?"

I crease my brow and take his hands in mine. "Don't say that. You're the best friend anyone could have! Absolutely the best!" I squeeze his hands tight, and in my drunken fog, I nod twice for emphasis.

Chet smiles. "I'm supposed to be protecting you. Come on, love. Put this on." He starts to unbutton his shirt.

"Why do you want me to wear your shirt?" I ask.

He shrugs off the shirt and puts my arms in the sleeves. "Because all you have on is a bra."

I look down at my chest. Hello, wow. There are my boobs. "Oh."

He pulls the shirt into place and buttons two buttons. "I'll have Clancy drive you home. I didn't realize you were this knackered."

"Knackered?" I say with a giggle. "Channeling your English forebears, are you?"

"Knackered is good," Clancy says. He pulls out the bag from underneath his shirt. "We're going to color your hair!"

I squeal. "Oh, goody! Did you get the lavender?"

"Not that much choice on a Saturday night," he says. "I have one box of bleach to strip the color from your hair, and then we're going...wait for it...blue!"

I gasp. Blue! How exciting!

Logan laughs. "You should probably remove that shirt. You don't want to get it all blue."

I totally agree. "Yeah, Chet. This shirt is expensive." I take it off and throw it on the floor.

Chet sighs. "Logan, my dear, I think it's time for you to go."

"But—"

"No buts," Chet says, steering him to the door. "Show's over."

"Call me!" I yell at Logan. "I'll miss you!"

Logan laughs and out he goes.

※

I wake up on Clancy's couch, and I'm amazed I don't have a hangover. And then I sit up. Ugh. I feel like a dry loofah. I need water.

I go to the kitchen and fill a glass from the tap. I down it. Then I get another.

"Morning, sexy," Clancy says at my back. I turn and smile.

"Morning. Sorry about last night."

He kisses my cheek. "Sorry for what?"

"Drinking so much," I say. "I was a little out of it."

Clancy leans back against the counter and raises an eyebrow. "You don't get out much, do you?"

"Not much," I admit. "But still…thanks for taking care of me."

Chet comes in wearing only boxers. "You haven't seen your hair yet, have you?"

My hand automatically flies to my head. I pat it. Sweet Jesus, my hair is practically gone!

I run to the bathroom and flip on the light. I just stare.

"Lady Strings," Clancy says behind me. "Ta da!"

My hair is about two inches long. All over. Sticking up in every direction. And it's a bright cobalt blue.

Chet hugs me from the back. "Remember, you have wigs. It's only hair. It grows."

My eyes sting. "If I hadn't been wasted last night, I…I never would have done this."

Chet squeezes me harder.

I turn in his arms and look at Clancy. He just stares at me uncertainly.

Then I launch myself at him and crush him in a hug.

"Thank you," I whisper. "Thank you. I never would have had the courage to do this on my own."

In the mirror behind him, I see Clancy smile at Chet. Chet swipes his hand over his brow.

Chapter 7

My phone rings as I'm trying to knit a baby blanket for Martika. I throw my needles beside me and answer the unfamiliar number.

"Hello?"

"Hey, Hope. It's Logan. The firefighter from last night?"

I laugh. "I remember. I wasn't that drunk."

"Were you drunk enough to let Clancy dye your hair?"

I laugh again. "Well, you got me there. How are you?"

"Good," he says. "I have tonight off, and I thought maybe we could hang out."

"Sounds like fun. What did you have in mind?"

"Some of the guys I work with are meeting for drinks," he says. "At the Brewing Company on Newport. I can pick you up. Say, 7?"

Another night of drinking. Just what I don't need.

"Great!" I hear myself say.

ଈଠ

Logan introduces me to his friends, and wow. Okay, not all of them have the face of a god, but their bodies? Make me want to light my house on fire just to have them come rescue me.

Logan buys me a pear cider without asking me. Whoa, it's kind of yummy. I know I should probably exercise my new-found voice and object, but he seems pleased with himself. No need to ruin the mood.

"Have you always had blue hair?" Fireman Aidan asks me. Logan has wandered down the bar, talking to some girl he knows. At least his buddies aren't that rude.

"I just dyed it last night," I say. "Kind of a spur-of-the-moment decision."

"That takes balls," he says. "Or have you always been that bold?"

I shake my head. "I was a little drunk," I admit. "Not as ballsy as you think."

He grins and looks down at Logan, then back at me. "How do you know Logan?"

"I'm friends with his neighbor. Just met him last night."

"And you agreed that fast, huh?"

I crease my brow. "You mean agreed to hang out?"

Aidan laughs. "Is that what we're calling it?"

"I don't follow."

"I mean the after part," he says. "Have you done it before?"

I'm thoroughly confused. "What after part?"

Aidan frowns. "You mean, he didn't tell you?"

"Tell me what?"

He looks suspicious, like I'm just playing dumb. "You're coming back to my place after this. Right?"

I glance down at Logan. He notices me and gives a little smile. "Logan didn't mention that."

Aidan scrubs a hand through his hair. "Shit. Sorry. I thought he talked to you—"

"About what?"

"Well…he said he was bringing the girl. I assumed it was you."

I slug back my cider. "Bringing the girl for what?"

Aidan leans in a little closer to me. "For a threesome. It's fun as hell. You should think about it."

I pause with my glass at my lips. "You want to have a threesome with me and Logan?"

"You're sexy," he says, lowering his voice. "We'll take care of you."

Uh…what? That's not happening. Not in a thousand years. But I don't say that out loud.

"And you're okay with another guy?" I ask. "I mean, I can understand the appeal of having two girls, but…another guy?"

He shrugs. "Don't knock it 'til you try it. It's fun to watch."

I nod slowly. "And do you and Logan…touch each other?"

Aidan smiles. "If the lady wants us to."

Okay, so my nipples harden at that. I have no idea why. I've never even thought about this stuff. But that doesn't mean I'm gonna do it.

"And how many ladies have you done this with?" I ask.

"A few," he says. "It's not always easy to find a willing participant, but you'd be amazed how many people are into it."

Yes, I would.

I look into my glass. The cider's almost gone, and my head is swimming. Now I know why Logan ordered it—it's twice as powerful as a glass of beer. Guess I gave him the wrong impression last night.

"So I guess you don't have a girlfriend," I say.

"I used to," he says. "Just broke up two weeks ago."

"I'm guessing your lifestyle would be tough for a girlfriend."

He laughs. "She got me into it."

Ooo-kay. I clearly need to get out more.

I rummage in my purse and pull out a ten-dollar bill. I throw it on the bar.

"Tell Logan I paid for my own drink," I say. I slide off the bar stool, and Aidan puts his hand on my arm.

"You're leaving?"

"Tell him I was gonna make him scream tonight," I say. "I was gonna suck his cock so hard he'd be seeing stars. But since he can't even be bothered to talk to me…fuck him."

Aidan's eyes go wide. "We can leave him here. We don't need him. We can go to my place."

I put my hand on his cheek. "I'm sorry, Aidan. You seem like a decent guy. But I only fuck people I'm attracted to."

And I head out the door.

Chapter 8

Martika laughs hysterically as I tell her about my "date" with Logan.

"Finally," she says. "You finally had a date with an asshole."

"What's that supposed to mean?" I ask.

"I've been amazed at all these guys," she says. "You've met one nice guy after another. Statistically, you were due for a clunker."

I laugh. "I guess you're right."

"You're coming to my Lamaze class tomorrow night, right?" she asks.

"Yep. I'll be there."

"Benny's pouting," she says. "He doesn't want to miss it."

I shake my head. "I'd think he'd be glad. Isn't it boring for most guys?"

"Benny's not most guys."

"True," I say. "Okay, I'll see you tomorrow."

଼ଚ

So Lamaze class. I don't know anything about Lamaze. I only know that when you're pregnant, you learn to do it. It's some kind of birthing technique, I think.

Martika signed up for a six-week class, and I'm glad I'm here on night one. Everyone in the room is as clueless as me.

The class is at St. Joseph's Hospital, in one of their teaching rooms. I didn't know hospitals have classrooms. Learn something every day.

We all sit on the floor in front of a projector screen, and I'm irritated immediately. Some of these women look ready to pop. I wonder how the hell they'll get back on their feet.

The instructor starts talking, and I glance around. Yikes. The lady sitting next to me has purple feet so swollen they look like they belong on an elephant. Poor thing. The woman next to her has a shirt on that's so tight it looks like the sleeves are cutting off the circulation in her arms. They all look happy, though. Even if they're bloated.

The lights go out, and a movie comes on, and I realize I haven't been paying attention at all. I lean into Martika's ear. "What's this about?"

"It's a live birth," she whispers back. "Just close your eyes if you need to."

Birth doesn't bother me. At least, I don't think it does. Only violence and blood bother me. I should be good.

We watch a doctor check the woman to see how much her cervix has dilated. Huh. The doctor figures this out with his fingers?

"Ten centimeters," he says. "You're ready to push."

The woman is doing some funny breathing stuff, panting like she's a banshee. Her partner bathes her brow and massages her shoulders. Wow. It looks like she's in a lot of pain.

The camera perspective changes. Now we're getting a full-on shot of her hairy hoo-hah. The woman actually agreed to make this movie?

The doctor sticks his fingers in and around and kind of stretches her out. We see the top of the baby's head. Oh my God, it's huge!

I sit mesmerized as this woman pants and pushes and groans. It takes about thirty minutes, but finally the baby's head slides out, and the doctor suctions the baby's nose and mouth, and then tells the mother to give one more big push. The baby slides out all the way with a squelch, and the class actually cheers.

I let out the breath I'd been holding, and a tear glides down my cheek.

That was the most amazing, wonderful, miraculous thing I've ever seen.

Class is dismissed, and Martika hugs me close to her side as we walk to the car.

"What did you think?" she says. "I'm proud of you, that you watched it."

"Will you let me watch when it's your turn?" I ask.

Martika stops walking, pulls away, and looks at me. "Are you sure?"

"I won't look," I say. "I mean, I won't look straight on—"

She throws her arms around me. "It would mean so much to me," she says. "And I'm not embarrassed. You know that."

"If I can't experience it myself," I say, "I want to experience it with you."

Chapter 9

I do another show at the Ugly Mug and collect more names for my not-yet-existent newsletter. When I get home and check my messages, I find Martika's left two.

"Don't get on the Internet, okay?" she says. "Just trust me. Let's do coffee in the morning."

"Just making sure you're going straight to bed. It'll be better coming from me."

I can't ignore that.

So I fire up my laptop and put my name in the search engine.

"Joe Cruz's daughter is expecting! Her lesbian love child is due this spring!"

Say what?

They know I went to that class, and they think Martika is my lover! Ha, ha, ha, ha, ha!

It's funny. So not something to get worked up about.

So I go to bed.

❧

"Twenty-eight weeks pregnant!" Benny announces when I come through their door. "We're in the third trimester!"

I give him a hug. "So exciting!"

Martika comes in from the bedroom, still in her robe.

"Are you feeling okay?" I ask.

She nods. "I'm just exhausted. I barely slept. My legs keep jumping."

"Restless leg syndrome," Benny says. "I'm gonna have her take a hot bath after this and see if she can get a nap."

I sit next to her on the couch and rub her back. "I can go. You rest."

"No," she says. "I'm fine. We need to talk."

"I already saw it," I say. "So you're having my lesbian love child, huh?"

She smiles. "Is that all you saw?"

"There's more?"

Martika sighs. "There's a quote in one of the articles. From Matt."

I cock my head. "Matt?"

Benny brings her laptop over to us, and Marti finds the article in question. She reads, "Matt Russell, Cruz's ex-husband, only had one thing to say about her bisexuality. 'Hope can't have kids of her own, and she and Martika have been close since junior high.'"

I swipe the laptop out of her hands and read it for myself.

"Why would he tell someone that?" I whisper. "It's nobody's business."

"I'm sorry, Hope," Martika says.

I stare at the screen. None of what Matt said is a lie, but it makes me feel icky, like I'm standing naked in front of a crowd.

"Are you mad?" she asks.

I shake my head. "I'm...baffled. Matt knows I wouldn't want him saying anything about this. And if a reporter did corner him, and asked about my visit to that Lamaze class with you, this isn't the right response. He would have said that my best friend is pregnant and I must have been helping out. I mean, why go to the part about me not having kids of my own?"

"That must not be what the reporter asked," she says. "Maybe they flat-out told him we're lovers."

I laugh. "Matt would never believe that."

Martika frowns. "So...you're okay with this?"

I stand. "I'll ask him about it. That's all I can do." I bend forward and plant a kiss on her head. "Bye, Lover."

ಶ

So I head to the university. Matt should be on campus right now, and I want to catch him off guard so he can't prepare a lie.

My body itches as I think this. While not particularly forthcoming, Matt's never been a liar. But this breach of trust has me doubting him. And I hate that I feel that way about him.

Oh, wait. He cheated on me. He did lie, even if it was only one time. How quickly I've forgotten.

I head down the hall to his office. His door is open. I walk in to find him sitting at his desk, a youngish beauty draped over his shoulder. Both their laughter stops and the girl straightens up when I enter.

"I need a word in private," I say.

The girl looks at Matt. He stands too quickly, awkwardly. "Uh…Hope, this is Hailey. Hailey, Hope."

Hailey raises an eyebrow. She obviously knows who I am.

"We're still on for lunch, right?" she asks.

"I'll call you," he says.

Hailey frowns and exits, careful not to brush me on the way out.

"What happened to your hair?" Matt says. "Have a seat."

"Why did you tell a reporter that I'm unable to have kids?" I ask without sitting.

He blinks. "I didn't."

"You're quoted in the article," I say. "Seems a long shot that someone would guess that outta the blue."

"I would never have said that, Hope. You know me better than that."

"Did you speak to a reporter?" I ask.

He scrubs a hand through his hair. "One of them approached me in front of the house. But I didn't say anything about anything."

"What did you say?"

"Fuck off, if memory serves."

"Then how would they know?" I ask. "The only people that know are you, Martika and Benny, my ex who's still in China, and my mother. None of them would talk."

"Maybe your ex did," he says.

"No. Never."

Matt narrows his eyes. "So a guy you knew for a couple of months…you have more trust in him than you do in me?"

"He didn't cheat on me," I say.

"Right. He only left with no explanation."

I grit my teeth. I'm gonna have to tell Benny to shut the hell up.

"He's in China," I say. "There's no way it was him."

"Who knows who your mother's told," he says. "She speaks without thinking."

True. "But they attributed the quote to you. Why would they do that?"

Matt shrugs. "I don't know what to tell you. Either you believe me or you don't."

"I want to," I say. "But I think that would be naïve."

And I turn around and walk out.

That Lamaze class movie lit something inside of me. Most likely, I'll never have a biological child of my own. But I want to grow something and take care of it.

I debate getting a pet. But I'm not at home that often, and I'm not certain I'm responsible enough. So instead, I decide on a vegetable garden.

I've never grown plants before. Sure, I have a yard, but I also have a gardener. I've never done the work myself.

I have a 10-foot-by-20-foot plot that runs along the back of the house. It has some random bushes in it, but if I clear those out, I'll have plenty of room to grow my own salad.

So I put some old clothes on and head to the yard. I grip the first bush and yank.

Nothing. This sucker must be in there pretty deep.

So I squat in the dirt and grab the main trunk close to the ground. The thorny leaves scratch my cheeks, but I grit my teeth, close my eyes, and pull. Puuuuulllll!

Nothing except some scratches on my palms. I need gloves.

Of course, I have no gloves except for some leather ones from my annual trips to New York with Mom. I can't ruin those. So I grab my oven mitts.

This is genius. The mitts even cover my forearms and save me from the pokey leaves. So I try again to pull the damn bush from the ground. I manage to strip an entire branch of leaves off, but that's it.

Maybe I can cut the bush down to size.

I grab a pair of scissors.

I spend two hours snipping whatever the scissors will cut through. Which is not much. But I do manage to denude the bush of all the leaves.

Hee, hee. I have a naked bush.

೫

With my bank account $500 lighter, I come home from the hardware store with a shovel, a pickaxe, giant tree clippers, a supposedly-easy-to-install drip watering system, a long hose with a special spray nozzle, fertilizer, ten bags of mulch, an orange tree, a lemon tree, some bible about gardening in the West, and about 20 packets of seeds.

I'm getting serious.

I wrap a bandana around my blue head and grip the shovel tight. I thrust it as hard as I can near the base of the bush.

It goes about half an inch into the dirt.

So I put a foot on the shovel and try to push it in.

Nope.

I stand on the shovel. I jump on it. Not working.

I spend an hour scraping at the dirt.

This is ridiculous! I can't be this weak, or this stupid. How the hell does a gardener do this?

I need to make the dirt easier to dig. Maybe if I watered it…

I set the hose on high and put it at the base of the bush. Then I go make a pitcher of lemonade and turn on HGTV.

I wake up two hours later, a pool of drool under my cheek. I didn't realize gardening was so tiring.

The dirt should be good and watered by now. So I go out to the yard…holy crap! My backyard is a lake!

I splish splash through the water and turn off the hose. Water oozes into my shoes and I feel my toes getting squishy. I spy the edge of something yellow under the water and realize that all of my purchases are under three inches of water.

Even the seed packets.

My entire mission was to grow something and lovingly take care of it. I cannot let these seeds die!

So I scoop everything out of the mud and set it on the dry patio.

It takes me two hours, but I manage to dig up two of those bushes.

Then I literally sit my ass in the mud as the sun sets and dig rows of holes. I plant my seeds.

And I say a prayer that they take root.

Chapter 11

My phone rings, and caller ID says Alec Chang & Associates. A wave of anger rolls through me, and I almost don't answer. But I miss Alec. I'm worried about him.

"Hello?" I say tentatively.

"Is this Ms. Russell?" a female voice says.

"Yes."

"This is Wendy Brae with Alec Chang and Associates. Is this a good time?"

"Sure," I say, breathing a sigh of relief and feeling a pang of disappointment at the same time.

"I have the paperwork ready for your estate," she says. "Mr. Chang passed it along to me, and I'd like to set up a time to go over it with you. Would you like to come into the office, or is it easier if I come to you?"

"I can come in," I say. "I'm free now."

"Great," she says. "Mr. Chang insisted that I make you a top priority. I'll be here."

"I'm leaving now," I say.

മ

I'm looking forward to this. I'm finally going to give my mother the things from my dad that she deserves, and I can stop feeling guilty for controlling her financially.

Ms. Wendy Brae doesn't keep me waiting. I don't even have time to sit before she appears, giving me a warm handshake and a smile.

"It's wonderful to finally meet you," she says. "Let's go back to my office."

I follow Ms. Brae's lead, and I can see Alec's office at the end of the hall. The door is open and the light is on.

I clear my throat. "Is Mr. Chang back from China?" I ask softly.

She nods. "He got back last week. Shall we say hello?"

I shake my head. "Maybe after."

She goes through the paperwork with me, and everything is in line with the plan Alec and I already discussed. My mother will be getting the two houses in LA that generate about $25,000 a month in rent, I'm setting up a trust account to pay for management and maintenance of the homes, and then I'm giving her $5 million in cash to do with as she sees fit.

I sign everything and thank Ms. Brae.

"Let me call Mr. Chang and have him come in," she says, reaching for her phone.

"No!" I say a little too loudly, and then I force myself to smile. "No. I'll just stop by his office on my way out."

I exit to the hallway and stare down in Alec's direction.

He's been home a week, and he didn't call me.

I don't have to see him. I can just leave.

"Is everything alright?" Ms. Brae asks as I stand shaking outside her office.

I smile at her. "Fine. Sorry. Thanks again."

And I force my feet to move.

∞

Have you ever seen that movie, *Poltergeist?* Scared the crap out of me as a kid, and there's a scene near the end where the mother is running down the hallway, trying to rescue her daughter from the ghosts, and the hallway gets longer and longer, and the more she runs, the farther away she is, and no matter how much she runs she can't get to the end...

That's what this is like. This fucking hallway stretches to forever.

But finally I'm there, at his door. I take a deep breath, knock on the jamb, and stick my head in. "Alec?"

He lifts his head at the sound of my voice, and he looks...tired. His eyes register pain that he doesn't hide quickly enough, but he plasters a small smile on his lips and stands.

"Hope."

I step into the doorway. "Hey. You're back."

He nods. "Did Wendy handle everything properly?"

"Why did you leave?" I blurt out.

Alec sighs.

He comes around his desk and shuts the door. We're standing a foot apart, and my heart pounds uncomfortably.

He waves me to a chair and we both sit.

"How have you been?" he asks.

"I'm not leaving until you tell me why you left."

Alec stares hard at his desk.

"It's long and complicated," he says, "but basically, my ex-wife returned to China to live with her parents about two months before I filed for divorce. We got married in China, but since I'm not a Chinese citizen, I could file for divorce here, and I did. She didn't contest it. Everything went through."

He takes a deep breath.

"But she was pregnant, Hope."

"You knew she was pregnant and you let her go?" I cry.

He shakes his head. "Of course I didn't know! She didn't tell me! But meanwhile, she contested our divorce in the Chinese courts, and I didn't know that, either. And then...I got a call from her mother. My wife was in a car accident and was in a coma. Her parents had been taking care of my daughter, but since it looked like my wife was about to die…they were going to put my daughter up for adoption."

I stare at him, but he still won't look at me.

"How could they do that?" I whisper.

He finally lifts his eyes to mine. "I had to go get her. I had to see to my wife. She died two weeks ago."

A tear slips down my cheek. "Did you bring your…daughter here?" I ask.

He nods. "She's eight months old."

I fight to keep my voice steady. "Why couldn't you tell me this?"

"I was still married, Hope," he says. "Technically. I was still responsible for her. If she'd survived, or was permanently disabled…it was my responsibility. I couldn't do that to you."

"I'm so sorry, Alec," I say. "That you had to go through that."

"You're not angry at me?" he asks. "That I was still married?"

I gape at him. "That's what you're hung up on? You didn't know, so no, I'm not mad at you for that. But I'm still mad."

"I didn't know how it would end," he says. "If it would end. I still care about you, Hope."

"Not enough to call and tell me you were back," I say with a forced laugh. "I care about you, too. And I know part of this was my fault. I had so little faith in myself...I guess it's not surprising that you had so little in me, too." I stand up. "Take care of yourself, Alec."

Chapter 12

Martika invites me over for dinner, saying she has something important to discuss. And I have something important to discuss with her, too. What should I do about Alec?

She gives me a hug at the door. "Is Benny working?" I ask. "I noticed his car's gone."

Martika nods as we head to the kitchen. She grabs a big bowl of salad and sets it on the kitchen table, and I grab the pitcher of iced tea from the fridge. I pour us both a glass while she sits.

"Benny's being deployed," she says, and I pause mid-pour.

"When?"

"Three days," she says, her voice breaking. I watch her blink hard.

"Oh, honey." I set down the pitcher and lean over her for a hug. She clings to me.

I pull away and carefully wipe the tears from her cheeks. "You're a warrior's wife, and you're a warrior yourself. We'll get through it."

She nods. "I know. I just...the baby changes everything. I've never worried about him before. I mean, not really. He's solid. The guys on his team are solid. But now...if something happens to him, Hope..."

I grab her hand and crouch down in front of her. "What do you need from me? Whatever you need, I'll do it."

She squeezes my hand. "You'll still go to Lamaze class with me, right?"

"Of course."

"And when I get closer to my due date, like a week away…will you stay here with me? Just in case?"

My eyes sting. "Of course."

"Will you be my lesbian lover?"

I blink. "Hell, no."

She laughs, and I join her.

"I'm here," I say. "I'll help you through it. You won't be alone."

"I knew that," she says. "I don't tell you enough, and maybe I've never told you at all, but…you're the best friend in the world, Hope."

That does it. Tears roll down my cheeks. "So are you, baby," I say. "So are you."

৪৩

We eat, and Martika brings out Benny's many lists, and we go over the plan for the next couple of months. Damn, there's a lot to do to prepare for a baby.

Which makes me think of Alec. He didn't have nine months to prepare. He barely had time to get used to the idea, let alone get his life in order.

"I talked to Alec today," I say as we wash dishes.

Martika turns off the faucet and raises an eyebrow. "He called you?"

I shake my head. "I saw him at his office when I went there to sign stuff. He got back last week and didn't tell me."

"Did he explain?" she asks.

I tell her the story, and we both sigh as we sink to the couch.

"So what are you going to do?" she asks.

I shrug. "I still love him. But I don't know if there's anything I can do."

"You can tell him that you still love him," she says. "Tell him you still want to be with him."

"I don't know if I do," I say.

Martika wrinkles her brow. "Why wouldn't you?" There's anger in her voice.

"Why are you mad?"

She shifts on the couch. "You're throwing away something really good. And why? What are you afraid of?"

I gape at her. "Afraid of? This doesn't have anything to do with fear. He left me, Marti. He left without even giving me an explanation. He didn't trust that I could handle it. Is that the kind of relationship that's good for me?"

"Hope, you have to be honest with yourself," she says. "We don't know if you could have handled it. You have these weird breakdowns, and you don't even have confidence in yourself—"

"You have confidence in me," I say. "You're counting on me to help you with this pregnancy. You didn't question me...did you?"

She shakes her head. "Never. But we've known each other practically our whole lives. Alec's only known you a few months. What if his wife had survived? He was saving you from something really painful."

"It was painful either way," I say. "He should have been honest with me."

"He should have," she concedes. "But nobody's perfect. You're asking him to deal with your flaws, but you're refusing to deal with his."

I sit back and close my eyes. She's right.

"Maybe it won't work out anyway," she says. "Who knows? But do you want to regret not trying? Alec is worth trying for. Isn't he?"

Chapter 13

Magician Martika manages to throw together a going-away party for Benny in two days. He's leaving in the morning out of Coronado.

This party is completely different than the last one they had. It's quiet, somber almost, as people whisper in small groups. Everyone fights to get time alone with Ben.

Then there's Benny's family, his mother weeping in the corner while his sisters comfort her. Martika spends some time with her mother-in-law, but then she drags me to the bathroom and locks us in.

"I can't handle this," she says, leaning on the counter. "Ben doesn't need his last memory at home to be of his wailing mother."

"He knows how she is," I say. "It's always been this way with her."

"But I've never been pregnant before!" she whispers furiously. "I don't need this!"

"And Benny doesn't need you hysterical, too," I say. "Buck up, little camper."

Martika cracks a smile at that. "Thank God my mom's not here. She'd be yelling at Ben for leaving."

"Mothers are crazy," I say. "There's a lesson here, you know that?"

She hangs head. "Dear God, I'm gonna be like them, aren't I?"

"I don't see you crying during a family party, but I could see you yelling at your daughter-in-law. Definitely something to guard against in the future."

Martika gives me a brief hug and steels her spine. "Okay, I'm better now."

We hear the doorbell ring.

"Oh," she says. "That might be for you."

I raise an eyebrow. "What did you do?"

She smiles and opens the door. We walk out to the foyer, and there's Ben, holding the front door open, and Charles standing on the steps.

"Charles!" I yell, and I run to him.

He laughs as I crush him in a hug. "I was hoping you'd be here tonight," he says, planting a kiss on the top of my head.

I look up at him. He's just as handsome as I remembered. "Did you just get in?"

He nods. "I couldn't miss this. Had to share a beer with my oldest friend before he goes off to protect us."

I step back. "Have your time with him. We can catch up later."

Charles gives me a soft kiss. "I'm counting on it."

As Charles walks away with Ben, I look up. Alec is standing in the doorway.

"Alec!" Martika cries, edging around me and taking his hand. "It's so nice of you to come!"

He kisses her cheek, but his eyes are on me. "Thanks for inviting me."

My head whips to Martika at that, but she refuses to look at me.

"Come on in," she says. "Hope can help you get something to drink." Then she rushes out to the patio, leaving us standing there.

"I guess you didn't know she invited me," Alec says.

"Martika likes surprises," I say.

"Do you like surprises?" he asks.

I ignore the question. "What are you doing here?"

"I was invited," he says.

"And?"

He looks around. "Is this the appropriate time? Honestly, I thought we could hang out and maybe talk later. But it seems like your later is occupied."

"Charles is an old friend," I say. "That's it."

"An old boyfriend?"

Well…we slept together the first night we met, and it was magical, but he lives in Texas. We've kept in touch, but that's it.

"Not really," I say.

Alec shakes his head. "Enough. I can't be upset. I broke things off. But the unfortunate part is…I want to fuck that guy up."

I laugh. Never thought I'd hear those words coming out of Alec's mouth.

"What are you doing here?" I say gently. "Really."

He blows out a breath. "I want another shot. I still love you, Hope."

My heart skips. "I don't know, Alec. You're right, this isn't the greatest time. But we can talk after."

His eyes soften. "You'll give me that time?"

I nod.

Alec opens his arms. I fall into them, and we hold each other tight.

And when I pull away and open my eyes…there's Matt standing at the door.

∞

I manage to corner Martika in the kitchen.

"Three of them," I say. "Three of them! Here. Tonight. Together!"

She sighs. "It's…awkward," she says. "I get it. But there's nothing we can do."

"But why did you have to invite all three of them?"

"I didn't," she says. "I let Charles know, but I never thought he'd show up. Ben invited Matt. Yes, I invited Alec, but that's only because you didn't have the guts to."

"Great," I say. "Blame me. Thanks a lot."

"It's fine," she says. "You and Matt know where you stand. Just be honest with Charles that you're seeing Alec. And then go home and screw Alec's brains out."

I throw back my Coke. "There's a plan."

Martika smiles. "See? Problem solved."

બ

Charles gives me a wave as I step out to the patio. I sit next to him on a bench, and he mashes his thigh into mine.

"Is something wrong?" he asks.

I smile. "How do you know that? You know me that well?"

He shrugs. "Those two guys are eyeing you, and you're trying too hard not to eye them back."

I bump my shoulder into his. "The big one is my ex-husband. And the other is a recent ex-boyfriend. And then there's you. Unfortunately…I have feelings for all of you."

"Shit," he says. "Guess you have some decisions to make. But I won't make it harder for you. I know you don't want a long-distance relationship."

"I don't," I say, "but I want us to stay friends."

Charles grins. "I'm a great friend."

≈

When I return from using the bathroom for real, I see Matt…talking to Alec. They both notice me and ignore me.

Shit.

So I hang out with Martika and Benny.

Benny's family finally leaves, and then Charles and a few other friends follow. Charles invites me out for drinks with the group, but I decline.

Matt tears himself away from Alec, and asks me if I'll show him out. I follow him to his car, and I'm dying to ask what he and Alec talked about, but I don't. How desperate would that make me sound?

We reach his car, and Matt palms his keys.

"I promised Ben I'd look out for Martika," he says. "I know you'll be the one here with her, so if you need anything, call me, okay?"

I nod. "Thanks. I will."

"This really sucks for them, doesn't it?"

"That's putting it mildly, I think," I say.

"You're gonna be an aunt," he says. "Exciting, isn't it?"

"I haven't thought about the baby much," I admit. "I'm more worried about getting Martika through it."

"That's why she's lucky to have you."

I smile at that. "Thanks, Matt."

He kisses my cheek. "Now go talk to Alec," he says. "The guy's dying."

ℴ

Alec and Ben are laughing when I return. Martika is cleaning up.

"Let me help," I say, but she shakes her head.

"Get out of here. Go be with Alec. I want some alone time with my husband."

I head to the patio and stop in front of the guys. "Time for me to wish you a safe journey."

Benny gives me a tight hug, the tightest, and I whisper a prayer in his ear.

"Vaya con Díos," I say, giving him one last kiss on the ear.

Alec shakes his hand, and then takes mine and leads me out to our cars.

"How late is your babysitter prepared to stay?" I ask him as we stand awkwardly in the street.

"She's staying with Auntie Ju-Ju overnight," Alec says.

"She...what's her name?" I ask.

"Mei," he says.

"Mei. That's beautiful."

He smiles. "She is."

I smile back. "My place or yours?"

"Let's meet at mine."

Chapter 14

Alec's house looks like a toy store exploded. My head swivels around, taking in the mess, and then I step on something that squeaks. A stuffed duck. I pick the duck up and hold it to my chest.

"Guess you've been a little overwhelmed," I say.

He laughs. "There's not enough time in the day. I'm still learning, and I haven't quite got our routine down yet. You want a beer?"

I didn't drink at the party. I wanted to be clear-headed for Martika. But now, I definitely need a drink.

"Please."

He grabs us each one, and we sit on the couch, not touching.

"So why didn't I tell you I was back?" he asks. "That's the big question, isn't it?"

"One of them," I say.

"First there was shame," he says, his eyes on his bottle. "Shame that I had a failing wife, that I was still married, that I didn't know I had a daughter. I physically couldn't tell you what was happening. My body wouldn't let me."

My initial reaction is that this is an excuse. But I've had moments where I wanted to say something and couldn't. My mouth simply wouldn't work.

I nod.

"Then…she might have lived. My wife might have survived. And even though I'd done everything I could think of to help her…I was obligated to do more. I didn't want you involved in that. And then…I knew I still wanted to be with you. But I didn't want you to think I just needed help. I was hoping to get a handle on everything, and figure out how to be a good father and still get to work on time…I needed to do all of that before I talked to you. I don't want you here out of pity, or because I have a baby. I want you here because you love me and only me."

"I would have stuck by you," I say.

Alec nods. "I know that. It wasn't about you. It was about me, and what I was feeling. It was about what I needed to do. And I know that hurt you, Hope. I'm so sorry for that."

"Like you said…we moved fast," I say. "We haven't had time to share everything, but all these things have been happening, and it's made us look like we haven't been honest, but that's not it at all. We just don't know each other yet."

He takes a deep breath. "I want to. I want us to know each other, inside and out."

"Me, too," I say. "That time without you…it was awful."

Alec smiles at that. "Awful, huh?"

"Awful."

"What about Matt?"

I cock my head. "What about him?"

"Do you still have feelings for him?"

I pick at the label on my bottle. "He was such a huge part of my life for so long," I say. "I think I'll always care about him. But I don't want to be with him."

"So how do we do this?" he asks.

I almost say, "I'll be whatever you need." Because, clearly, Alec has the tougher life right now.

But I catch myself.

"Let's date," I say. "Let's continue to get to know each other. And we'll see how it goes from there."

Alec nods. "I've missed you. We have until eight in the morning. That's when Auntie Ju-Ju is dropping Mei off."

I scoot up close to him. "And what do you do with Mei while you work?"

"I have a nanny."

"You need to tell her to clean up."

Alec smiles. "If it's a choice between spending time with Mei or cleaning up, I choose time with Mei."

"Sensible."

Alec puts his hands on my cheeks. "Kiss me already, will you?"

෨

I'm out of the house at seven. I told Alec I had an early appointment.

Which I do if you count eleven o'clock as early.

I just didn't want to see Auntie Ju-Ju so early in the morning when it was obvious I spent the night.

Okay, okay. So I'm a little nervous about meeting Mei, too.

I don't know how to hold a baby. I don't know how to change a diaper. Alec will see what an incompetent mother I'd be, and he'll want nothing more to do with me.

I wonder how long I can put him off.

Chapter 15

I put my music on the back burner, and I rearrange my life to help Martika. Not that I had much of a life to rearrange, let's be honest. Sunday activities with my mother, Wednesday nights playing at the coffeehouse until they get tired of me…that's pretty much the extent of my schedule.

Now I have Monday night Lamaze class, Tuesday night parenting class, and—at Martika's urging—Thursday morning workouts with a trainer.

It had to be done.

My trainer's name is Sadie, and she was in the Navy with Martika. Enough said.

We spend the first session getting a handle on my current fitness level. Sadie puts me through the paces, trying to determine where I'm weak. I could have saved us a lot of time by telling her "everywhere."

"It's not as bad as you think," she says as I throw myself on the floor and run a towel over my face. "Arm strength needs work, but your cardio's decent."

"I've had some pretty good sex lately," I say, and we both laugh.

"Sex is great exercise," she says. "And it's good for your relationship, too. I recommend once a day."

"My boyfriend will love to hear that," I say.

She pulls me to my feet. "You're gonna be sore, but you have to work through it. Do the arm exercises I showed you three times a week. Light cardio four times a week. We'll start slow and add stuff over time."

"That's starting slow?" I ask.

Sadie grins. "Yes, this is slow. I want to hear from your doctor before I really push you."

Right. My appointment's tomorrow afternoon.

"Drink lots of water," she says, "and call me if you have any questions."

Right.

❧

Alec offered to come to the appointment with me, but I opted for Martika. Whatever the news about my heart—if there is any news—I want some time to think about how to tell him.

I've known Dr. Parsa for fifteen years. She greets me with a hug. "Where's that gorgeous husband of yours?" she asks.

"This is my best friend, Martika," I say. "Matt and I divorced last year."

Dr. Parsa grabs my hand. "Hope, I'm so sorry."

"Thank you," I say. "It was tough for a while, but I'm good now."

"Then let's take a look," she says. "The nurse said you're not experiencing any negative symptoms?"

I shake my head. "Nope. No pain, no shortness of breath."

"Let me look at the echocardiogram we did."

Martika and I sit patiently while she examines my test results.

Dr. Parsa finally looks up and smiles. "Everything looks good, Hope. No changes from last year. Are you getting much exercise?"

"I just hired a trainer," I say. "The focus is gonna be on my physical strength, but I'd like to do more cardio, too. Can I?"

She nods. "You should. There's no need to push yourself to the max, but a few times a week where you get your heart pumping is great. Like I said, don't push it. Listen to your body. If you feel out of breath, stop."

"I do have one other question," I say. "I know in the past, you've recommended that I don't get pregnant. But if I did…if it's something I really wanted…"

Her eyes soften and she takes my hand. "I thought you'd decided not to have kids."

"That's what Matt and I had decided," I say, "but Matt's gone."

She rolls her stool over to me and sits down. "It would be a high-risk pregnancy. I can't predict how your heart will take it. Everything might be fine, or it might strain your valve to the point where you need a replacement. But you will need a replacement at some point. I've told you that. The fix you had at birth...nothing lasts forever. This is really something you need to discuss with your partner, Hope."

"I don't mean to be rude," Martika says, "but that wasn't very helpful. She knew all that."

I cringe and swat Martika's arm, and Dr. Parsa sighs. "Many patients with your condition have successful pregnancies. The mechanical valves today are much better than the valves of ten years ago, even five years ago. Our surgical procedures are better. Right now, I'd say you're an excellent candidate for pregnancy. You don't even have a heart murmur. But there are no guarantees. I can't make the choice for you, Hope."

Tears gather in my eyes. "You think I'm an excellent candidate to have a baby?"

She smiles. "As far as your heart goes, yes."

"What's that supposed to mean?" Martika asks.

Dr. Parsa narrows her eyes. "You will have health issues, Hope. You have health issues. You can't just think in terms of having a baby. You'll need a strong support system, ideally a strong, committed partner. If you choose to get pregnant, I'd want all of us working together—me, your neurologist, your OB/GYN, a mental healthcare provider. From beginning to end, we should all be involved."

"I'm finally seeing a psychiatrist," I say. "He's really helping me."

"Excellent. And do you have a partner?"

I nod. "It's new, and he knows about my heart, and we haven't actually discussed getting pregnant, but I wanted to know my options."

Dr. Parsa gives me a hug. "You're doing the right things. Take care of yourself, and keep me in the loop."

⁊

"So what do you think?" Martika asks when we get in the car.

"I can't think," I say. "It doesn't seem real."

Martika shifts to face me. "This is something you really need to think about, front to back. I mean, I'm happy for you, so happy...but there are consequences."

I nod as I drive. "I know. I'm not gonna run off and get pregnant."

"And you should tell Alec everything the doctor said—"

"I will," I say, feeling a little irritated.

"You should talk to Dr. Steinburg about this," she presses. "Like she said, all your doctors should be involved—"

"I get it!" I turn and glare at her. "Why are you up my ass about this?"

"I'm not up your ass," she says. "I just want you to think hard about this and do the right thing."

"And what do you think the right thing is?" I ask.

Martika stays silent.

"Well? You seem to know what's best for me. What should I do?"

"Hope."

"Don't Hope me," I say. "You don't think I should have a baby, do you?"

"I never said that."

"But that's what you think, isn't it?"

We pull up to her house, and Marti pushes her door open then looks back at me. "Aren't you coming in?"

I shake my head. "I should go."

"Please, Hope," she says. "Please come inside."

I sigh, turn the car off, and march inside. "What do you want?" I ask her.

I follow her to the kitchen, where she picks a manila folder up off the counter and hands it to me.

"Ben and I had Alec create a trust for us, with a will and stuff," she says. "We'd been meaning to do it, but it's not like we have any assets beyond the house, and even that's mortgaged to the hilt. But when he got called back out, Ben's first thought was that we needed to protect the baby, just in case."

I open the folder.

"It's on page four," she says, and I flip to page four.

I blink hard as I read, then my eyes whip to hers. "You named me guardian of the baby?"

Martika nods. "If you'll do it."

"But you have family, both of you. One of your sisters, your moms…they'll never let me—"

"It's not up to them," she says. "It's up to me and Benny."

"They'll fight it," I say. "I have too many health problems."

"But you have enough money to fight them," she says. "And we spoke with Alec and several people in his office, and they all know our wishes. We're trusting you with the thing that matters most to us."

I choke on a sob. "You think I'll be a good mother."

She smiles and takes my hands in hers. "I know you'll be a great mother. But…should you get pregnant? I don't know, Hope. I don't want to lose you. I don't know if it's worth the risk. But I want you to know that my opinion has nothing to do with your ability to be a good mom. That's a given."

Chapter 16

Alec invites me over for dinner to meet Mei, and since it's been two weeks since we started dating again, I know I can't continue to hide. I decide to just come clean.

"Um…you know I've never been around babies, right?"

"Is that why you've been avoiding coming over here?" he asks.

"Well…yeah. I'm nervous."

Alec laughs. "Don't be. I'll help. I'm not exactly a pro myself. Plus, this is great opportunity to be ready for Martika's baby, right?"

"I guess," I say. "Okay. What should I bring?"

"An overnight bag," he says, voice low. "And that massage oil. I can use a massage."

I laugh. "Okay. See you soon."

₮

I can hear Mei wailing as I walk up to the front door. Oh boy.

I can do this.

I take a deep breath and open the door. "Alec?"

He's pacing in front of the couch, clutching a sobbing bundle of blankets to his shoulder. "Just in time."

I smile. "I don't know that I'll be much help."

"If you can take her for five minutes while I heat a bottle, I'll love you forever."

I close the door and walk over to them. "Hey, Mei."

The baby doesn't seem to notice me. She's got herself all worked up, her face scrunched and her lungs bursting.

"What's wrong with her?" I ask.

Alec bounces on his toes. "Who knows? Sometimes babies just cry. I haven't figured out a surefire way to soothe her yet. I'm hoping a bottle will help."

He lifts Mei into my shaking arms, and I hold her tight to my chest. "Hey, you."

She cries harder.

"Oh, let's not cry," I say, shifting her up to my shoulder. I bounce around the room. "I want to meet you. I want to talk to you. My name's Hope. I love your daddy, you know that?"

I watch Alec fumble with a bottle. His sink is full of dirty dishes, the counter, too, and he seems completely off balance.

"It's okay," I say to him with a laugh. "Take a breather. I've got her."

He puts his hands on the counter and leans forward. "She's been crying for an hour. Makes you feel like shit."

"Then get the bottle and grab a beer. Or go for a walk. Seriously, I'm fine."

He smiles at me and continues with the bottle. "I wouldn't leave you here alone, but I appreciate the offer."

"Does she like you to sing to her?" I ask.

"You've heard me sing," he says. "I'm pretty sure me singing would be considered child abuse." He comes out of the kitchen and holds out his arms. "I'll feed her."

I pluck the bottle from his hand. "Get a beer. I'm doing this."

I settle on the couch and move a squirming Mei to my lap. I try to give her the bottle, but she wriggles around and pushes it away.

"I prefer a little entertainment with my dinner, too," I say. And then I sing *Twinkle, Twinkle, Little Star.*

At first, Mei screams louder, seemingly in an effort to drown me out. And then she hiccoughs. She turns her bright brown eyes on me and blinks.

I sing softer, and I bring the bottle back to her lips.

She sniffles, then opens her mouth, and her tiny hands help guide the bottle in.

Bingo.

Alec comes to the couch with two beers, and he sits right up next to me.

"You're a genius," he whispers.

A tear glides down my cheek.

I watch this beautiful little girl fall asleep with her fingers wrapped around my pinkie. My heart is so full it feels ready to burst.

∞

"You're always so hard on yourself," Alec says as we eat pizza on the living room floor. "When are you going to start believing in yourself?"

I take a bite of my crust. "How can I be confident in something I've never done? This baby thing is uncharted territory."

"Didn't look that way to me," he says.

I duck my head. "She's precious," I say. "You're so blessed."

Alec sighs and rolls to his back. "She's got me. I'd do anything for her. But I'd be lying if I said it was easy."

"It's still new," I say. "But you're lucky. You have lots of family to help out."

He flips over to his stomach and props his head in his hands. "How does this change things for us?"

"It makes it a lot more serious, doesn't it?" I say. "I mean, we have Mei to think about. Whatever happens between us will affect her, too."

Alec nods. "Is that a problem?"

I shrug. "You and I have always been serious."

"But?"

I throw my crust in the pizza box. "What if I get close to Mei, and then you and I don't work out? What then?"

"It's the same as getting married, having kids, and then divorcing," he says. "There's always the possibility of disaster. But we can't assume disaster."

"Except that if Mei were really mine, I'd still get to see her. Now...I have no claim to her. I'm already falling in love with her, and there are no guarantees."

Alec sits up and pulls me into his chest. "What do you want, Hope?"

I look into his eyes. "I want us to work out. And I guess we just have to take a leap of faith."

He leans in and kisses me, but I pull back. "What do you want, Alec?"

"You," he says. "I just want you."

I smile and kiss his nose. "Come on. I'll help you clean the kitchen. There's no way I can have a satisfying orgasm until the work is done."

Alec laughs and pops to his feet.

ॐ

We share a lazy morning, coffee, news, and Mei. Alec surrounds her with pillows in the middle of the floor and encourages her to sit up by herself.

He has a book that tells you all the milestones a baby is supposed to hit every month. I flip to the section on "Eight Months Old," and it says that most babies are crawling or scooting, and they should be able to sit up.

"Have you read this?" I ask him as he sits a falling Mei up again. "She should be able to sit up on her own."

He nods. "Her gross motor skills are behind the curve. Her pediatrician said there's nothing physically wrong with her. Most likely, she was in a crib all day and didn't get a lot of opportunity to use her muscles. He thinks she'll catch up quickly."

I read some more. "And you should be introducing new foods to her. One a week."

"She'd never eaten solid foods except for rice cereal," he says. "We're doing peas this week."

"Peas?" I say, scrunching my nose. "You want her to like vegetables. Why start with peas?"

"The doctor suggested it. He said to start with the green vegetables, otherwise she won't touch them at all. Carrots and squash and everything not green are much sweeter."

"Damn, babies are smart," I say. "It says she should know a few words. Does she talk yet?"

"She can say 'Ma.' I've been trying to get her to say 'Da.'"

I sit in front of her and smile. "Dada. That's your Dada. Can you say Dada? Dada."

Mei blows a raspberry at me and laughs.

"I wonder if this is confusing for her," I say. "She's used to hearing Chinese, not English."

Alec pulls me up into his arms. "I love that you're concerned about her."

"Of course I am," I say. "It doesn't sound like she got the best start." He kisses me, and I pull back. "Do you think we should be doing that in front of her?"

Alec laughs. "I think it's good for her to see people being affectionate. I didn't have that, and I want her to have it."

"How is it that you're so affectionate if you didn't have it?"

He cocks his head. "How did you know it's wrong to hit your child?"

I close my eyes. "You just know, in your gut, when something feels wrong."

"Exactly."

I open my eyes. "So what was wrong with our parents?"

Alec pulls me back against him. "I guess we'll never know."

Chapter 17

Dr. Steinburg offers me a cup of coffee, and I take it. With Mei up twice last night, my ass is dragging.

"So why the yawning?" he asks as I try to discreetly cover my open mouth with my hand.

I tell him all about Alec and Mei.

"And then Alec and I were talking about how to raise kids, I mean, some things specifically, like he wants to show Mei a lot of affection since he didn't get that as a kid, and of course, I would never hit my child, and I just wondered…what was wrong with our parents? Why didn't they see they were hurting us?"

He sits back. "One reason is how they were raised. If, for example, you are hit as a child, you are more likely to hit your own children. And not because you think it's good or right, and not because you don't realize you're hurting them, but because that is what you were taught. That is how things are done. You lived through it, so your children will, too."

"But Alec and I will never repeat the abuse," I say. "Never. So why are we different?"

"In Alec's case, it's more a cultural difference," he says. "He was raised here, where hugging and kissing your child is pretty standard. And it sounds like he went through a marriage that didn't have a lot of affection, and since he's an intelligent man, he decided he wanted something different. With you, I think a big part of it is the absence of substance abuse. Both your parents spent decades in a drug-induced haze, and you are clear-headed. But beyond that…I'd say your relationship with Matt has a lot to do with it."

"One more thing I owe him for," I say.

Dr. Steinburg raises an eyebrow. "Has something happened between you two?"

"No," I say. "Well, you know we decided to just be friends, and he and Alec both showed up at a party and they got to talking…I have no idea what they actually talked about, but Matt sorta gave me his blessing to be with Alec. And I've been feeling guilty about that. I don't know why, though."

"I think you know you need to let go of the guilt," he says. "By having an affair, Matt was pretty much letting you off the hook for any imbalance in the relationship."

I blink. "He was letting me off the hook?"

"Subconsciously," he says. "He committed the greatest sin against you that he could live with. That way he was the bad guy. Even if he didn't realize what he was doing, it was very calculated."

"Why didn't you tell me this before?"

Dr. Steinburg eyes me over his coffee cup. "This information changes something for you?"

I shake my head. "I don't know. I just…I never thought of his affair as something that was actually motivated by his care for me."

"It was, and it wasn't. He wanted out, but he wanted to make it easy on you. You can't take this as a sign of love, Hope. That's not what I was getting at."

I nod.

"My point was about guilt. Let it go. Focus on Alec. How do you feel about him being a father?"

I try to focus on the question, but all I can think about is Matt, compromising himself, so I didn't have to feel bad.

"Wait. If Matt wanted to make it easy on me, he could have just left. He didn't have to have an affair."

Dr. Steinburg sighs. "This is more complex than I've made it. Matt needed to feel appreciated, according to what he told you. So he found that in a grad student. He was confused, he wasn't sure if he wanted out of the marriage…and then he told Benny about the affair, who told Martika, who told you. Why do you think he told Benny? He'd already gotten away with it. He wanted a way out without having to take responsibility, without having to say, Hope, I'm leaving because of you. Ultimately, he made you do the dirty work, and he got to wallow in his own guilt. Win, win."

"Men," I say, and he smiles.

"And they say women are the more complex gender. Let's go back to you and Alec. How did your cardiologist visit go?"

I pick at a hangnail. "I can have kids. She told me I can get pregnant."

"That's wonderful, Hope. How did Alec take it?"

"I haven't told him," I say. "And he didn't ask. But I don't blame him. He's completely overwhelmed right now."

"Do you intend to tell him?"

"Someday," I say. "I just…don't you think it's a lot of pressure right now? A year from now, my doctor might say it's not safe to have a baby. Hell, tomorrow it might not be safe. I don't want Alec to feel like I'm pushing him."

"I think that's wise," he says. "Are you feeling pressure yourself?"

"Of course," I say. "It's all I can think about. But then I spent time with Alec and Mei…I know it's not easy. And I know it's not something I want to do on my own, raise a kid, I mean. I want that perfect partner first."

"I agree. How goes the music?"

I tell him about Lady Strings, my new persona, and that it's coming along.

"Lady Strings," he says. "How'd you come up with that?"

"It's a nickname Matt gave me in high school," I say. "All my close friends called me Strings, although I made them stop when Matt and I separated."

Dr. Steinburg smiles.

"What?" I ask.

"You realize this means you're not really hiding. If more than one person knows, you'll be outed."

I smile back. "Yeah, I kinda figured that."

I spend the night at Alec's again. I was worried about getting close to Mei too soon, but I just decided to jump.

We make love after Mei falls asleep, and I decide to jump further.

"I didn't tell you about my appointment with the cardiologist," I say.

"I forgot all about it," he says. "I'm so sorry. How'd it go?"

I smile. "Great. Everything's fine. And she…she even said…I can get pregnant."

His eyes widen. "Really? It's safe?"

I nod, and Alec pulls me down to his chest and wraps his arms around me.

"Wow. So what are you thinking?"

"Nothing," I say. "I don't want to screw this up. I don't want you to feel like I have to get pregnant. This doesn't change anything. Let's just keep going."

"Hope," he whispers, and the emotion in his voice makes me shiver. "I have to be honest with you."

I lift my head in alarm. "What?"

"This…Mei has changed everything for me, and I don't want to make any absolutes, but I…I think…"

"What?"

"I don't think I want any more children."

I sit up, too fast, and turn away from him.

"I don't know for sure," he says, "but I'm pretty sure."

"Do you think, maybe, you're just overwhelmed?" I say without looking at him.

"Probably," he says. "But that doesn't change anything. I can't imagine it'd be easier with more kids."

"But you're doing it all alone now," I say, my voice rising. "And if we ever...I mean, hypothetically, if we got married, we'd be doing it together."

"You were prepared to never have kids," he says, "and suddenly you're angry that I don't want more?"

"I'm not angry," I say. "Or maybe I am. I just...you're making a huge decision without even discussing it."

"Mei is one more child than you thought you'd ever have," he says. "You can't be happy with that?"

I climb from the bed and search for my clothes. "If Mei was all I ever had, yes, I'd be happy. But it's in God's hands. Whatever happens...I just want the chance for it to happen. And you're deciding for me."

"We have to agree, or one of us decides," he says. "If we don't agree, one of us has to compromise."

"I don't know if I can compromise on this," I say. "Not after I've been given a chance."

I pull on my jeans and shove my feet in my tennis shoes.

"Don't go," he says. "Nothing's changed. We haven't even decided to have a baby."

"But you've decided not to," I say. "Alec, I love you. I want a life with you. But if you're dead-set against this...neither of us should waste our time."

"I don't know what I want," he says quietly.

"There seems to be an epidemic of that running around. And I don't want to catch it. Goodbye, Alec."

To Be Continued…

BOOKS BY ANDREA RING

Stand-Alone Contemporary Romance

High Maintenance

Young Adult Contemporary Romance

Under Water (A Yellow Wood Series Book 1)

Breaking the Surface (A Yellow Wood Series Book 2)

Romantic Fantasy

The Go-Between (Nilaruna Cycles Book 1)

The Princess (Nilaruna Cycles Book 2)

Goddess (Nilaruna Cycles Book 3)

Science Fiction

Nervous System (The System Series Book 1)

Systematic (The System Series Book 2)

Operating System (The System Series Book 3)

Honor System (The System Series Book 4)

Systems Go (The System Series Book 5)

Note to my readers: I'm humbled and grateful that you read my work. I hope it touched you. I'd love to get to know you, hear your thoughts, and learn what makes you tick. Send me an email. Write a review on Amazon. Comment on my blog. You're the reason I write, and I'll never forget that.

Read a chapter from the next episode in
The String Serial,

String Theory
The String Serial
Part Four

String Theory

I help Martika into the car after her doctor visit. She's clearly uncomfortable and trying not to show it.

I pull out of the parking lot, and she sighs.

"Okay. First thing I do is try to contact Benny. Then I need to pack my bag for the hospital. You have my list of contacts, right? All the people who need to be called when I go into labor?"

"Yes, dear," I say.

She rolls her eyes at me.

"We can finally put the sheets on the crib…and remind me to sleep with a towel under my butt. If my water breaks in the middle of the night, I don't want to deal with the clean up."

"Got it."

"Then a power walk. Three miles oughta do it. We can walk again after dinner."

I've lost five pounds in the last three weeks. Martika is on a mission to get this baby out as soon as possible.

"I can't believe you're already dilated two centimeters," I say. "With any luck, you'll be most of the way there before you're actually in pain. Nervous?" I ask.

She smiles. "No. I know I should be, but no. I can't believe it's finally here."

"She said you might still be a week away."

Martika shakes her head. "No way. Two days tops. My uterus is scrunching itself up as we speak."

I laugh. "It's your cervix that needs to do the work, not your uterus."

"Look at you," she says. "Miss Pregnancy Expert. Take a guess. When is this little guy coming?"

I reach a hand out and put it on her belly. "Tonight. After midnight. You're gonna wake me up, and we'll rush to the hospital, and he'll be here by sunrise."

"My son wouldn't be so rude as to interrupt my last night of rest. I say tomorrow morning. I wake up, my water breaks while I'm in the shower, I arrive at the hospital ten centimeters dilated, and I push for ten minutes, and boom. I'm a mama."

"You're dreaming," I say with a laugh.

About the Author

Andrea Ring was born and raised in Orange County, California. At age eight, she wrote an essay proclaiming she wanted to be an "auther" when she grew up. It only took her thirty years to realize her dream.

She enjoys beating her four children at Boggle, reading science fiction and fantasy, and eating bacon. She hates to exercise, but loves taking walks with her family through Old Towne Orange. She's lucky to be married to the love of her life.

She thinks every book should contain a love story.

Did we mention her love of bacon?

www.ingramcontent.com/pod-product-compliance
Lightning Source LLC
Chambersburg PA
CBHW031414240626
47154CB00001B/32